SEWING THE
SHADOWS
TOGETHER

SEWING THE SHADOWS TOGETHER

ALISON BAILLIE

Matador
9 Priory Business Park
Kibworth Beauchamp
Leicestershire LE8 0RX, UK
Tel: (+44) 116 279 2299
Email: books@troubador.co.uk
Web: www.troubador.co.uk/matador

ISBN 978 1784623 555

British Library Cataloguing in Publication Data.
A catalogue record for this book is available from the British Library.

Printed and bound by CPI Group (UK) Ltd, Croydon, CR0 4YY
Typeset in Garamond by Troubador Publishing Ltd

Matador is an imprint of Troubador Publishing Ltd

This book is dedicated to my lovely sons and granddaughter
— Alec, John and Akira

BAT

By DH Lawrence

At evening, sitting on this terrace,
When the sun from the west, beyond Pisa, beyond the mountains
   of Carrara
Departs, and the world is taken by surprise...

When the tired flower of Florence is in gloom beneath the glowing
Brown hills surrounding...

When under the arches of the Ponte Vecchio
A green light enters against stream, flush from the west,
Against the current of obscure Arno...

Look up, and you see things flying
Between the day and the night;
Swallows with spools of dark thread sewing the shadows together.

A circle swoop, and a quick parabola under the bridge arches
Where light pushes through;
A sudden turning upon itself of a thing in the air.
A dip to the water.

And you think:
"The swallows are flying so late!"

Swallows?
Dark air-life looping
Yet missing the pure loop…
A twitch, a twitter, an elastic shudder in flight
And serrated wings against the sky,
Like a glove, a black glove thrown up at the light,
And falling back.

Never swallows!
Bats!
The swallows are gone.

At a wavering instant the swallows gave way to bats
By the Ponte Vecchio…
Changing guard.

Bats, and an uneasy creeping in one's scalp
As the bats swoop overhead!
Flying madly.

Pipistrello!
Black piper on an infinitesimal pipe.
Little lumps that fly in air and have voices indefinite, wildly vindictive;

Wings like bits of umbrella.

Bats!

Creatures that hang themselves up like an old rag, to sleep;
And disgustingly upside down.

Hanging upside down like rows of disgusting old rags
And grinning in their sleep
Bats!

In China the bat is symbol for happiness

Not for me!

'Bat' from *Birds, Beasts and Flowers* by DH Lawrence
reprinted by permission of Pollinger Limited
(www.pollingerltd.com) on behalf of the Estate
of Frieda Lawrence Ravagi.

PART I

I'm alone in the park. The September moon rises over the Forth and a chill breeze rustles through the branches of the old trees. I pull my cardigan round my shoulders and feel the rough wood of the bench through my thin skirt. In the stillness, the water of the burn gurgles through the bushes. Shona hasn't come back. I'm late, I'll be in trouble. I feel a mixture of betrayal and anxiety. My best friend told me to wait and didn't come back.

Behind me, a crackle of leaves. A movement in the shadows, a long black coat, the blur of a white face shining pale in the moonlight. Logan Baird. I am breathless with panic. I try to run but my legs won't move.

Sarah lay in her bed shaking, her skin clammy. The duvet had slipped off and Rory's side of the bed lay empty. It was more than thirty years since Logan Baird had murdered Shona, but in that grey void between sleep and consciousness the memories still haunted her.

CHAPTER I

Tom McIver walked along the empty promenade. Portobello had not changed much in the last thirty-seven years: the same wide sweep of the bay, the faint distant coastline of Fife and the huge pale sky. Although it was nearly ten o'clock at night, the daylight was still dissolving slowly into darkness.

He'd forgotten how long the summer evenings were in Scotland; so different from South Africa, where the evening sun sank quickly, the southern hemisphere darkness dropping like a cloak. He thought briefly of drinking sundowners, watching the sky change colour over Plettenberg Bay, but the image melted and the fishy Scottish air brought him back to the present.

He never thought he'd come back to this place where he'd spent the first sixteen years of his life. But when his mother clutched his hand and begged him to scatter her ashes on Eriskay, the island of her birth, he'd made the promise to come back to Scotland. He'd planned to go straight to the Western Isles, but the nearer the trip came, the more he realised he couldn't avoid Portobello. He had to come back to confront the memories he'd tried to bury for the whole of his adult life.

The buildings that edged the wide pedestrian walkway were still distinguishable in the grainy evening light: the grim bulk of the Free Presbyterian Church, the red stone of the municipal baths where he'd learnt to swim, the run-down row of cafés and shops. Then he saw the looming shadow of Brunstane High, his old school, the playground walls topped with broken glass shards. He shuddered; he was glad the school reunion he'd impulsively signed up for was not being held in this building.

Sooner than he expected, he found himself at the more residential end of the prom. Abercorn Park stretched back from the shore into the darkness, fringed by a row of large, late Victorian villas. A group of teenagers lounged on the roundabout in the children's playground. Behind them, the stark silhouette of the slide stretched up in front of a cluster of old trees and in front of him the waters of the burn disappeared into the dark hole of the culvert which ran under the prom. He felt a shudder run through him; it was where Shona's body had been found.

He forced himself to go further and after only a few yards saw the red-stone tenement where his family had lived. The door at Number 28 was newly-painted, with entry phones replacing the brass bell pulls, but otherwise it seemed almost unchanged.

Looking up to the third floor, he saw the window of his old room and memories of those nightmare days came flooding back: Shona's empty bedroom, the police questions, the journalists on the doorstep. His chest tightened. He couldn't stand and look any longer. In the gathering darkness he hurried back to his small room in the Regent Guesthouse and lay down on the floral bedspread. He'd known it would be hard to come back, but it was even worse than he'd imagined.

He reached for the remote control and pinged on the television, not caring what was on, just wanting to blank out his thoughts. It was some kind of chat show, where the guest,

6

an attractive red-head, was wiping tears from her cheeks and smiling bravely for the camera.

The shot cut to the interviewer. The voice attracted Tom's attention first and when he looked more carefully there was something familiar about him. The well-cut suit and the perfectly-groomed grey hair threw him off track at first, but then he was certain. The smile, the smooth sympathetic tones, the angle of the head as he leant towards his guest took him back to his school days.

The host turned towards the camera and gave an intimate smile. 'So that's all for tonight. I'd like to thank my guest, Mara O'Callaghan, for speaking to us so openly, and to you all for watching. It's good night from me, Rory Dunbar, and keep safe until we meet again next week.' With a final dazzling smile the interviewer turned towards Mara as the picture faded.

Rory Dunbar! He'd been in his class at school, lived in the next stair and they'd mucked about together. Tom had been glad to be part of Rory's golden circle, because even back then Rory had been the one all the girls fancied and all the boys wanted to emulate. Tom wasn't surprised he'd been the one to succeed.

Rory would probably be at the school reunion tomorrow. Tom wondered, not for the first time, if it had really been such a great idea to sign up for it. When he'd looked at the school Facebook page and seen it was on this weekend it had seemed like fate, but now he wasn't so sure.

*

Sarah clicked off the TV as her husband gave his trademark sign-off and felt the intense quiet in the high-ceilinged

Georgian drawing room. She looked at the school photos of the twins on the tall mahogany chest. She'd been so happy when they were growing up; her life was full and she'd almost forgotten what had happened when she was young, but now they'd moved out into their own flats, the house was so empty and there was no escape from her memories.

As she walked into the darkness of her bedroom, she wondered if Rory would be back tonight. No doubt he would have to comfort Mara in her distress.

The phone rang. Sarah wondered whether to answer it. It wouldn't be Rory, he never phoned but perhaps it was her mother, or one of the twins. After hesitating over the handset, she picked it up and instantly regretted it, hearing the chirpy tones of Patsy Mills.

'Oh hi, how are you? All ready for tomorrow?'

Her heart sank. The school reunion. She didn't want to go and, as Patsy kept reminding her, it wasn't even for her year – just the four classes that had started Brunstane High in 1971. She was only being allowed to attend because she was married to Rory.

'Oh, Patsy, I'm fine. Just going to bed, actually. How are you?'

'Is Rory there? I just wanted to check that he'll be at the Craigie Arms at six for the pre-dinner drinks.'

'He's not back yet – but I'm sure we'll be there on time. I'll remind him as soon as he gets in. But Patsy I'm going to have to go now because… ' she hesitated as she searched around for an excuse, 'I've got something on the stove. See you, sleep well.' She put the phone down, still hearing Patsy squawking until the final click cut her off.

CHAPTER 2

Tom hesitated at the wide front door of the Craigie Arms Hotel. It was in Joppa, the more upmarket end of Portobello, one of a row of residential buildings in Scottish baronial style with turrets and towers and a long garden leading down to the seafront. It seemed familiar; he had a vague memory of being there once, perhaps at a wedding or an eighteenth birthday party.

Inside, the decor showed it had fallen on hard times. The function room was set up with five round tables, each seating eight, but the white tablecloths didn't distract from the drab wallpaper and the stained carpet. On the left there was a small bar with a group of men holding pints and laughing. Small clusters of women were scattered about the room, talking earnestly, heads close together.

He thought back to the class photo he'd found among his mother's things. Strange that she'd packed that last frozen image of him in his school uniform, blond hair down to his shoulders, surrounded by other sixteen-year-olds with seventies glam rock hairstyles. Looking towards the bar, he hoped that some of the faces would seem familiar, but he didn't recognise anyone.

'Tom.' A very small woman in high-heels and a low-cut dress tottered towards him. She flung her arms round his neck and pulled his head down to kiss him. 'Lovely you could make it. You look just like your Facebook photo.'

This had to be Patsy Mills, organiser of the event. She bore only a passing resemblance to her youthful photo on Facebook and he couldn't remember her from school at all.

'We have a reunion every year, but this one's special because of the school's centenary, so it's great you could come.'

Taking his hand, Patsy led him towards the group at the bar and introduced him. There were a few muttered greetings, and one of the group stepped forward and offered Tom a drink before melting back into the comfort zone of his friends. Nobody else spoke to him. Tom stood on the edge of the laughing crowd, sipping his pint and trying to look as though he belonged.

Patsy, who'd been keeping an anxious eye on the entrance, ran towards the door, squealing 'Rory!' A hush fell over the room and all eyes turned towards the door as Rory Dunbar strode in. He bent to kiss Patsy on the cheek and then flashed a dazzling smile round the room, joining the group at the bar with much back-slapping and laughter. A woman – who Tom guessed was his wife – tall and graceful with shoulder-length dark hair, stood a few paces behind him.

Patsy stood on tiptoes and whispered in Rory's ear. He looked round and nodded to her before coming over to Tom. Pumping Tom's right hand with his left arm round his shoulder, Rory greeted him effusively. 'Tom! Tom McIver. How great to see you! When did you get back?' Without waiting for an answer he turned to the others. 'Remember Tom? He was in our class, great footballer! Do you still play football, Tom?'

'Not any more. I do a bit of running though.'

'Still support the Hibees, I hope. You'd better – they

need all the support they can get. Tragic how bad they've been this season.' Rory turned to the group who started talking about scores and disappointments and how they 'were robbed'; Tom felt the conversation drift away and fall into the void of the years separating them.

Patsy clapped her hands, her voice rising above the hubbub. 'Now it's time to eat. We want everyone to talk to each other so you'll all have to move around. You've got a card with the four courses you chose, the table number and the seat number. Now don't sit in the wrong seat or I'll get very cross. Might have to spank you!' There was a loud whooo from the bar.

Patsy giggled. 'You know, we've got people jetting in from all over to come to this reunion. Jennie's come from Singapore,' a thin, short-haired woman with an expensive-looking dress and a lot of gold jewellery waved both arms, 'and Tom's come all the way from South Africa. The first time he's come back and just for our reunion.' Someone started clapping and others joined in raggedly. Tom gave an embarrassed smile.

'And, of course, as always, we're fortunate to have our very own Rory Dunbar here today.' She broke off for a few appreciative cheers from the crowd and Rory gave a practised wave. 'So find your places and, if you're very good, there's a special after-dinner treat for you.'

Tom was trying to decipher the information on his card when Patsy appeared at his elbow. 'I chose the menu for you because you signed up so late. Hope that's OK. Anyway, come along. I've put you at the same table as Rory for the first course.'

The seating was traditional – alternate men and women.

11

Tom found his place between two well-preserved women, whose neatly-styled hair showed they'd been at the hairdresser that day. They introduced themselves briefly, explaining they were primary school heads, and then continued a conversation across him about children growing up too quickly these days. Tom tried to place them but their names meant nothing to him.

Rory leant over one of them. 'Tom, so great to see you. What's life like in South Africa? Went there once, to Cape Town, loved it. Where do you live?'

'A place called Plettenberg Bay.'

'Is that near Cape Town?'

'Not very. It's a small town on the south coast, on the Garden Route.'

Rory shrugged to indicate that he'd never heard of it. A man across the table asked what it was like meeting all those beautiful women and Rory turned towards him. 'It's great. I've got them knocking at my door all the time – but I never let them out!' Tom watched as a burst of laughter erupted from the table at this lame joke. Everyone wanted to be part of Rory's magic circle.

Tom finished his lukewarm carrot and coriander soup and sat back as they joked amongst themselves. Most of the men looked their age, with thickening waists or balding heads, but Rory still had the large dark eyes and sculpted cheek-bones that had made him so popular with the girls when they were young.

Tom's light trousers and his pale blue cotton shirt seemed exotically casual compared to the dark suits and white shirts of the others. He didn't fit in. In South Africa he was always recognised as Scots, but here he felt colonial,

12

his accent and identity worn away by the years in Plettenberg Bay. His skin was tanned, his hair thinner and bleached colourless by the years of sun and salt. He adjusted his long legs to fit under the table and tried to smile and nod as conversations flowed around him.

After what seemed like a very long time, Patsy tapped her glass with a spoon. 'Time to move again. Hurry up, and no changing the seating plan, or else!'

Rory winked as he moved to his next table. 'Catch you later, Tommy boy.'

'Now, Tom,' said Patsy as they settled down to their Waldorf salad. 'I especially put you next to me for this course because I want to hear all about you. Are you married?'

'Haven't met the right girl yet.' Tom cringed as he came out with the clichéd answer.

Patsy pressed on, undeterred. 'So, what do you do?'

Tom felt her attention wander as he told her about his aimless career of odd jobs and messing about on boats. He started to tell her about the sculptures he made out of driftwood, but she turned away to a stocky man on her other side, who started joking with her, fixing his eyes on her cleavage.

Tom stabbed at a walnut; even the narrow single bed and the rose-covered wallpaper of the Regent Guesthouse were beginning to seem attractive.

He looked up from his half-eaten salad and round the room. At the next table he saw Rory Dunbar's wife looking in his direction. Her eye caught his. She smiled and he felt a slight twinge of recognition. Had she been in his class? He couldn't really place her, but the smile touched him.

When Patsy stood up again and gave the order to move,

Tom was relieved to see Rory's wife waving in his direction. 'You're over here, Tom, next to me.'

He slid into the chair next to her.

'Do you remember me? Sarah, Sarah Campbell, Shona's friend.'

Tom caught his breath. Beneath her graceful figure, he did recognise her. Sarah Campbell, the gangling thirteen-year-old with long dark hair who'd always been at Shona's side. Images came flooding back: Shona and Sarah, one so blonde and the other dark, giggling in their new school uniforms, setting off arm in arm for their first day at secondary school, playing on the beach, dancing to Radio Forth in her bedroom. They were inseparable.

Tom realised there'd been a long silence. Looking at Sarah, an image of Shona as an adult formed in his mind. It was a shock. When he thought of his sister, he'd always seen her as a little girl. But she'd be an adult now, perhaps a wife and mother. His voice cracked, 'Sorry, it's been a bit strange coming back. And you're the first person who's mentioned Shona's name.'

'It was a long time ago and maybe people don't want to rake up painful memories.' Sarah hesitated. 'But I think of her all the time. I turned fifty last month and it does make you look back over the years. My most vivid memories are of the time with Shona.' She paused as Tom didn't reply. 'I'm sorry. Should we talk about something else?'

'No, please talk about Shona. I haven't even said her name for years. My mother avoided the subject – it was just too painful at the beginning and then it became taboo. Nobody else in South Africa had ever met her. I used to pretend I was an only child – it was just easier that way.'

Sarah raised her wide grey eyes and looked at him. 'Shona was such a lovely girl – the only real friend I ever had. I miss her so much.' Her lip trembled. 'Things were always so much fun with her. I was such a wimp back then and she was so daring! Nothing scared her, she'd talk to anyone, do the maddest things. It was always an adventure being with her.'

Tom felt a part of himself that had dried up through lack of use quivering into life; here was someone he could talk to, someone who had known Shona. Listening to Sarah, he could see his sister again in his mind's eye; so bright, so beautiful and so wild. In fact, he'd sometimes worried about her, because nothing seemed to scare her.

'Yes, she was always getting into scrapes – but she usually managed to put the blame on me.' Tom laughed as he remembered; Shona could get away with anything, but he often ended up with a slap round the head from his father. 'She could twist everyone round her little finger, especially my dad.'

Their eyes met. Sarah flushed slightly and lowered her eyes. Tom wanted to say much more, but not here. These were things too precious to be shouted above the superficial chatter in the room around them.

Sarah seemed to sense this and changed the subject. 'How are your mum and dad?'

Tom cleared his throat. 'Both gone. My father didn't last long after we went to South Africa. Never really settled… and he had a few problems.' He swallowed as he remembered how his father, who'd always liked a drink, had descended into full-blown alcoholism after they arrived in Plett. 'Mum died two months ago.'

He looked up. 'That's why I'm here, actually. In the hospice my Mum made me promise to scatter her ashes in Eriskay, the island where she was born. Do you remember Shona and I used to go back to the Outer Hebrides every summer?' He smiled, remembering those long sunny summers of freedom. 'I'm going up on Monday.'

'So you're going on Monday…' Sarah took a sip from her wine glass. 'Are you doing anything tomorrow? There's an open day at the school to celebrate the centenary. Would you like to come?'

'There are some things I should do tomorrow.' As he said this Tom wondered what they were. Sitting in the guesthouse or mooching around the shops? Looking at Sarah he realised he'd have the chance to talk to her again, and see more of Rory, too. He glanced round and saw him talking to Jennie from Singapore, who was dabbing her eyes with the corner of her table napkin.

Sarah leant forward. 'Please come. I've got to go because the group has bought a present for the sixth-form common room and Patsy has persuaded Rory to make some kind of dedication. They've built a new school on Duffy Park, but our old school on the prom is still used as an annexe, so you could see our old classrooms too.'

Before he could answer they were interrupted by Patsy's voice. 'Now don't all get too comfortable, because it's time for dessert. Last person seated has to pay for the drinks.'

There was a sudden good-natured rush of musical chairs and Tom found himself next to Jennie. Beneath the facelift he recognised her. Jennie Howie… An old schoolboy chant echoed in his memory. '*Jennie Howie – any way you likie.*' She was famous at school – lots of his pals had their first experience with her. He shuddered, remembering the last time they'd met, on that most terrible day.

'So you're Tom,' Jennie leaned forward, her eyes glistening. To his relief, Tom saw absolutely no hint of recognition in them. She held out her glass and indicated that he should fill it.

'You've come all the way from South Africa, have you? Are you by yourself?' Jennie's Scottish vowels were modulated by a mid-Atlantic twang. She brought her face close to his; Tom drew back from her stretched tanned skin and the high fly-away eyebrows and nodded.

'So am I. My so-called husband had to stay in Singapore.' Her head flopped forward and she put a bejewelled hand on his forearm. 'There's a woman. Half his age. She's only interested in his money. These Chinese girls may look very sweet, but they're crafty.'

Tom nodded, not knowing how to reply. Jennie gave a skeletal smile. 'So, Tom, we're both in Scotland on our own. We should spend some time together.'

Tom recoiled from the look of desperate need in Jennie's face. It reminded him of the weekday widows in Plett, the ones whose husbands flew up to Johannesburg to work during the week. Sometimes one would ask him to do some 'odd jobs' around the house, but when he arrived he realised this was just a pretext. He knew he was just another diversion when golf, bridge and lunch became tedious, but he usually just went along with it – it seemed easier that way. But there was no way he was going to say yes to Jennie.

Patsy's voice cut across his thoughts. 'Now, I told you I had a treat for you... and here it is.' She turned round with a flourish. 'It's our surprise guest and after-dinner speaker,

HJ Kidd, or, as you probably know him better, Captain Kidd! You'll remember him, as I do, as the most inspirational English teacher, but he's also a published poet and he's come along to talk to us tonight.'

There was a ripple of applause and a tall distinguished-looking man in a black polo-neck and corduroy jacket moved over to Patsy's table and smiled round the room. An older-looking woman with short grey hair and a comfortable soft face stood behind him. The room fell silent.

'I've been invited to a lot of school reunions over the years, but I've always resisted up to now. However, I've made an exception this evening for several reasons. Firstly, I have just retired and it does make one feel a little nostalgic and sentimental about the passing years. Looking back, I remember my early years of teaching, and your class was among my first. Also, my dear wife Hannah, who's here with me tonight, says she's tired of my sitting around the house. Finally – and this is the clincher – Patricia is very persuasive. There's no saying no to this lady.'

After a burst of laughter, HJ gave a witty speech, recalling some of the characters who had taught at the school in the seventies, the dragon of a head of English, who had treated him like a naughty schoolboy, the staffroom gossip. He then moved on to describe his retirement project, a poetry workshop to encourage aspiring young writers.

'Now, having a captive audience, I cannot resist the opportunity to read one of my poems from my latest slim volume, *Fragments*. It's called *The Seagull*.' He cleared his throat and held the book up to the light.

Above me
A lone seagull
Battling against the wind.
A single screech, primeval scream
Rips out my heart.
He is memory:
A flying fossil, harbinger of the past
Of our guilt and fears.
What lies buried in our collective consciousness?

Kidd finished with a dramatic pause. There was silence, followed by a smattering of puzzled applause. Tom felt a shiver run through him – the single screech, the primeval scream of memory and guilt. It touched something deep inside him. Looking over to Sarah he saw her sitting motionless, staring straight ahead. She felt it too.

Patsy's breezy voice brought him back to the present. 'Come on, now it's time to dance. I want to see everyone getting up, mind.' The lights dimmed and coloured strobe lights began to circle the ceiling. The Stones' 'I Can't Get No Satisfaction' creaked out from the speakers at the back of the room. A few couples stood up; Rory took Jennie's hand and led her to the dance floor.

Tom wished he could feel a little drunker. Around the room there was a kaleidoscope of images in the swirling lights: laughing groups, beer glasses raised, couples with their heads together, reliving memories. He made his way to the bar, looking around for Sarah on the way. When he saw her sitting by herself at a table in a dark corner, he fought his way through the scrum at the bar and asked her what she was drinking.

When he came back with her glass of white wine, Sarah was staring into the centre of the room. He followed her eyes and saw Rory supporting Jennie in the semblance of a dance. Sarah smiled. 'School reunions, eh? Don't you love 'em?' Her lip trembled. Turning to Tom, she asked, 'So where are you staying exactly?'

'In a guesthouse in Regent Street – absolute vintage boarding house kitsch. Do you still live in Portobello?'

'We've got a flat on Great King Street. We've been there since we got married, and I love it. It's near the centre so we can walk up to Princes Street and there are good local shops down in Stockbridge.'

Tom remembered that Great King Street was in the centre of Georgian New Town Edinburgh. 'I thought it was all lawyers' offices there.'

'There are a lot,' she smiled again. 'We're lucky to have one of the few flats.'

'And your mum and dad?' Tom remembered Sarah's father, a huge stern bear of a man, a lay preacher at the Free Presbyterian Church, and his tiny, well-groomed wife. They were an incongruous couple.

'My father died suddenly when I was nineteen, a heart attack. A real shock because he'd always seemed so healthy. Mum's still going strong, though. In fact, she's thrown herself into Edinburgh society and has a much more active social life than me. Widowhood really suits her.' Sarah gave an ironic smile.

'I'm sorry to hear about your dad. He terrified me, you know.'

'Me too, actually.' Sarah laughed, but Tom detected a tremor that made it sound strained.

Tom wanted to say more when a roar of laughter made them turn round. Rory was now surrounded by a group hanging on his every word. Jennie was slumped over the back of a chair beside him, her eyes fixed on him. 'Rory seems to have his fan club over there.'

'He just loves being the centre of attention.'

Tom was just about to reply when Patsy tapped him on the shoulder and dragged him onto the dance floor. Mud's 'Tiger Feet' blasted out from the tinny speakers while Tom attempted to follow the triangular moves, wondering how quickly he could make his escape. He looked through the dancing couples to where Sarah was sitting. Her chair was empty.

To his surprise tears pricked the back of his eyes. Being back in Portobello, seeing Sarah, imagining what Shona would be like now... Together with the beer and the music he was transported back to his sixteen-year-old self. And Sarah had gone without saying goodbye.

The music came to an end and Tom disentangled himself from Patsy. He looked around for Sarah in the shadows cast by the flashing coloured lights, but he couldn't see her. Without her there was no reason to stay, so he decided to slip quietly away back to the guesthouse.

He became aware of a presence next to him. Sarah. 'I'm going now, but I just wanted to remind you to be at the new school at two tomorrow. There'll be a group of us, and Captain Kidd may be there, too.'

'I'll be there. It'll be interesting to see the old place.' He wanted to see Sarah again, even if it meant having to endure a trip round the school. He raised his hand to stifle a yawn. 'I'm going to leave now too. Been a long day.'

'I can give you a lift.'

Tom protested that Regent Street was only a short walk away, but Sarah took his hand and led him to where Patsy was standing with one of the bar-crowd's arm round her shoulders, his hand wandering close to her cleavage.

'You can't go yet!' yelped Patsy. 'We've got a late license until one.' She looked around the room. 'And where's Rory?'

'He's gone. He had to take Jennie back to her hotel. She was a bit upset.'

Patsy shot Sarah a doubtful look. 'Well, don't be late tomorrow. Remember Rory's making the speech and I've phoned the *Evening News*. I hope they'll send a photographer down.'

Sarah kissed her on the cheek and promised they'd be on time. Tom extricated himself from Patsy's enthusiastic embrace and followed Sarah into the car park.

After the embarrassingly short drive to the guesthouse, Tom hesitated. He didn't want to get out of the car. Putting his hand on the door handle he said, 'I'll see you tomorrow – but I haven't contributed anything to this presentation.'

'Don't worry. We put in plenty. Apparently the budget doesn't cover things like a coffee machine and water-cooler – that's what the students said they wanted. Of course, Rory's intrigued by the water-cooler effect; hopes they'll all stand round talking about him.'

She laughed and turned towards Tom. Their eyes met. Sarah leant forward and her lips brushed his. 'Goodnight, Tom. See you tomorrow.'

The softness of her mouth and the touch of her hair made Tom feel almost paralysed. He didn't want to go, to say goodbye. But he had to. He opened the car door and quickly stepped out. Standing at the edge of the pavement, he watched the lights of her car disappear round the corner into the High Street, his lips tingling with the memory of her kiss.

PART 2

The blurred outline of the classroom comes into focus. Mr Kidd stands book in hand, a shaft of pale morning sunlight capturing him in its spotlight, dark hair curling to his shoulders, academic gown slung over his velvet jacket... the very image of a poet.

He's reading a poem about Florence, the Ponte Vecchio at twilight, with swallows catching insects in the gathering dusk. He describes their path with his slender fingers and I see, with him, the swallows weaving in the air, sewing the shadows together.

A knock at the door. The burly figure of the headmaster enters, whispers to Kidd, their heads close together. They both turn in my direction. I touch the empty seat beside me and hear the name, Shona McIver. Through the doorway I see the dark shape of a policeman and everything swims in front of me.

CHAPTER 3

Sarah sat bolt upright in bed. In the half-world between waking and sleeping she was back in her old classroom, every detail in heightened definition. She shivered; she hadn't thought about that day for years. The school reunion, and seeing Captain Kidd and Tom had triggered the memory. She reached over to Rory's side of the bed. It was empty. She rolled over, trying to blank the classroom from her mind. Shona had been gone for so long but the memories still came unexpectedly, sometimes like a video from the past, sometimes distorted dreams, but she was always there.

The phone rang. Reaching for it, Sarah saw the morning sunshine through the cracks in the shutters.

'Hiya!' It was Patsy's chirpy voice. 'How are you? Wasn't it great last night? Is Rory there?'

'Hi, Patsy. He's just popped out. Can I give him a message?'

'I wanted to tell him the Head Girl is going to be at the school to accept the presentation, and the photographer from the *Evening News* is coming at 2.30.'

'I'll let him know – and we'll be there. We're meeting at the front door at two, aren't we?'

'That's right. Don't be late. See you soon. Take care.'

Sarah rubbed her eyes and went through to the kitchen. Sultan strolled over, his tail erect, and rubbed his sleek black fur on her legs, hungry as always. She fed him, made a coffee and sat down at the long wooden kitchen table, holding the cup in two hands. No word from Rory, not that she was surprised. He would turn up for the presentation at the school because he loved any kind of publicity, but he'd probably arrive at the last minute as usual.

She paced the kitchen, impatient to set off. She'd see Tom again at the school. She thought of his face, so like Shona's, with light brown eyes and a wide full-lipped mouth. She wanted to see him again, get to know him better, share more memories of Shona. How could she see more of him before he disappeared off to the Outer Hebrides?

She had an idea – Sunday lunch. Her mother and the twins always came and what could be more natural than inviting Rory's old friend? Pleased to have a plan, she picked up her car keys and looked around for a scrap of paper to leave Rory a note. *Gone to the school. Photographer coming at 2.30. Don't be late.*

He'd get a taxi. Rory had never driven since the day he knocked down an old man after a long drinking session in the Buckie Bar. The old guy survived, but was on the critical list for several days. Now it was just another facet of Rory Dunbar's public persona, always taking taxis. 'Don't ask a man to drink and drive', he loved to say.

*

Tom opened his eyes. A momentary feeling of disorientation. Where was he? He saw the floral wallpaper and counterpane and then remembered – Portobello, the Regent Guest House. He rubbed his eyes. There was the tour of the school today, which really didn't interest him, but it was a good excuse to see Sarah and Rory again.

He looked at his watch. He'd missed his full Scottish breakfast but wondered if he could at least get a cup of coffee. His must be the only guest house in Scotland without tea-making facilities. The sound of a hoover downstairs told him Mrs Ritchie must be around.

He showered and got some crumpled but clean clothes from his case. The vacuum cleaner stopped, but the sound of the television came from a room at the bottom of the stairs. The door was ajar so he tapped gently. It swung open and he saw Mrs Ritchie, an overall tied round her ample figure, standing in front of the screen.

'Oh, Mr McIver, it's yourself. You've missed your breakfast.'

'I'm sorry, late night. Any chance of a cup of coffee?' Tom attempted a winning smile.

Mrs Ritchie turned back to the television. 'I'll just watch the end of my programme and then I'll see what I can do.'

Tom looked at the screen and recognised Rory's show. The landlady turned and smiled, her eyes shining. 'Yon Rory Dunbar, he's my favourite. I taped it because I was at the bingo last night. Cannae miss his programme. He's from here, from Porty, you ken.'

Tom nodded. 'Yes, I was at school with him and, in fact, I saw him last night.'

'You know Rory Dunbar? Could you no get me his autograph?' Mrs Ritchie smoothed her pinny. 'It's too late for a full fry-up but I can give you a wee cup of coffee and some toast.'

*

Twenty minutes later Sarah parked on the wide street outside the grey stone façade of the Regent Guest House, willing Tom to come out. She was about to knock at the door when it opened and Tom stood there, tall and lean in a navy-blue Helly Hansen jacket.

'Thanks for coming, Sarah. I'm not exactly sure where the new school is.'

Sarah drove the short distance, chattering about the school, inviting him to Sunday lunch, very aware of Tom's presence next to her. She knew she was talking too much, but he smiled at her and said he'd be delighted to come to lunch.

As they drove into the car park in front of the modern school building, Patsy came running over. 'Sarah, thank goodness, you're here.' She stopped abruptly and Sarah could see the disappointment on her face when she realised who was in the car. 'Where's Rory?'

'He's coming here directly. Isn't he here yet? I just went to pick Tom up because he's never been to the new school.'

'The photographer's going to be here any minute and the Head Girl is waiting.'

Sarah was just about to say something conciliatory when a taxi drew into the car park and Rory leapt out. Patsy rushed towards him. 'Rory, everything's ready. So glad you're here.'

'Wouldn't miss it for the world, Patsy my love. You've done such a great job organising all this.'

'I've got an engraved plaque for the machines. '*Presented to the Senior Common Room on the occasion of the school centenary by the Class of 1977*'. Because that's the year most of us left.'

'Nice touch, Patsy.' Rory put his arm round her narrow

shoulders and they walked towards the entrance to the school, where a small group of revellers from the night before was gathered.

Sarah walked behind with Tom. Rory hadn't even acknowledged her presence, but she was used to that. Hearing footsteps behind her, she looked round and saw a crumpled-looking figure in his forties, with a camera round his neck and a cigarette hanging from his mouth, walking across the car park.

Rory's face broke into a wide grin. 'Archie, you old reprobate. What are you doing here?' He punched the reporter on the shoulder. 'No exciting crimes for you to chase?'

Archie's drooping eyes glinted. 'Bit quiet on the murder front today. Saw this request for a story, starring my old mate Dunbar, so thought I'd have a little trip down to Porty and get a bit of sea air.'

'Which you're polluting with your smelly fags. Don't you read the government health warnings?'

'Nonsense, they're good for you. Clear the tubes.'

Patsy pushed between them and stood on her tip-toes. 'Hello, I'm Patricia Mills, I contacted you.'

Archie and Rory exchanged looks over her head. Rory gave a mock bow. 'Patsy, my apologies. Allow me to introduce the one and only Archie Kilbride, senior reporter at *Scotsman Publications*. We are honoured indeed.'

Patsy simpered. 'Thanks for coming, Mr Kilbride. If we just go upstairs to the Senior Common Room, Rory can give the presentation and let you get away.'

The ceremony passed quickly. Rory gave a speech about water being good for the brain and coffee keeping students awake. The Head Girl smiled appreciatively and thanked him on behalf of all the seniors, and Archie Kilbride took a photo with Rory drinking a symbolic plastic cup of water in front of the shining apparatus, his arm loosely round the Head Girl's shoulders.

Afterwards, while Rory was surrounded by a group of school girls armed with pens and autograph books, Sarah saw Archie draw Patsy to one side; Patsy flushed with pleasure as she chattered to him, turning round and pointing in the direction of the old students.

They were still talking when Captain Kidd hurried up the stairs, followed by his wife Hannah; Patsy indicated him with a nudge of her shoulder and whispered something to Archie, before tottering off to greet her old teacher. Archie looked at Kidd carefully, nodded his head and then ambled over to Rory, who looked up from his autographing session as Archie approached.

'I'll be off now, Rory, my old son. But we must have a chat very soon. Come and see me in my office – aka the Cafe Royal – Monday lunchtime?' Archie raised his eyebrows, looking for assent. Rory nodded, before turning back to the group of excited girls.

Archie took a cigarette out of the packet. 'Better not hang around here too long or they'll think I enjoy this kind of work. See you!' And with a brief wave he shambled towards the stairs, his cigarette hanging out of his mouth and his lighter poised in his hand.

Captain Kidd greeted the group of old pupils. He was wearing the same corduroy jacket as the night before, with a pale blue shirt that picked up the bright blue of his eyes. His hair was still thick and black, shot through with strands of grey and worn a little longer than was normal. Sarah had to admit he was still a most attractive man.

The Head Girl obviously thought so. She beamed in his direction. 'Mr Kidd, how wonderful that you've come. We really miss you at the school. English just isn't the same without you!'

'I just had to come and see you – and look around the school with this group of reprobates. They were my first ever class.'

Patsy clapped her hands. 'Super. Thanks so much, HJ, for coming along.'

'You're a very hard lady to refuse, Patricia. Now I'm going to show you the new library and the English block, and then we'll go down to the old school and relive our misspent youth.'

Sarah followed as HJ Kidd, Patsy and Rory led the group along the shiny new corridors, smelling of plaster and cleaning fluid, past classrooms where teachers gave demonstration lessons. Sarah brought up the rear with Tom, not talking but conscious of his every movement next to her.

After about twenty minutes, HJ suggested walking down to the old school. Sarah had walked past the building several times, but had never been inside since she left it so many years before. She felt a shiver, and looking at Tom, noticed his jaw clenching.

In through the heavy wooden doors. The dark wood and uneven maroon tiles of the entrance hall. The double stairs leading up to the first floor. The smell of history, dust and decay. HJ was talking about how much he loved the old building, but his voice seemed to recede into the distance as Sarah was swept back forty years.

35

He opened the door of room 23, his old classroom, like something out of the nineteenth century, with fixed desks stepped up to the back of the classroom. Smelling the familiar mix of wood and polish, chalk and dust, Sarah was transported back to the day Shona disappeared, seeing the young Captain Kidd caught in the sunlight shining through the high ecclesiastical windows. The walls began to blur and sway.

She would have fallen if Tom hadn't caught her, and she allowed herself to be led outside. She sat on the sea wall, gulping in the salty air. HJ Kidd stood over her, his face full of concern. 'Sarah, my apologies, that was thoughtless of me. I'm sorry. Please come and have a cup of tea at my house – it's just five minutes away. Tom and Rory, please come too.'

The rest of the group started to melt away, muttering farewells, but Patsy hovered anxiously. When HJ grasped her hand and asked her if she'd like to come too, she bobbed up and down with relieved excitement.

Hannah appeared at HJ's side and the small group walked slowly along the prom towards his imposing grey-stone house on the edge of Abercorn Park. As they walked up the short garden path, the heavy smell of the old rose bushes triggered something in Sarah's memory. The wide front door with the brass step leading into the mosaic lobby, the inner door with the stained-glass window – it all seemed so familiar. Had she been there before, or to another similar house?

A memory floated in her mind, like a half-remembered dream. Then it came to her: the After School Writing Club. Captain Kidd had organised this for pupils in the junior classes interested in creative writing. Lots of the girls in her class had gone along, because it was given by their handsome young teacher. And sometimes they'd come to his house. She'd been here before.

As they went into the large drawing room on the left, the feeling of familiarity intensified; she recognised the large piano, the Chinese silk carpet, occasional tables and chairs with antique bowed legs.

HJ moved to the mahogany inlaid drinks cabinet. 'Brandy, Sarah?' She shook her head, but he poured a glass anyway. Patsy held out her hand too. 'Tom, Rory, would you rather have whisky? I'm having one.' They nodded and he poured out generous measures as Hannah appeared at his elbow with ice and a small crystal glass jug of water on a silver tray.

'I hope you're feeling better now, Sarah? Tom? I can understand that the visit to the school brought back unsettling memories for both of you.' He raised his glass. 'In memory of Shona. A delightful girl, whose life full of promise was cut tragically short.'

Everyone raised their glasses, but the toast was interrupted by the sound of the doorbell. Glancing out of the bay window, Sarah was surprised to see the journalist from the school, still with his camera slung round his neck. Captain Kidd went into the hall and, after a whispered conversation, ushered him in.

HJ Kidd looked pale. He looked around the room and said, 'This journalist has got something rather shocking he wants to tell us. I think we should hear him out as it concerns all of us.'

All eyes were on Archie, who cleared his throat noisily. 'I'm sorry to burst in on your gathering like this, but seeing you all together seemed so incredibly opportune I just had to seize the chance. I've got something I think you all should hear.' Sarah sensed a warning in his voice. 'This isn't common knowledge yet, but it's going to break soon and I think it's better you hear it from me, rather than reading it in the newspaper.' The room was silent as all eyes were fixed on the journalist.

'Logan Baird is going to be released from Carstairs in the next few days.'

There was a collective intake of breath. Sarah felt numb with shock. Logan Baird, the monster who'd killed Shona, was going to be set free? HJ Kidd was the first to find his voice. 'But we were told that he'd never be released. He's criminally insane.'

Archie shook his head, 'There's no doubt that he's completely loony tunes. He's one of the longest-serving prisoners in Scotland and most people think he should stay locked up until he rots.' He cleared his throat. 'But new information has come to light which makes his original conviction unsafe. He's always insisted he wasn't responsible for Shona's death, but nobody was interested in his case until some holy Joe started visiting him and persuaded the police to review his case.'

Nobody spoke, everyone's attention fixed on Archie. Sarah realised she was holding her breath, afraid of what was coming next. 'I've been tipped off by a mate in the SCCRC that they've uncovered evidence which proves beyond doubt that Baird couldn't possibly be the killer.'

There was a stunned silence, until it was broken by Patsy's shrill voice. 'The SCCRC? What's that?'

'The Scottish Criminal Cases Review Commission. They

look at cold cases where a miscarriage of justice is suspected. Apparently Baird's lawyers are going to appeal against the sentence, based on their findings. The Appeal Court won't sit until next year but they're going for interim liberation, pending the appeal.'

Sarah couldn't believe what she was hearing. The one comfort they'd all had was that Shona's killer had been found quickly and imprisoned for life. 'But he confessed.'

'He did, but that was after eleven hours of questioning, and he withdrew his confession afterwards. I'd never put this in print, but to me it seems obvious that he was fitted up by the police. They had to find a suspect – the case involved the rape and murder of a teenage girl, the press was baying for an arrest – so they picked up the local weirdo and leant on him until he'd say anything to get out.'

'But they had other evidence as well,' Kidd's face had gone from pale to flushed.

'Apparently that's what it all hinges on. His blood group matched semen found on the cardigan,' the journalist paused as Sarah sat down heavily on the Chesterfield and buried her face in her hands. She remembered that pink cardigan so well; she could see it flapping as Shona ran away. She heard Archie's voice as if in the distance. 'But, to put it briefly, modern DNA techniques have shown that it couldn't possibly be his.'

Sarah looked over towards Tom. He hadn't said a word since Archie came in. He was staring at Archie as the journalist continued. 'This is going to be a big story: Scotland's longest-serving prisoner to be released. The police are trying to bury it – it doesn't exactly show them in a good light at a time when confidence in the force is at an all-time low – but there will have to be a statement when Baird is released and I'm going to be ready with my story then. I'll be able to do an insight piece, maybe even a book. And I was hoping I might be able to get some input from you, people who knew Shona.'

'So you thought you'd come sneaking in here to get our stories? Well, you'll get nothing from me.' Tom stepped forward, his eyes blazing with fury.

Archie raised his hands in surrender. 'Peace. I just came down to Portobello to get a few background photos and a bit of local colour. I thought the school presentation would make a good cover so none of the other papers could get a whiff of the story. It was only when Patsy so kindly identified you all that I realised that most of the surviving big players were fortuitously all gathered together.'

Patsy went scarlet. 'You only asked me if there was anyone who might have known Shona! I was just trying to be helpful. You didn't tell me that monster was being released.'

Tom looked straight at Archie. 'I remember the press at that time, always on the doorstep, tricking photos out of schoolfriends… the lurid, lying articles and the sackfulls of mail that followed. All those letters to my parents saying they didn't deserve to have a daughter, if they couldn't look after her. Spiteful, illiterate rants saying we should have watched over her better. That was the last straw, the thing that drove my parents to South Africa. I won't give you anything.'

Archie nodded, 'I can understand that this is a shock for you. Journalists can be a slimy bunch, but I like to think that I've still got some integrity. I tried to trace your family, Tom, but I'd got nowhere so I don't think any of the other papers will be able to find you as long as we all keep quiet.' He glanced towards Patsy. 'If you grant me an exclusive for my book, I'll keep you out of the story now.'

Sarah looked up, her cheeks wet with tears. 'That isn't the worst thing. The question is: if Logan Baird didn't kill Shona, who did?'

CHAPTER 4

They left Captain Kidd's house in silence. Rory slung his arm round Tom's shoulder. 'I think we need a drink. Tom, come to Paddy's Bar. Remember he was the only one who'd serve us when we were sixteen?'

'No, Rory, I've had enough. I need to go back to the B&B.'

Rory threw his hands up in mock horror, 'What for? You're not going to sit around by yourself this evening, brooding over the past, are you? We haven't had a real chance to talk. We've got lots to catch up on after the last forty years. Come on!'

Tom hesitated. It was true it would be better to be with people tonight. He nodded towards Rory and fell into step beside Sarah. She moved her head close to his. 'Remember lunch tomorrow, 1.30 at 95 Great King Street. Please come.'

Tom's step faltered. 'Aren't you coming to the pub?'

Sarah indicated Rory, striding ahead. 'Not invited.'

Patsy pulled her arm. 'Come for a drink in the Wine Bar with me.'

Sarah shook her head, 'No, Patsy, I'm going home. I've got things to do – six people for lunch tomorrow.'

Patsy's face fell and she looked hopefully towards Rory. Ignoring her, he took Tom by the arm and led him away. Tom followed him, but looking back he saw Sarah's eyes fixed on him.

Paddy's Bar hadn't changed much over the years. The darts board had gone and had been replaced by a huge television screen showing a football match from Sky Sports. There was a small group of locals sitting in front of it, eyes glued to the screen, clutching their pints. Paddy, who used to serve anyone who had the money to buy a pint, had long gone. Behind the bar was an attractive girl with high Slavic cheekbones and a tight top. She poured the pints and dispensed the whisky chasers with an air of disdain.

Rory and Tom sat down at a dimpled copper-topped table at the back of the bar. Tom was relieved that Rory didn't mention Logan Baird straight away – he needed some time for the enormity of Archie's bombshell to sink in.

Rory started reminiscing about the old days and Tom felt himself falling into the easy friendship of their teenage years. They talked about football, teachers, the scrapes they'd got into.

'Do you remember the day we set fire to the Fun Palace?' Rory laughed.

Tom winced. That was another thing he'd attempted to blank from his memory. At first it was only a small bonfire behind the run-down amusement arcade on a frosty evening. But a winter wind had sprung up and the fire had quickly spread to the peeling wooden fence. They'd tried to beat the flames out with their jackets, but the fire spread inside the amusement park and when it reached the rides some oil or gas exploded.

'God, it was like a firework display!' Rory's eyes sparkled at the memory.

Tom relived the horror. The whole complex had caught fire, flames and sparks floating high into the night sky. As

43

the fire engines arrived, Rory and Tom had fled to a nearby street and cowered in the darkness, watching with awful fascination as the firefighters raised their ladders and tried to drench the blaze.

'I was shaking in my boots for the next few days,' said Tom. 'Every time the door bell rang I thought it was the police coming to get me.' Amazingly, the dreaded knock at the door had never come, although it had been the hot topic of conversation on every street corner for weeks, and the smell of the charred wood was a constant reminder of what they'd done. How fortunate they were that the Fun Palace was so badly run and dangerous that the firemen had put it down to an electrical fault without deeper investigation. Nobody had been hurt, thank God, and once the site was bulldozed and new flats built, the fire was soon forgotten.

'We were lucky, damn lucky,' Rory slurred slightly. 'If we'd been caught we'd have been marked men, given a police record, sent to Young Offenders, started on the slippery slope to crime.'

Tom was cautious. 'We shouldn't even talk about it. I've never mentioned it to anyone. Couldn't we still be charged now if they found out about it?'

'Nah, there's statute of limitations or something. You can't be done for old crimes. I think we've got away with it, Tommy boy.'

There was a cheer from the football-watchers and they both looked up at the large screen as the goal was replayed. Emboldened by the pints he'd drunk, Tom changed the subject. 'Sarah's a lovely girl.'

'She is.' Rory leant forward. 'She's my rock. A clichéd

expression but true. A real earth-mother and I know she'll always stay with me.'

Tom felt a wave of annoyance. Here was Rory married to this beautiful, empathetic woman and was that the best he could say? Suppressing his anger, he carried on. He wanted to talk about Sarah and find out more about her. 'You know she was Shona's best friend? They were always together until…'

'Yes, she said that to me when we first met, but I couldn't remember her from school at all. She can't have been very noticeable then. But she was certainly noticeable when we met at the *Scotsman* offices.'

'When was that?'

'She must have been about twenty. Gorgeous-looking girl. Tall, slender, those long legs, long dark hair. Irresistible. You know, the cool exterior and the fire beneath. And what was really attractive was that she was totally unaware of how beautiful she was.' Rory paused and took another gulp of beer. 'She's put on a bit of weight since then, of course.'

Tom felt another surge of anger. 'Still very good-looking, though.' Did Rory not appreciate what he had? 'Did you get married soon after that?'

'Well, not that soon. I was already married when we met, of course.'

Tom looked up, astonished.

'Didn't you know? It must all have happened after you left. You remember Babs Barrowfield, the Drama teacher?'

Tom did remember her. She had caused quite a stir when she'd arrived at the school, small and vivacious, with dramatic curves and only a few years older than them. Drama Studies and school plays had suddenly become very popular.

'She used to invite some of us older students to her flat and she certainly taught me a few things that weren't on the school curriculum. It would probably just have been one of those rite of passage things, but then she fell pregnant.'

Tom felt his jaw drop.

'She said she was going to have the child adopted but I persuaded her to marry me. I was still at school, but I was nearly eighteen and it was Captain Kidd who really helped me then, encouraged me to go to university, helped me get a scholarship. Just one of the reasons that I think he's such a great bloke.'

Tom was still digesting the shock information about Rory's first marriage. 'So you have an older child? Not just the twins?'

'Yes, Abigail. She's in her thirties now. Babs wasn't keen on me seeing her when she was young, but we re-established contact when she was older.' Rory stared reflectively into his pint. 'Always saw Babs though. A very temperamental woman. Spiteful in many ways, but very passionate.' He drained his drink, before standing up and walking carefully to the bar. He leant over it as he ordered the drinks and even the ice maiden seemed to be thawing under the influence of his charm. She smiled as she pulled a couple more pints. Rory brought them back to the table.

Tom looked at the pint. 'I really shouldn't have any more.'

'Come on. We've got forty years drinking to catch up on. And you never said no to a drink in those days.'

'Forbidden fruit when we were sixteen. Made it more exciting. But I saw the way drink affected my dad...'

'Aye, your dad could really put them away. I saw him

46

really steaming several nights. In fact, I saw him that night.' Rory put his glass down and looked directly at Tom. 'He was in the park the night your sister disappeared. He was in a right state.'

'He was out looking for Shona. He was upset, we all were!'

'No, this was earlier.'

Tom sipped his pint and realised that Rory was much drunker than he was.

'I was in the park, looking for you. Remember, we were supposed to meet up. Where were you?'

Tom blushed beneath his tan. He thought he'd got it made when Jennie Howie agreed to meet him that night. They'd met at the other end of the prom by the bandstand but... even after nearly forty years he cringed at the memory. It had all gone so well at first. She'd let him feel inside her bra and had guided his hand under her skirt. He'd felt inside her lace-trimmed panties, the warm moistness. All the anticipation, the whispered boasts of his friends – he was going to join the club, going to be a man.

Then the excitement had peaked and he'd felt the dampness in his jeans. He tried to carry on, but the moment had passed. Jennie had pulled up her knickers in scorn, snapped that he was no use to her and stamped off into the night, leaving him feeling humiliated, frustrated and uncomfortable.

But the worst thing was, after he'd slunk home, his mother had asked where Shona was. She'd asked him to keep an eye out for his sister, but he hadn't been there when she needed him and... he'd never seen her again.

Rory was persistent. 'Where were you? Were you with a lassie?'

Tom tried to steer the conversation away from all that. 'You saw my dad that night in the park, but you testified you'd seen Logan Baird there?'

Rory slumped towards him, still with his boyish charm, but slurring his words. 'Well, Tommy, I was in the park looking for *you*. There were quite a few people around. I definitely saw your dad and Captain Kidd. And I think I saw Logan Baird, hanging about in the trees. When the police came round and asked if I'd seen him I told them I had.' He shrugged his shoulders. 'I knew other people had said they'd seen him – there were even some lassies who said he'd exposed himself to them. I didn't go as far as that but I did beef it up a bit.'

He knocked his whisky back and looked at Tom again. 'I remember now! You were trying your luck with Jennie Howie. But where-y, when-y and howie exactly we don't know-y!' He laughed uproariously at his own joke. 'She was a generous girl in those days, all right. Still is, mind you, but her head's a mess.' He took another slurp of beer and wiped the foam from his mouth. 'Last night was miserable. I took her back to her hotel room. She could hardly stand. And then she just lay on her bed and lifted up her skirt. Begged me to shag her. I just didn't have the heart to say no. I just had to stop her crying. She's suffered so many knock-backs.'

Tom stared at Rory. 'But you're married to Sarah!'

'Ah, Tommy boy, I am. But there are so many women out there, vulnerable, lonely women. They throw themselves at me. It would be ungentlemanly to refuse. I don't want to hurt their feelings. You must know that, being a wild young bachelor, as you are.'

'Well, hardly.' Tom didn't know what to say. Rory had

been a womaniser when they were young; it was easy for him because he was so good-looking. He'd always had an eye for the girls – in fact, Tom remembered the time he'd punched Rory in the nose when he'd leered at Shona in her shorts, saying she was a wee cracker and was going to be a goer in a few years' time. He'd been furious that day.

Rory leant forward and waved his hand in Tom's face. 'Just grab your opportunities. There are so many of them, especially in my business. Like that Mara O'Callaghan the other night. A bit of sympathy and she went like a rabbit.' He caught sight of Tom's shocked expression. 'Don't feel bad, Tommy boy. It's just part of the job.' He gave his mock-rueful little boy smile.

Did Sarah know what Rory was like? She seemed so composed and in control. Tom didn't trust himself to say much. 'Your job must be very exciting.'

Rory shrugged. 'It's getting boring, always the same interviews. People coming on to push their new film or book. I need a new challenge. I'm looking out for something new, something real, meaningful journalism.'

A cheer from the football crowd signified another goal. Tom took the opportunity to stand up. 'I'd better be going but I'll see you tomorrow anyway. Sarah has invited me to lunch.'

Rory groaned. 'Oh God, the famous Sunday lunch. Her mother will be there, and the twins too – but they usually push off as soon as they can. The food'll be good, but don't say you haven't been warned about the conversation. Her mother talks all the time – can't listen, not that she ever did, mind.'

Tom stood up and pulled on his jacket. As they went out

into the crisp night air, the moon hung heavy over the water of the bay. Rory pointed to the sky, 'Nearly full moon – still romantic. And I know you won't say anything to Sarah, will you? It would only hurt her.'

The diesel whirr of a taxi saved Tom from having to reply. Rory leapt out into the street, hailing it. 'There's my Joe Baxi. I'm away off home, Tommy boy. You must be a good influence on me.'

The taxi driver switched off the yellow sign and Tom was left standing in the road, watching it rolling away into the night, the image of Sarah's face imprinted on his brain.

PART 3

The room is airless, silent except for the tick of the clock. The heavy curtains are drawn, the weak ceiling light sending shadows across the gloom of the best front room.

My father looms over me, thick steely hair combed severely back from his heavy face, deep-set eyes boring into me. His meaty fist is on the Bible. I'm sitting on the edge of a hard chair, my hands clutching the table through the harsh cut velvet of the tablecloth.

'This was the work of the devil.' His voice booms harsh and resonant. 'You will leave that school. You will bring no one to this house. You will go to the homes of no other pupils. You will not go out in the evenings. You will work at school and do the Lord's Will.'

Sarah's eyes opened. She was in bed with her husband beside her. Although her father had been dead for more than thirty years, his voice rang through the darkness of the bedroom and his eyes looked down on her, condemning her. She sunk her head in the pillow, trying to bury the shame and guilt she still felt so keenly.

CHAPTER 5

Sarah busied herself in the kitchen, peeling potatoes and preparing the Sunday roast. Rory had got up and left early, and she had a few hours before her mother and the twins arrived. And Tom, too. She smiled despite herself, but then shuddered – thinking of him brought back the memory of Shona and that awful night. Should she have followed her? Could she have done anything to save her?

She'd waited in the park for what seemed like hours, until the air turned cold and the last rays of evening light disappeared. Walking home slowly, she'd looked round every time she heard footsteps, hoping they were Shona's. Her friend running off had made her feel angry at first, but as the darkness fell she started to feel scared. Shona had never left her alone before.

By the black front door of their granite house next to the Free Presbyterian Church, she'd hesitated. She'd be in trouble; she was not supposed to stay out after dark.

Her mother was waiting at the door, crying. Her father had gone out looking for her. Sarah became even more frightened. Her distant, silent father always had an air of barely-suppressed anger, but when this broke through, he could be terrifying.

When he'd come back, he was trembling, angrier than she'd ever seen him before, his stern face dark with rage and his deep-set eyes red-rimmed. She'd been only too glad to retreat to the sanctuary of her bedroom. As she lay quaking in bed, the phone rang. Her father didn't like people phoning the house at an hour he considered 'unsuitable' and had answered sharply: 'Yes, Sarah is at home. No, nothing at all,' and replaced the handset firmly. Sarah was sure it was Mrs McIver. Did that mean that Shona hadn't gone home?

Sarah hadn't slept well that night.

She basted the meat and went through to lay the table in the high Georgian dining room, going through the comforting ritual of making the table beautiful, laying the cutlery, polishing the glasses, folding the napkins and arranging the freesias as a centrepiece. She must concentrate on today, making it a lovely day for her family, and for Tom. She smiled, despite herself.

*

Tom woke up with a start and looked at his watch.

12.20.

With the long journey, the beers, and the emotional whirl of the last two days, he must have slept for nearly twelve hours. He heard Sarah's voice in his memory: *'Lunch 1.30 at 95 Great King Street'*.

He showered and dressed quickly, and hurried down the stairs.

'You've missed your breakfast again, Mr McIver.' Mrs Ritchie stood at the door of her sitting room in her good Sunday coat.

'Sorry, got to rush.' Tom ran out into the quiet Sunday street, his landlady's voice ringing in his ears, still reminding him about Rory Dunbar's autograph.

Up at the High Street, he remembered the 26 bus used to go up to the centre of town. Checking at the bus stop, he saw it still ran. So many things were just as he remembered them. The long gardens leading up to the solid Victorian houses, the cracked pavements, the trees overhanging the grey stone walls; the familiarity washed over him with a strength that hurt almost physically. He willed the bus to arrive.

When it did come, he went upstairs to his old favourite seat at the front. As the bus made its way slowly through the centre of Portobello, he saw that there were changes; the power station and the open air pool had disappeared, and the old Fun Palace area was now replaced by regular rows of neat housing. He winced again remembering the fire – but it was better really that it had been razed to the ground. It had been an awful place. He remembered trying to keep Shona away from the amusement park, which was filled with Elvis look-alikes hanging on the back of the dodgems, and shifty-looking men bent over the slot machines. She ignored him, of course; she always thought she knew best.

As the bus approached the centre of Edinburgh, he saw the massive hulk of the castle rising above Princes Street Gardens and the timeless silhouette of the churches and high buildings stretching along the Royal Mile. Getting off in George Street, he was surprised to see the crowds of shoppers. Sundays were obviously very different from when he was young.

He had the feeling Great King Street was in the lower section of the New Town, so he set off down Frederick Street. When he saw the Forth glittering in the distance, and the huge outline of St Vincent's Church at the foot of the hill, it all came back to him, and he was soon turning into the wide cobblestones of Great King Street on his right.

Number 95 was the large grey-stone building on the corner, with wide stone steps leading up to a black door with an arched Georgian fanlight above. He saw DUNBAR on the top brass plate and, after a moment's hesitation, pushed the buzzer. The door creaked open without any questions from the entry system and he climbed the worn stone steps to the top floor.

The door was open and Sarah stood waiting, silhouetted against the light from the hall. Her dark hair framed her face and the soft heather-coloured pullover moulded beautifully to her body. She reached out her hand and kissed his cheek. A soft breath of perfume. Tom felt aware of his heart thumping, his movements awkward. He regretted being so late and the lack of a bottle of wine or a bunch of flowers.

'I'm so glad you found it. Come in, you're just in time.' Sarah leant forward and whispered in his ear. 'Don't say anything about Logan Baird, please. Just keep smiling.'

She led him into the dining room where a long table was set for six. Nearest to him was a smartly-dressed lady in her seventies. Her thin white hair was elaborately styled into a candyfloss halo and her face was carefully made up, with rouged cheeks and arched pencilled eyebrows.

'Mum, this is Tom McIver. He was at school with Rory. He's just over from South Africa. Tom, this is my mother, Flora Campbell.' The old lady looked carefully at Tom and extended her bony hand.

'You've certainly travelled a long way. What do you do in South Africa?' Tom muttered his stock answer about odd jobs here and there and the old lady visibly lost interest. 'Rory isn't here, you know. Working again. He has to work so hard. He's on television, you know? Meets all kinds of interesting people.'

Tom nodded and Sarah led him round the table to an attractive, dark eyed young man with floppy brown hair. 'This is Nick.'

'Nice to meet you.' His smile and charm made him very much his father's son.

Next to him sat his sister Lottie, similar but somehow less attractive. Her long brown hair shone, reflecting the light, swinging like a curtain when she moved. Definitely her best feature, thought Tom, like a shampoo advert. Her boyfriend Liam, blond with pale lashes and eyebrows, held her hand under the table. Rory was nowhere to be seen.

As Sarah began to serve the traditional Sunday lunch Mrs Campbell fixed her gaze on Tom again. 'Why are you here?'

Tom started to explain about going to the Western Isles to scatter his mother's ashes, but she interrupted him. 'I mean, why are you here today? Rory isn't here.'

Tom didn't know what to say. He wondered himself. Sarah hesitated and then said carefully. 'Tom is Shona McIver's brother.'

The old lady looked blank at first, but then leant towards him and tapped his forearm. 'Shona McIver, yes, I remember – dreadful business. Most upsetting at the time. But it's a long time ago now and life goes on.'

Nick raised his eyebrows and tactfully asked how long Tom was staying. Tom gratefully seized the opportunity for small talk, and found out that Nick and Lottie both worked for the Royal Bank of Scotland, Nick as a project manager, whatever that was, and Lottie in Human Resources. Liam didn't say much and seemed to do something with computers.

Flora sat twiddling her fingers and looking bored during this interchange, but as soon as there was a gap in the conversation she seized the opportunity to explain what had happened at her Bridge Club on Wednesday. The back-stories of all the main participants were carefully explained, especially if they had aristocratic connections or successful lawyers in their families. The young ones were obviously used to stories like these as they all nodded attentively. When her mother paused for breath, Sarah offered more vegetables, but Flora carried on as if nothing had been said.

Tom soon lost track of the conversation and his thoughts returned to Shona. What would she be like today? He imagined her as a mother like Sarah, serving her family roast potatoes on a Sunday afternoon. The image was unbearably poignant.

Sarah and Lottie began to clear the plates and Sarah came back with a dish of apple crumble – his favourite. Mrs Campbell was telling the table about the difficulty she had finding a blouse to go with the new autumn suit she had just bought at Jenners.

Lottie patiently gave some suggestions and her grandmother turned her attention to her. 'You really should do something about that hair – ridiculous for a girl of your age.' She patted her lacquered white halo. 'I go to Ricki at the same time every week and it just shows breeding to have a good cut and regular care. Of course, it is very difficult to get an appointment with him. All the best people use his salon, but if I put a word in for you I might just be able to get you an appointment.'

Lottie winced, but answered politely in an even tone. 'Thanks, Granny, but actually I like my hair as it is, and so does Liam.' Her grandmother gave a little snort of disapproval and began to push her crumble round the plate; it didn't look as if she'd eaten any of it. She looked up and raised her empty wine glass, which Sarah patiently refilled.

When everybody else had finished Tom helped gather the dishes and followed Sarah to the kitchen. She poured boiling water into the cafetière. 'I'm sorry. Mum does rather tend to dominate any conversation. She lives alone and I think she saves up a week's worth of conversation for Sunday lunch.'

'It must have been hard for her when your father died.'

'Everyone thought she would be lost without him, but she immediately got her life very well-organised – always out shopping and going to lunches. And she's a wizard with finances. That must be where Nick gets it from, because Rory's hopeless with money – and I'm not much better!' She laughed. 'Anyway, we'd better get back and rescue the young ones!'

When they got back into the dining room the conversation had turned to problems with Flora's drains, complete with a word for word account of the conversation between her and the plumber. She wanted to start at the beginning again for Sarah's benefit, but her daughter reassured her she'd heard it all from the kitchen.

After they'd drunk their coffee, Nick stood up. 'Right, Gran. I'll give you a lift home.'

'Oh, are you going already, Nicholas?' His grandmother looked disappointed.

'Yes, can't hang about here, places to go, people to see…'

He flashed his grandmother a smile, so like his father's, and she visably melted.

'I'm sure you're going to meet a girlfriend. Why don't you bring her along to lunch?' She looked round and fixed her eye on her granddaughter's boyfriend. 'Liam comes.' She managed to say Liam in a tone that left nobody in any doubt of her distaste for him. Liam blushed and Lottie stood up, still holding his hand.

'We'll be away too, Mum,' Lottie said, leading Liam emphatically towards the door. Sarah raised her eyebrows at her mother, who, totally impervious to the atmosphere she'd created, moved towards the hall, waiting for Nick to help her on with her coat.

Tom hesitated. Perhaps he should say his goodbyes too. He wanted to stay and talk to Sarah, but Rory wasn't here and he wondered if Mrs Campbell would think it odd if he stayed.

Sarah seemed to sense this. 'Tom, Rory should be back any time now and I know he wants to see you before you go up north so could you hang on for a while?'

CHAPTER 6

Sarah leant on the door and closed her eyes. 'That's it over with for another week. Don't get me wrong, it's lovely that everyone comes, but Mum's such a strain. She doesn't mean to be rude, she's just spent too long alone – and she's such a dreadful snob.'

Picking up a couple of glasses and a half-finished bottle of wine from the table, she led the way into the drawing room, a typical Georgian room, with high casement windows on two sides and an ornate corniced ceiling. She sat down on the Chesterfield sofa. 'We'll finish the wine off before I face the clearing up.'

'Do you know when Rory will be back?' Tom asked. He was surprised that the family had accepted his absence with so much equanimity.

'Who knows? He often has to work on a Sunday, strategically I think, to avoid my mum. The irony is that she absolutely adores him. He can do no wrong in her eyes. Of course she loves being able to talk about Rory Dunbar, her son-in-law, star of *Chats with Rory* to all her pals at the Bridge Club.'

Tom thought back to Rory's conversation the night before, but realised that nobody would ever say anything to Sarah. She seemed so calm and content.

A look of sadness crossed her face and she turned to

him. 'I can't stop thinking about Logan Baird. I can't believe it wasn't him. And if it wasn't him, who was it?'

'Captain Kidd suggested yesterday it must be someone from outside. There were other serial killers around at that time.'

'But she was hidden in the culvert, with the grating replaced. Only a local would know about that.' Sarah shuddered. 'It's so frightening to think there's been a killer on the loose all these years.'

'Nothing's happened for over thirty years. I'm sure there's no danger to us, but as soon as I get back from the Hebrides I'm going to find out who's leading this investigation and what's going on.' Tom spoke calmly in order to reassure Sarah. But it did cross his mind that the real murderer could have thought he was in the clear for so many years and, with Baird proved innocent, and suspicion falling on other people, perhaps the murderer would feel the need to act again.

He changed the subject carefully; he didn't want Sarah to worry. 'I have to scatter the ashes first – I want to lay my mum to rest before I start raking up the past.' He cleared his throat. 'When my mother was dying, she talked a lot about her childhood. I think she reverted in her mind to a happier time. She made me promise to take her ashes back to Eriskay.'

Tom looked up and was surprised to see a tear running down Sarah's cheek. 'Sorry, I don't know why I'm crying, it's just… ' She started to sob. 'I think back to happier times too, with Shona…'

She took a paper hanky from her pocket and wiped her eyes. 'I never had a real friend after her. My father took me away from Brunstane High immediately after it happened and sent me up to town to St Margaret's. No boys.' She smiled wryly. 'My mother was pleased, because it was her old school and she thought I'd meet a better class of girl there. But my father wouldn't allow me to bring friends home, never let me go out after school. I travelled up to Edinburgh on the bus every day and came straight back.' She twisted the tissue in her hand. 'I was so lonely. I didn't have contact with anyone in Portobello any more. Girls avoided me, as if I was tainted by what had happened...'

Tom moved closer, nodding to encourage her to go on.

'I wanted to go to university. My teachers said I should. I wanted to study History, but my father wouldn't allow it. He made me go to McAdams Ladies Secretarial College, because he considered it safe and my mother thought it suitable.'

The sobs subsided and her breathing became more even. 'And then my father died. It was so sudden. He'd seemed so healthy, no one could believe it. My mother moved away from Portobello and started her new life, and suddenly I had freedom too.' She straightened herself and smoothed her skirt. 'I don't know why I'm talking about all this. I never do. I just feel I can talk to you.'

Tom leant over and said softly, 'I know how you feel. It was also difficult for me to get close to people or talk about what happened to Shona.'

Sarah took another sip of her wine. 'People think Rory and I are an odd couple in some ways – he's so outgoing and I'm shy. But he was the first person I could really talk to.' She looked up at Tom. 'I met him when I got a job at the *Scotsman*. He listened to me. He understood me and didn't judge me. When I was with him everything seemed better.'

Tom watched her, filled with conflicting emotions. From the first moment he'd seen Sarah he'd been attracted to her. He'd felt a connection with her that he couldn't remember experiencing before. When Rory had talked about his other women he'd felt so angry, and he'd wanted to rescue Sarah from him, but now he realised that, despite everything, there *was* something between Sarah and Rory.

Sarah blew her nose. 'Right, I'm better now. Thank you for listening.' She poured out the last of the bottle and drank it in one gulp. 'Now, how about a cup of coffee? And please tell me about you. I've been talking about myself all the time.'

Sarah swept up the glasses and walked towards the kitchen. Tom followed her with the empty wine bottle and watched as she ground the coffee and prepared the cafetière.

Sarah smiled. 'So what's South Africa like? I've never been there.'

'It's a beautiful country. When we first went there Plettenberg Bay was just a small fishing village by a long beach. My mum's Uncle Gus lived there; he'd been a captain on the tankers for years, travelling all over the world, but when he met Betty, a South African widow, they got married and he settled down. Everyone was amazed because he'd seemed like a confirmed bachelor, but I don't think I've ever seen a couple so happy with each other.'

Tom cleared his throat. 'After what happened he offered us a house, and a job for my father. It seemed too good a chance to miss, to get far away from everything that had happened.' He drank from his coffee cup. 'My Aunty Betty's family owned an old fisherman's cottage, very simple, just a wooden shack on the sand dunes, with four rooms and a corrugated iron roof. But it had a veranda looking out over the sea and you could stand there and watch the dolphins leaping through the waves. It seemed like paradise after...' He swallowed. 'It is beautiful; warm sun, fresh wind from the ocean and the ever-changing shades of blue in the sea and sky.'

Sarah smiled. 'It sounds idyllic.'

'In some ways it was, but it was also really hard. I was a sixteen-year-old from Portobello and suddenly I was thrown into a completely different society. The students at the school I went to were mostly Afrikaans speakers. They played rugby and cricket, not football, and we had almost nothing in common. I never fitted in.' Sarah watched him, sympathy in her wide grey eyes.

'I dropped out pretty quickly and spent my time with the hippies on the farm over the hill, smoking dope and learning peace and love.' He gave a rueful smile. 'That's before I graduated to being a beach bum, working on the whale-watching boats, teaching surfing, and being a general handyman.' He paused again. 'I don't know what's happened to the years, they've just flown past.'

'Didn't you ever meet anyone? Did you never want to settle down and have a family?'

'Not really. I never felt close enough to anyone.' Tom thought about Layla, the one girl he'd ever loved. After that had turned out so badly he'd been cautious, never exposing himself to the hurt of losing another girl the way he'd lost Shona and Layla.

His thoughts were interrupted by a click at the front door and Rory came in, clutching a bundle of manila files.

'Hi, Tom. Glad you're still here. Something fantastic's happened. Remember I told you last night that I wanted to do something different? Well, something's come up which will make a great programme.'

Tom was surprised that there was no word of explanation or apology to Sarah.

'I'm going to make a programme on Captain Kidd, scion of one of the great Edinburgh families, who spent his whole career teaching in a comprehensive school. Now he's a published poet, but spends his free time encouraging young writers. He's part of the new Edinburgh Renaissance.'

He held up the files. 'I was down in Porty today and got some great things from the Captain. Early unpublished poems and…' He selected a folded handwritten sheet with carefully crayoned illustrations. 'Look at this. It's is a comic he wrote with his sister Antonia when he was about eight. Amazing stuff!'

Tom felt he had to respond to his exhuberance, 'Sounds great.'

'Yes, I'm getting fed up with all those interviews, massaging egos. I want to do real journalism.' He put the files on the table and looked at Tom. 'So when are you off to the Isles?'

Tom stood up. 'Actually I'd better be going. I've got to leave really early in the morning to pick up the hire car and catch the ferry.' He walked into the hall, followed by Rory. Sarah remained in the sitting room, collecting coffee cups.

'Keep in touch, Tommy boy. We'll have to have another night out when you're back.' Rory lowered his voice slightly. 'Perhaps we'll ask Jennie to come along. Saw her this afternoon and she mentioned that you and she might have a bit of unfinished business. I can tell you she still knows all the tricks.' Rory gave Tom a wink and disappeared into a room which appeared to be his study.

Sarah appeared next to Tom. He had no way of knowing if she'd heard what Rory had said. She stood in front of him, almost as tall as he was. Her skin was pale and she looked beautiful, ethereal. Tom looked into her grey eyes and a charge seemed to flash between them.

To his surprise, she moved towards him and kissed him, softly at first but then harder as she held him tightly. He felt passion flood through his whole body.

After a moment he pulled back. He was torn: he felt so attracted to her in every way, physically, emotionally, intellectually, but she was married and her husband was on the other side of the door. Rory was unfaithful, Sarah was vulnerable, and he had to go to the Western Isles tomorrow. He took her head in his hands and kissed her gently on the forehead. Then he left, closing the door quietly behind him.

PART 4

We're in Shona's bedroom. The Bay City Rollers' 'Keep on Dancing' is playing on her blue Dansette record player. Posters of the band in their tartan denim outfits plaster the wall; we love them all, especially blue-eyed Eric. They really are the boys next door for us – everyone has a connection – Woody's aunty is even one of our dinner ladies at school. We are dancing, throwing our arms in the air, when I feel eyes watching us. I look round and see Tom at the door, leaning against the doorjamb, swaying and singing along with the record 'Keep on dancin' and a prancin''. He's tall and slim, in skinny bell-bottomed jeans, blonde hair hanging on his shoulders, fringe falling to his pale brown eyes.

We freeze. Shona picks up the pink teddy from her bed and throws it at him. Tom catches it and throws it back. Soft toys fly through the air. We collapse laughing together. Tom joins in singing 'Shake it till the break of day', dancing a parody of the Rollers' strut. The music fades.

Sarah lay in bed and felt the rhythm of the Rollers' music going through her head. The image of the sixteen-year-old Tom merged with the man she kissed at the doorway of her adult house. She still felt the imprint of his soft lips on hers.

CHAPTER 7

Tom stood at the helm of the *Lord of the Isles* as it sailed away from Uig in the north of Skye towards North Uist. The sea was calm and the sun shone, twinkling on the islands and promontories that reached out into the shining water.

After a couple of hours he saw the outline of the harbour at Lochmaddy. Although it was more than thirty years since he'd last been there, he recognised it all. He drove off the ferry and through the treeless landscape, feeling a mixture of apprehension and excitement as he got closer to the place where he'd spent so many happy holidays. Images of Shona, running on the springy heather hills and along the long white beaches, came into his mind. Nostalgia pulled at his intestines, a physical response to coming back.

The sky was huge, almost colourless, with the sun glistening on the water with a pale, almost Scandinavian glow. Through Benbecula to South Uist, the single-track road wound past the sandy bays on the right and the three hills of ancient rock on the left, and as he approached Eriskay he saw the new causeway which had replaced the ferry they'd always used before.

Driving slowly over it, he passed the bay where they'd hunted for cockles when he was a boy. The tide was far out and the low sun glistened on the wet sand. Then he turned inland up the valley towards his aunt's house, heather-covered hills rising on both sides. Where his grandmother's croft had stood, there was a scattering of white modern houses, all of a similar design with satellite dishes on the side. He narrowed his eyes into the low evening sun and saw a figure sitting on the bench in front of one of the houses. His aunt. She stood up and waved, running towards him as he parked the car.

Opening the car door, he was enveloped in warm arms. 'Tom, you've been a long time away, but now you're back. Annie's boy has come back!' Mary Agnes, his mother's youngest sister, spoke in the soft tones of a native Gaelic speaker. Like many on the island she had two names to distinguish her from the many other Marys.

She pulled him close to her. 'I've always been waiting for you to come back, to come home.' She led him into the modern kitchen. 'You'll be ready for a cup of tea, or would you rather have something stronger?'

Tom took tea and they sat on the bench, gazing out over the silver water of Eriskay Sound. Tom gave an upbeat account of their life in South Africa, skirting over many of the details of his mother's slow death from liver cancer to make it seem as peaceful and painless as possible. He described how her Uncle Gus and his wife, Betty, had been so good to them.

Mary Agnes reciprocated with news of her children, who were just toddlers when Tom had last seen them. His cousin Donald was a surgeon in Glasgow, very successful but unfortunately divorced. Mary Agnes didn't see those grandchildren at all now. She gave a sad smile. That happened so often these days. She brightened when she talked about her daughter, Kirstie. She was married to a very nice man and lived in the south of England. She came up to visit quite often with her children, two girls in their early teens now.

'It's lovely to see them on the beach, digging for cockles and collecting mussels from the rocks. I remember back to those days when you were all young, playing together.' She looked at Tom. 'Shona was such a bonnie wee lassie. It was a terrible thing that happened, a wicked terrible thing. That your poor mother had to suffer that – the loss of a child.'

She laid her hand on Tom's. 'The pity is she didn't come back here. I think it was your father who wanted to go to South Africa. Kenny always was a wanderer, him being in the Merchant Navy and all. I suppose Gus's offer just seemed the best thing to do at the time.' She paused and smiled wistfully. 'And your father never did want to come back to the islands.'

Tom thought back; he remembered his father had always stayed in Edinburgh when they came up in the summer holidays. He said something about having to work. Tom couldn't even remember ever visiting his father's parents on Lewis.

Mary Agnes continued in her gentle tones. 'Our mum and dad were so pleased when Annie met a man from the Islands. They'd worried when she went away to Edinburgh to do her nursing that she'd meet the wrong kind of folk. But because your father was a Lewis man they thought he'd treat her right. Of course, he was that wee bitty older, having been away on the tankers, but he gave that all up for her when she wanted him to settle in Edinburgh.'

She paused, obviously wondering whether to say more. When she did, she sounded sad. 'Of course, it was difficult for him, her being a Catholic and all. I think it caused some problems with his family. You know what the church is like up on Lewis, they think Catholics are the anti-Christ. Be that as it may, Kenny never talked about his family and he never went back. Annie said often enough that you bairns should know all your grandparents, but Kenny wouldn't have any of it.'

Tom thought back. What did he know about his other grandparents? They were just never mentioned. Tom was astonished how unquestioning he had been when he was young. He couldn't remember ever asking about them or even thinking it was odd that they never visited. It was just the way it was.

Mary Agnes pulled a handkerchief from her sleeve and dabbed her deep-set eyes. 'But what a lovely wee family you were. Until, that monster…' She paused and took a deep breath. 'I still cannae believe it. I cannae believe that any man would do that to a wee lassie like her.' She tucked her hanky back in her sleeve and smoothed her skirt. 'I think we need that dram, now.'

'I think we do, Aunty Mary.' He hugged her to him and held her tight. Then they sat, watching the sun sink into the sea, and drank a glass of whisky, silent in their own thoughts.

Tom wondered whether he should mention the news about Logan Baird's release, but he realised he had to. It might hit the national news any day and it was better his aunt heard it from him. When he told his aunt she nodded and sighed. 'It's a bad business.' There were no tears, no histrionics. The islanders were stoical, used to tragedy and accepted that life was hard and unfair.

Later, eating roast chicken, he caught up on some island

news and then they sat and watched the huge television. Mary Agnes was knitting the complicated design of the seamless Eriskay sweater when she turned to her nephew.

'What happened to you, Tom? You were so clever at school – I always thought you'd be a doctor or a lawyer. I hoped you'd meet a nice girl and have your own wee family. New life would have made it easier for everyone to move on.'

Tom didn't know what to say. These were thoughts that sometimes came to him, but it was easier to bury them, to drift along and live from day to day. His mother had never asked difficult questions like these. 'I don't know. I don't know what's happened to all the years.' He looked down.

His aunt, seeming to sense his discomfort, turned the conversation to her sister's ashes. They decided on Thursday evening for the ceremony, enough time for Mary Agnes to contact all the relatives and the local priest. Tom hadn't thought of involving the church, but he was more than willing to leave the organisation in his aunt's hands; he could see she was gaining comfort from being able to say goodbye to her sister in this way.

After the late news finished, Mary Agnes folded up her knitting and kissed him goodnight. Tom climbed up to his narrow room under the sloping eaves, feeling a turmoil of emotions: being with his aunt made him think about his family and the lack of contact with his father's relatives. Why had they never visited his home island? Why had his father changed so much after they went to South Africa? What lay behind his drinking, his dark depressions, his anger at the world? Of course, Shona's murder affected all of them, but was there something more behind his smouldering rage? As

Tom tossed uneasily in the narrow bed, he made a decision. He was going to Lewis – he needed to find out more about his father.

Eventually he managed to drift off, but slept fitfully. Memories of summers in South Uist mingled with images of Sarah, her grown-up wide grey eyes looking at him tenderly, her sensitive mouth hovering above his saying something he could not hear. He opened his eyes, remembering the taste of her kiss on his lips and the soft curve of her breasts as she held him close.

*

Sarah sat at the high sash window watching the evening sky darken over the roofs of Stockbridge. Her thoughts kept going back to Tom. A flush of embarrassment spread over her face. *That kiss*. It was so unlike her – she'd never had any kind of relationship with a man since she met Rory and here she was almost flinging herself at Tom. She hoped he wouldn't think badly of her.

What had got into her? He was attractive, so tall and lean, with a beautiful sensitive mouth and full soft lips, so like Shona. But it was not just a physical attraction, it was the ease she felt with him. Although they'd only just met again, it was as if he'd always been there. And now he'd gone away and she was amazed how much she missed him.

She looked at her phone again. She wished she'd asked for his mobile number when she'd given him hers at the reunion. No message. Why hadn't he contacted her?

Tom woke next morning to find the house swathed in low white cloud. The smell of bacon wafted up the stairs and when he went down he saw Mary Agnes standing at the cooker.

'Good morning, Tom. I trust you slept well.' She paused and cracked an egg into the frying pan. 'I've been phoning the family. They all want to see you, Tom. We were worried you might never come back.' She turned the bacon and looked round at him. 'I hope you'll no have to run off again too soon.'

Tom put his arms round his aunt. 'I'm sorry I can't stay all that long. I'll have to leave after we've scattered the ashes because there are things I've got to do.' He didn't add that he was going to Lewis, because he was not certain himself if it was a wise thing to do. He allowed the thought to remain in her mind that he was going back to Edinburgh to see the police.

After breakfast Tom changed into his running kit and ran up the track away from the house. He felt happy to be running again. In South Africa he went every day, pounding along the firm sand at the water's edge and through the soft dunes. He'd missed that and was pleased to feel the damp air in his lungs as he forced his way up the path and into the springy heather. There was a drizzle in the air and his vest was damp by the time he reached the top of the hill. As he stood there, surrounded by the peat pools, the air lightened and the sun shafted through the cloud like beams pushing through a window. The view opened up over the island, showing the long white beaches and smaller islands dotted in the sparkling ocean.

As he stood, feeling his heart swelling with the beauty of the view, his phone beeped. A text message. His first thought was Sarah and he took his phone out of his pocket with excitement. When he saw it was from his South African provider, asking if he wanted to sign up for an overseas package, he felt a sense of disappointment and isolation. His only contact since he arrived in Scotland – an automated message from a mobile phone company.

In the distance he saw the beach his mother had loved so much, where her ashes would be scattered. He remembered her sitting in the hospice, eyes sunken, her hair colourless, and her face covered with white papery skin. She'd reached out and clutched his wrist, using all her strength to ask him to bring her ashes back to 'her' island. He was glad he could fulfil this last request. Soon she'd be at peace.

Running down the hill, he passed the shell of his grandmother's croft. He and Shona had stayed there when they were young, collecting water from the well, washing in the stream. Mary Agnes explained that nobody lived in the old buildings now, since the Highlands and Islands Development had paid for the new houses. They could choose from a very limited number of designs, which explained why nearly all the houses looked similar, strangely modern and out of place in the wild countryside.

When he arrived back at the house, cousins had arrived, bringing a bucket of crabs' legs. They all sat down on the bench in front of the house and exchanged family news. The whisky bottle was brought out and they had the customary dram.

This set the pattern for the next days. A run in the morning and then a succession of visitors arrived, or he was taken by Mary Agnes to visit other relatives. He seemed to be related to nearly everyone on the island.

The days were full, but as he lay in the narrow bed at night he found it hard to sleep, his mind crowded with thoughts of Shona, Logan Baird and Sarah.

Thursday dawned clear and after Tom's run up the hill they drove to St. Michael's Church, at the highest point of the island, overlooking the main village. It wasn't that old, about a hundred years or so, but it had a timeless Scandinavian feel, rectangular with a rounded north end, steep blue roof, grey stone with the windows picked out in white bricks. It would not have looked out of place on a Norwegian fjord.

Eriskay, South Uist and Barra had always remained Catholic when the other islands had become protestant. St Michael's Church was surrounded by a memorial garden, with a statue of the Virgin Mary, overlooking the Sound of Barra. They went inside. It was bigger than Tom had expected and was dominated by the altar in the form of the prow of a boat.

A priest stepped out from the shadows under the gallery and held out his hand. 'I'm Father Eric McNeill. Bless you, my son.' Tom felt awkward; he had never been a church-goer, but Father Eric smiled and soon put him at his ease. 'I'm sorry to hear of your loss. Your aunt has told me about your mother and I'll be happy to say a few words when her ashes are scattered.'

Tom grasped his hand, 'Thank you.' Although his mother worshipped at the ecumenical One World Church in South Africa, she'd asked for a priest before she died and was comforted by the ministering of the Last Rites. 'That would make her very happy.'

Afterwards Tom and Mary Agnes made their way round the island, stopping at white houses dotted on the treeless headlands and bays. Herds of wild white Eriskay ponies wandered freely over the roads, knowing that every car would stop for them. At each house they were welcomed in, food and drink appeared and, after a few minutes, the whisky bottle.

As the evening drew in they made their way down to Bonnie Prince Charlie's Beach, where the Young Pretender had landed. It stretched in a wide curve, backed by dunes and tussocks of coarse grass. From every direction cars came and parked on the road. Groups of dark-clad people made their way through the dunes onto the beach. Tom was touched by how many people came, standing in a horseshoe, silhouetted dark against the setting sun. Father Eric was one of the last to arrive and greeted the members of his congregation with a small inclination of his head. Tom stood next to him with his casket of ashes.

When the priest started his address in a clear sonorous voice Tom was astonished by how much he knew about his mother. From information given by Mary Agnes, he'd captured her quiet character, her unassuming manner, her dedication to helping others, as a nurse, a mother and a friend. The sadness of her last years, the loss of her daughter and husband, being so far away from friends and family in South Africa, were referred to briefly, but then much was made of her ashes returning to the place of her birth.

The priest blessed the casket and Tom scattered the first handful of ashes into the sand. Silently his mother's cousins stepped forward to take part of her and share in her homecoming. The tableau of dark figures was silhouetted on the evening sky as the sun melted huge and glowing into the sea, leaving the sky ablaze with lilac, dusty pink, red and golden yellow.

*

The next day Tom woke in his narrow bed, his head throbbing. It had been a fine night back at the house and all his new-found relatives had taken him into their arms and their hearts. It was tempting to stay here in the warmth of family, but he knew he had to go – and quickly. The longer he stayed here, the more he began to feel a sense of belonging that he could never remember feeling before. He packed his things into his bag and went down to where Mary Agnes was standing in the kitchen, cooking breakfast. He ate quickly and threw his bags into the boot of the car.

Mary Agnes held him close and he could sense rather than see tears in her eyes. 'Haste ye back', she whispered.

'I'll come again, Mary Agnes.' As he said it, he hoped that it was true.

CHAPTER 8

Sarah paced around her front room, a duster in her hand, wiping the furniture in a random fashion. As she turned to the coffee table, she saw the manila folder with HJ Kidd's material. Rory was never around much, but he was at home even less than usual at the moment. He seemed obsessed with the Kidd programme, poring over the material the poet had given him. He was especially delighted with the handwritten comic 'The Blue Moon' (*because that's how often it appears*) which HJ had written with his older sister Antonia. Sarah picked it out of the folder. Between crayoned adverts and family news items was a poem called *Tibby the Cat*.

Tibby tiptoes across the carpet
White socks on each paw
Whiskers like wires
Eyes like marbles
I love you Tibby
Come and sit on my knee.
By Horatio J. Kidd

Sarah smiled. So his name was Horatio. Now she knew why he was always known as HJ.

There was a yellow post-it note attached to the comic. On it Rory had written in his surprisingly beautiful handwriting *First of the animal poems? A link to the metaphorical language of later works?*

'Have you got that folder from HJ?'

Sarah started at the sound of Rory's voice. She hadn't heard him come in. She looked up and saw Rory standing in front of her.

'Yes, I've been looking at 'The Blue Moon'. That's a lovely starting point for the programme.'

'That's what I thought.' He sat down on the arm of the sofa. 'I'm so glad to get out of the studio. My guests tomorrow are that body-waxed apology for a footballer, Greg Muldoon and his anorexic WAG. He's *written,*' he signified quotation marks, 'an autobiography and I'm supposed to promote his book – oh sorry, question him about his fascinating life. I've got that dim new researcher girl to read the drivel and write up a few questions. All he's famous for is dating a few talentless models or members of girl bands. Oh yes, and his exciting collection of tattoos.'

Sarah smiled. She liked it when Rory had his rants, as he called them. She was pleased if he could use her as a safety valve when pressures at work built up.

'These modern day so-called sportsmen are just not like the real footballers we used to have – like Donald Ford, for example. A genius and a gentleman.' He gave an ironic smile. 'Well, unfortunately he played for the Jam Tarts, but you can't hold that against him forever.' Rory picked up the folder. 'I just want to get on with this programme. We've got a great provisional title – *Kidd down with the Kids.*'

Sarah smiled, 'It's wonderful to see you so enthusiastic.'

'I have to be, because the programme planners aren't that keen. They don't see poetry as a great hook, so I have to get another angle to sex it up a bit.' He looked thoughtful. 'Anyway, I'm just going to see HJ's sister, Antonia – or Lady

Moncrieff as she is now. A widow, I think. She lives not far from here, in Ann Street.'

'Great if you can get some of HJ's family to contribute.'

'Yes, I think the family's a great angle. Actually the idiot researcher was supposed to make an appointment, but she couldn't pin Antonia down to a time, so I'll just pop round and dazzle her with my boyish charm.'

Rory jolted as if something had just occurred to him. He took the folder, patted Sarah on the top of her head, and was making for the door when the phone rang. Rory picked it up as he was passing. Patsy's high-pitched voice squawked at the other end of the line.

Rory turned on his charm. 'Yes, I saw the photo. It was great, well done you!' He kept walking as Patsy said something else and then he replied. 'I'm sorry, I'm just going out. Work, you know – no rest for the wicked. But Sarah's here – she's not doing anything, so just pop round.'

Sarah grimaced and indicated wildly to Rory that this was the last thing she wanted, but it was too late. Rory put the phone down. 'Patsy's just coming round. She's a good kid. It'll be good for you – you spend far too much time by yourself.' Without waiting for Sarah to reply he continued into the hall and the door slammed behind him.

Sarah groaned. Patsy was good-hearted, but Sarah wasn't sure why she was so keen to be her friend – because of her sparkling personality or because she was married to Rory?

Moments later the door-bell rang and Sarah heard Patsy's voice on the other end of the intercom and then her heels clicking up the stairs. She arrived, panting and clutching a bottle of Pinot Grigio. 'I've just taken it out of the fridge, so it's cold.'

She stopped and looked round. 'Wow, this flat is lovely. Such high ceilings and all those lovely original features. Could I just have a little nose round? Gavin and I have a few properties so I'm always interested in seeing other people's houses.'

Sarah mentally checked that all the beds were made and then showed Patsy the rooms. She was effusive in her praise. 'Lovely, lovely Georgian rooms, so much character – and in such a great location, too. You're so lucky!'

Sarah nodded and got two glasses and some olives from the kitchen before leading Patsy through to the drawing room.

Patsy raised her glass. 'Well, cheers. It's really nice that we can have a drink together like this.' She took an olive. 'We didn't really get a chance to talk the other day because of that horrid news about the murderer, so I thought it would be a good idea to have a catch up now.'

Sarah sighed. 'It was so awful. I can't stop thinking about it and wondering who could have done it, if it wasn't Logan Baird.'

'We don't want to talk about that now. It was terrible but it's such a long time ago and, as Captain Kidd said, they'll probably find out that it was one of those serial killers. Anyway, we don't have to worry. It's not as if we have a murderer in our midst.'

Sarah shuddered. The killer had thought he was safe for all these years. What might happen now the case had been reopened?

Patsy was oblivious to her mood. 'Let's talk about something more interesting. I still go out with some of the girls from the class sometimes. We have such a laugh and it's always nice to catch up on a bit of gossip. Wasn't the reunion great?'

'Great,' Sarah said weakly and took a gulp from her wine glass.

Patsy leant over confidentially. 'But someone, I won't say who, made a pass at me at the end of the evening. The cheek of it!' Her small face twisted with disapproval. 'Everyone knows I'm married, and Gavin had just arrived to pick me up.'

Sarah thought of Patsy's slight, sandy-haired husband. He always seemed to be delighted just to fetch and carry for his vivacious wife, happy to stay in the background and gaze at her with total devotion.

Patsy continued in an affronted tone. 'I do flirt sometimes but I've never been unfaithful to Gavin. He understands there's a line I would never cross. But I think a few things do happen at these reunions,' she gave a sly smile. 'Some of the girls were wondering what happened between you and the lovely Tom.'

Sarah felt herself blushing. 'Absolutely nothing. I just gave him a lift home.'

'He is rather dishy though, isn't he? So attractive and so mysterious. I wonder why he never got married? It's a bit funny him coming back to Scotland after all these years. Did he say why?'

Sarah was going to mention Tom scattering his mother's ashes but then stopped. She didn't want Tom's plans to be Patsy's next hot topic of gossip. 'Not really.'

'And what about Jennie? She left with Rory, didn't she?'

'You know what Rory's like. Can't bear to see a damsel in distress. He took her back to her hotel.'

'It must be difficult sometimes, being married to someone as attractive as Rory, isn't it? I mean he must have loads of women after him.' Patsy gave Sarah an encouraging smile.

Sarah drew back in her chair; she was used to women fishing for information about Rory, usually more subtly than Patsy. 'Of course, he does have to meet a lot of women, but that's part of the job.'

Patsy reached over and patted her hand. 'You know, it's nice we're friends. It's important to have someone to chat to, share things with.' She shot Sarah another encouraging glance. 'If there's ever anything you want to talk about, you know, about men and things, I'm always just a phonecall away.'

'That's nice of you,' Sarah replied. She knew a lot of people, women especially, couldn't understand their relationship, but Rory had chosen to be with her, and had stayed with her for nearly thirty years. She looked around for a way to change the subject. 'You know, I don't think I know what it is you do, apart from organising reunions that is.'

'I don't really do anything, now. I was Gavin's PA, but now we're married he says we shouldn't work together. I do help a bit with our property portfolio, which is why I was so interested in your lovely flat. We've got over forty flats now, but that's just a hobby really, separate from Gavin's main business.'

So that's where the money comes from. I wonder what attracted Patsy to millionaire Gavin? Sarah thought, and felt ashamed of her bitchiness.

'What do you do, Sarah? Apart from looking after Rory, that is,' Patsy giggled.

'When the twins were at home, looking after them did take up all my time.' Sarah smiled; she'd loved that time, looking after the house, doing activities with the twins, making a home for her family. But now the twins had left, and Rory was always so busy. 'Now I work part-time in an office. Not very interesting.'

Patsy carried on brightly. 'Perhaps we could do something together one evening? I belong to White's Health Club. Would you like to come along as a guest sometime? They have super trainers and the Zumba class is amazing.' She simpered and leant forward. 'You know, I've got so flexible since I started Zumba, we've managed positions we haven't tried for years – Gavin loves it.'

Sarah tried to block the unwelcome image of Gavin and Patsy in unusual positions and wondered how she was going to get rid of her. She looked at her watch. 'Oh is that the time?' Her voice sounded hollow and unconvincing, even to her. 'I'm sorry, Patsy, I've promised to give my mother a lift to the Bridge Club. I didn't realise that it was so late already.'

She stood up and passed Patsy her coat, ignoring the look of disappointment on her face as she opened the door. 'I'm sorry it's been so rushed, but you know how it is with mothers.' She smiled. 'Thanks for the wine.'

She closed the door. She knew she was being rude, and, although the thought depressed her, Patsy was the nearest thing she had to a friend. But she didn't want to get too close to anyone, didn't want to have to explain her relationship with Rory. She wanted to keep up the façade of the perfect family life and didn't want to have to explain why she would always stay with Rory.

*

The front door slammed and Rory stamped in. 'Stupid woman!' Sarah looked up from her book.

'Kidd's sister is impossible!'

'In what way?'

'You'd think that she'd be pleased to be the sister of Scotland's greatest living poet, but no. She wouldn't even discuss him. Said she couldn't remember anything about 'The Blue Moon' comic – and refuses to have anything to do with the television programme. Said she hasn't spoken to her brother for over forty years.'

'She must be getting on a bit now, so perhaps she really can't remember.' Sarah tried to be conciliatory; things must be bad, because Rory never usually admitted defeat in anything.

'Bollocks. She's only about sixty-five – and I must say, a damn fine-looking woman for her age. Of course, she can remember and she'd be great on television. A great character and a real looker.'

So that's it, thought Sarah, *a woman who didn't succumb to his charms.* No wonder Rory was so furious. She laid her book down. 'Perhaps there was a falling-out. HJ doesn't seem to fit the mould of the rest of his family.'

'You're right there. They're all law lords apart from him. And Antonia, Lady Moncrieff, must be rolling in it – that house in Ann Street's worth millions.'

'Perhaps he's a black sheep of the family? Maybe they think he should have done something more prestigious than be a teacher in a comprehensive?'

Rory stood up straight and gathered his folders together. 'You're right. I think there is something behind this. And I'm going to find out what it is.'

He turned round and went out again, the door crashing

behind him. Sultan climbed onto Sarah's knee and Sarah stroked him behind the ears in the way she knew he loved. The house was peaceful again.

She took out her mobile phone and looked at it, for perhaps the thousandth time since Tom had left. She knew Tom had her number. She couldn't stop thinking about him. Why didn't he send a message?

PART 5

The kitchen at Shona's. A sink unit in front of the sash window looking out over the Forth. Dishes hidden on shelves behind red gingham curtains. The smell of mince cooking on the range. Mrs McIver is stirring with a wooden spoon, wearing her long pinny with a ruff up the sides. She is asking us about school and the teachers in her melodic Hebridean tones.

Then a crash at the door and Mr McIver, red-faced, dark hair tousled, stumbles in. Everyone freezes. He lurches towards his wife, knocking over a chair. Shona grabs my hand and pulls me out of the room. I see Mrs McIver shrinking back over the formica kitchen units as her husband puts his red face close to hers. The door closing muffles his roaring curses. Shona and I stand outside the door, not daring to look at each other. Tom appears beside us and gently puts his arms round our shoulders, leading us to the front room.

CHAPTER 9

Tom drove along the straight empty roads to the north. There wasn't a ferry due at Lochboisdale so there was little traffic. As he approached the more mountainous skyline of Harris he realised that he was just driving, not knowing where he was going. He hadn't been in contact with any of his father's relatives for years. The only thing he knew was that his father had lived in Nigg so he was going there and hoped he'd find someone related to him.

As he drove through Lewis, the landscape became flatter and bleaker. He saw the circle of standing stones at Callanisch, gaunt against the skies, with dark clouds shot through by shafts of silver sunlight. Driving towards Nigg, slightly lower but still exposed to the unrelenting wind on the barren treeless landscape, Tom hoped he'd find a pub with a roaring fire where he could chat to the locals at the bar while sipping a welcome pint. But when he arrived the streets were empty and lifeless, reminding him of a town in a film he'd once seen, where all the inhabitants had been spirited away by aliens.

Beside the road he saw a bungalow with a sign *Nigg B&B* and *vacancies*. He was tired, had to stay somewhere, so he went in. Terry and Maureen, the proprietors, were very welcoming. The room was comfortable, but they couldn't help him with his quest because they'd only recently moved up from Coventry and didn't know many locals.

The next morning Tom walked to the local shop, which doubled as a post office, and, Tom was sure, the hub of all local knowledge. A shiny round face peered from between stacks of tins of beans, cereals, washing powder and shoe polish, everything that villagers might need.

'Nearly everyone here is called McIver,' the shopkeeper said with her sing-song lilt, in response to Tom's question.

'My father was called Kenny, he joined the Merchant Navy.'

'So many of the young boys did then. If they couldn't go to the university, that was the only thing to do. The fishing was not enough to support all the sons.' She paused. 'Kenny, did you say? Went to Edinburgh and never came back to the island?'

Tom felt a surge of excitement. 'Yes, that's the one. He was my father. Do any of his relatives live nearby?'

The round face hesitated. 'It's a long time he's been away from the island. I'm no sure.'

Tom sensed she was holding something back. 'We never used to come here as children. I know there must have been something of a falling-out.'

The shopkeeper removed her round glasses and rubbed her eyes. 'Mary McIver at the church may know. But I'm not sure she'll want to talk. Those were hard times.' She paused. 'And now, if you'll excuse me, I have work to do.' Her head withdrew behind the piles of tins and Tom knew there was no use asking anything else.

He drove the hire car over the flat, bleak landscape. The clouds travelled quickly over the huge skies but there were few trees or landmarks until Tom saw an enormous church dominating the landscape. A thin woman in a faded dress was sweeping the doorstep.

He approached her slowly and coughed. She raised her head and stared at him. Her eyes were deep-set in her care-worn face.

'Excuse me, I'm looking for Mary McIver.'

'Who wants to know?'

'I'm Tom McIver and I'm looking for relatives of my father, Kenny. He joined the Merchant Navy. I think he came from round here.'

'There's many that came from here and are long gone.' A cold wind swirled round Tom. The woman turned away and continued vigorous sweeping.

Tom knew he had to persist to get anywhere. 'My father died many years ago in South Africa and I want to find out something about the rest of my family. He never spoke about them.'

The woman rested on her broom and looked round. A flicker of recognition crossed her face and she pursed her mouth in disapproval. 'As well he shouldn't. Such wickedness.'

'You knew him?' Tom felt a sliver of hope, although the woman had turned her back to him again.

'Kenny McIver was a wicked young man. It's no surprising that he would never show his face here again.'

'Please tell me about him. It would help me understand him better. I'm the only one left of our family now and I want to know where I came from.' Tom waited.

There was a long pause before the woman turned again and lifted her head. 'I'm Mary McIver. I'll be your aunt.' She looked carefully at Tom with her deep-set eyes. 'So you're the son of Kenny – you have a look of your father about you, sure enough.' Tom looked at Mary; he could see nothing of his father in this grim-faced woman, but he was glad to have found a relative.

Mary pursed her lips again. 'You'd better come back to the house. But first I have to lock up the church.'

Tom followed her into the enormous bare building. Mary indicated the space with pride. 'It can hold 1400 people but there were 2000 for the inauguration of the minister.' Tom stared at the stark white walls and the bare pews in amazement. There didn't seem to be a thousand people living in the whole area.

Mary locked up the church and led Tom to a small modern house a few hundred yards down the road. She unlocked the door and Tom followed. They'd not exchanged a word since they were in the church.

The old lady showed Tom into the bare front room and disappeared into the utilitarian kitchen. There were no pictures, no plants, nothing to alleviate the stark chill of the atmosphere. Mary came back with two cups of tea and sat down.

'I moved here with my parents when they built the new houses. The croft where we used to live is up the road. My parents are both gone now, and the rest of the family have all gone to Glasgow or further, so I just have the church now. And Duncan has gone too.' She stared past Tom far into the distance through the bare square window. Tom waited for her to say more, not daring to break her flow.

'Kenny was the oldest. He was the apple of our mother's eye. A wild one he was, always in trouble. But then he joined the Merchant Navy and never came back. Lied about his age he did, he was only fifteen. Broke his mother's heart.'

There was a long pause. Mary looked down and fiddled

with the edge of her cardigan. 'And then we found out why he had run away.'

Tom looked at her. He was longing to ask questions, but knew he had to let her tell her story in her own time.

'He was always a fine-looking lad was Kenny, and popular with the girls.' Mary stared out of the window. 'A girl falling pregnant in those days was a scandal. Poor wee lassie, she was just a child herself.'

Tom gasped. 'My father had a child?'

'Aye, Duncan.'

'I have a brother?' Tom felt a rush of excitement. He wasn't totally alone.

'He was a fine boy, not unlike yourself. But he was taken by the sea, like so many others.'

'What?' Tom gasped. 'When did this happen?'

'Many years ago. He was nineteen when the fishing boat went down.' Mary's harsh features softened.

Tom felt a sense of loss. 'I never knew anything about him.'

'Your father was a coward. He ran away and left that poor wee lassie to face the music alone.' Another long pause. Mary's dark eyes began to glisten. 'It was a terrible wicked thing. She was only fourteen and the birth was too much for her. She was taken by the Lord the next day. But she left the boy, Duncan.'

She sniffed. 'The lassie's parents were broken by the shame and the loss of their wee girl. Could never abide the sight of the boy. Our family took him in and your grandmother loved him so. It was something left of Kenny. A fine boy he was, Duncan, but cursed by his birth.'

Tom felt quite disorientated. 'Are there any photos?'

Mary sat still for a long time and then stood up slowly. She opened a drawer in a cheap ugly sideboard, lifting out an envelope with a few yellowing photos. She looked quickly through them and selected one. 'Here is Duncan with my dear mother and father. He will be about seventeen in this picture.'

Tom took the photo. He saw a small white-haired couple and a smiling youth standing between them, with his arms protectively over their shoulders. He felt a shock of recognition; Duncan did look like him. He'd had a brother and he never knew. His father had never said anything about him.

Mary interrupted his thoughts. 'There's a chest. Kenny left it when he went. I wanted to throw it out but my mother would never allow it. She was always waiting for him to come home.'

Tom's head was reeling with what he'd heard. It explained the deep, hidden part of his father he'd never been able to understand. He nodded. 'Can I look at it?'

'It's in the outhouse. You can take it away with you. I'll no be wanting it.'

Mary stood up and led Tom out into the pale late afternoon sunshine. Tom shivered. The house was cold, both in temperature and the sparse signs of a joyless life.

Mary led Tom into a dusty outhouse and he saw an old-fashioned trunk in the corner wreathed in cobwebs. 'Take it,' said Mary. 'I'll be glad to see the back of it.'

Tom staggered as he carried it to the car. It was heavier than he'd expected.

'You'll be wanting to get away now.' Mary stood with her arms folded and her mouth pursed. Tom felt uncomfortable.

Did she want him to go or was she disappointed he was going? Her air of disapproval was evident, but Tom couldn't make out why.

'Can I take you for a meal this evening?'

'There's nowhere I would eat here. Only for tourists and incomers.' Her thin mouth was set grimly over her prominent chin.

Tom stretched out his hand. 'I'm so grateful that you've given me this and filled in some of the gaps in my history. Are you sure that there's nothing I can do for you?'

'I'm just glad that I can put an end to that time. Now I must go and prepare. It's the Lord's Day tomorrow and I must make everything ready.' She nodded her head and turned away. Tom withdrew his hand. She was his aunt, but she was not the sort you could hug.

'Thank you, Mary,' he said to her retreating back, but she didn't turn or acknowledge that she'd heard.

Tom lugged the trunk into his room at the bed and breakfast. He'd waited until the owners had gone out shopping before bringing it in from the boot of the hire car. He wiped off most of the cobwebs, out of respect for the cream carpet, and looked around to see if any neighbours were watching from their windows. Anyone would think that he had a body in it.

He looked at the trunk with a mixture of apprehension and curiosity. He realised that he hadn't really known his father. Had he ever had a conversation with him? The whole family had tiptoed cautiously around him, careful not to trigger one of his rages. His mother had spent her life making sure that nothing annoyed him; that his dinner was ready when he came home, that the family only ate the food that he liked, but he could still lash out at her, especially when he'd been drinking. Tom had felt helpless.

He'd felt his father's belt on many occasions, often not knowing what he had done to incur his wrath. His mother always excused his father, saying he'd had a hard life; conditions in the Merchant Navy were severe in those days. Shona could do no wrong, though. His little princess. And after she died, he'd drowned in sorrow and alcohol.

The trunk was an old-fashioned one with metal bands round it and a rusty lock. He looked at the trunk with distaste. Perhaps Mary was right. Maybe there were some secrets that should not be disturbed.

CHAPTER 10

Sarah looked at her phone again. Was it working? No messages. She rarely heard anything from the twins between Sundays, as they were firm subscribers to the 'no news is good news' school of thought – and her mother only phoned when she wanted something. The door flew open and Rory bounded in.

'I knew there was something!' he looked jubilant. 'My journalist's nose is still able to sniff out a story. I went to meet Archie Kilbride in the Café Royal and who should I see there, propping up the bar, but this old guy who's always rambling on about his schooldays at Fettes. I just happened to mention that I was doing the programme on HJ Kidd and wondered if he was at the school about the same time.'

Rory beamed. Sarah smiled, encouraging him to go on.

'Well, he did know him, and once he started on his tales I just couldn't shut him up. Apparently, old HJ was a star student, the golden boy of his family, but then something happened. He left the school early, moved into digs and, instead of going to Cambridge as expected, went to uni in Edinburgh.'

Sarah nodded, waiting for him to build up to whatever was making him feel so pleased.

'And who was his landlady?' Another dramatic pause. Rory could hardly contain his delight, 'the fragrant Hannah.'

Sarah frowned. 'I thought she might be a bit older than him, but I didn't think there was that much of an age difference.'

'There isn't really – it just sounds good. She was a student at the uni and her parents bought her a flat in Marchmont with a spare room. She was already in her third year when HJ moved in, aged seventeen, and the rest, as they say, is history.'

'So what happened to make him leave school and home?'

Rory tapped his nose. 'I don't know – yet. But I'm going to find out!' He swept up his coat and moved to the door. 'Might be late – don't wait up!' A final grin and the door slammed again.

Sarah turned up the music – Brahms' Poco Allegretto. How long had he been in the house – five minutes? She lay back.

Tom, please contact me.

Another glance at the phone.

Nothing.

*

Tom prised the lid of the trunk open. A fusty smell. A teenage boy's treasure trove from those troubled war years. Tom lifted the contents out slowly, hoping for some clues into the enigma that was his father.

The top layer was mostly paper: deeply creased football posters, bundles of old cigarette packets, Craven A, Players Navy Cut and Woodbine, bound together with a stiffened rubber band that snapped as he pulled it. Then he saw a yellowing newspaper with news of the sinking of a Merchant

Navy convoy by U-boats. Tom skimmed the article and laid it to one side. Then he felt a clutch of milky marbles, a packet of Rizla cigarette papers and a cigarette machine with two little rollers and a loop of paper. This was like a time capsule, capturing life in the war years.

Reaching down, he found a fishing knife, a rusting box with a cycle repair kit, and a medal. Tom lifted it up: *Winner of the Junior 100 yards dash.* Tom felt a strange emotion; so his father had been an athlete; he had run too. Tom had never seen him do any activity more physical than lifting a pint glass. He felt a sense of pride in the father he did not know at all.

Tom delved deeper into the chest. Next he lifted out a large cardboard book with the resplendent tail of a peacock on the cover. Tom opened it and saw a colourful sticker on the first page. Carefully written in copperplate hand: *Presented to Coinneach McIver. Annual Painting Prize. Nigg School June 1938.*

His father painted – and he kept this book among his treasures. Tom felt a sense of regret which clutched his heart like a physical pain. So much lost potential. His father had been a runner and a painter; he'd been a teenager with hopes and aspirations. Tom had never known him like this, only as a resentful glowering presence with a beer can in his left hand and a short temper.

Then a bundle of photographs. His father, tall and handsome, standing squinting into the sun with a harbour wall in the background; a school class showing kids in long tweed shorts, the ill-fitting collars of fathers' cut-down shirts, and girls with bows in their hair; a group of boys dressed in their best, leaning together, arms over their friends' shoulders.

And then a well-worn photo of a girl with long blonde hair and a pale summer dress. Tom smoothed the curled corners and looked at the photo carefully. A very pretty girl of about thirteen, smiling shyly at the camera, a smile that showed attraction. Was this the girl he'd made pregnant? The mother of his half-brother? Tom felt a rush of revulsion. She was just a little girl, only about the age of Shona.

He looked further into the box. There were some pencil drawings, harbour views, a fishing boat, the silhouette of a tree, a few awkward figure compositions. Tom was surprised. His father had talent, better at drawing landscapes than figures, though.

Then he saw a thick roll of papers tied with a bit of string. He unrolled them carefully and straightened them out. There were about fifty pieces of paper and they all seemed to be of naked women. Or one naked woman. They were all the same prepubescent girl with small breasts and the beginnings of pubic hair. The face was sometimes blank, but where there were features it was recognisably the girl in the picture. Although they were drawn so many years ago, Tom felt an uneasy sense of embarrassment. This was too intimate.

As he leafed further down the pile of papers the pictures became more stylized, the breasts sharper, the private space between her legs larger and cruder. And then there were other images etched on the drawings with thick, heavily-drawn lines; ropes, knives, bleeding wounds, giant phalluses violating the purity of the images, crushing every part of the sketched figure. Tom screwed the papers together in disgust.

So, seeds of the violence and aggression that had characterised his father's behaviour when he was older were there in his youth. Tom tried to think back to when he was that age. He'd fantasised about girls, of course, but this was something different. He thought of that poor girl. What indignities had his father subjected her to? Was this why he'd run away? He looked at the photo again. Her long blonde hair, her childlike innocence… there was definitely an air of Shona about her.

An unthinkable idea began to form in the back of his mind. He didn't allow it to take shape at first, blocking it out, but it diverted and found other ways to force its way into his conscious thoughts and solidify. If it wasn't Logan Baird who'd killed Shona… and Rory had said he'd seen Tom's father in the park that night…

No, not his father… no!

It was impossible, unnatural… Tom wrestled with the thought in his mind. But, after Shona's death, his father had really fallen apart, and they say most murders are committed by a family member…

No. it couldn't be. His father loved Shona, he adored her, his little princess. He loved her sitting on his knee… No, these thoughts couldn't go any further…

Tom was shaking. The walls of the small bedroom seemed to be closing in. He felt suffocated, nauseous. He had to get out, he had to get this wicked, evil chest out of the room. He dragged it back to the car, panting guiltily. A nosy neighbour really would think it was a body, he thought, as he looked furtively in every direction before lifting it into the boot of the hire car and slamming the lid shut.

The owners of the B&B didn't seem to be around so he left the key with a note and payment for the next night. Still breathing heavily, he drove as fast as he could away from the village in the opposite direction from the church and Mary McIver's pursed-lipped disapproval. Had she any idea of the secrets in the chest?

Tom sped on into the gathering darkness, down a long road, past an isolated churchyard seemingly in the middle of nowhere. He had no idea where he was going, he just had to get away. The road seemed to peter out as he reached a deserted cove. The beach was different from the ones on Uist and Harris, rockier with piles of marbled stones, smooth and regular from the sea, with swirling lines and colours of years of prehistory.

There was not much fuel around, but Tom managed to gather some driftwood, which had been caught between the stones and piles of dry seaweed and built a pyre on the beach. He found the book of matches he'd picked up at the B&B in his pocket and as the first stars appeared in the sky he managed to get a fire started. He watched as the flames grew higher and the logs glowed red in the gathering darkness before dragging the wooden chest over and heaving it onto the fire. At first, it was difficult to get the chest to burn, but once the ancient wood caught and the dry papers inside started to burn, there was a rush as sparks floated high into the night sky.

The flames started to subside into a red-gold ember glow and Tom poked it with a stick until there was nothing left but the twisted remains of charred metal.

He looked up at the sky. Without the light pollution of the city, the sliver of moon shone brightly in a vast dome of stars. The Milky Way was clearly recognisable and also some constellations he could remember from comics when he was young. He breathed deeply; it was almost as if he had been holding his breath since he opened that poisonous chest. He must never tell anyone what he had seen. He must keep it a secret.

He felt tears prick his eyes. Who would he tell? There was no one. His parents were both dead; his sister, and the half-brother he'd never even known, also gone far too soon. He'd led too superficial a life in South Africa to form close friendships. He shivered, although the air was not cold. He felt so lonely, so totally alone.

He put his hand in his pocket and felt his mobile phone. Sarah. He had Sarah's number. He'd forgotten, until this moment, that she'd given it to him that first evening. She was the one person in the world he wanted to talk to. He typed in a text message.

*

Sarah was sitting in her favourite chair, flicking through the television channels and half-reading the *Evening News* on her knee. She felt restless, in limbo, waiting for something to happen.

A beep sounded. She leapt up. Where was her mobile phone? She patted her pockets and looked into her handbag. Not there. After keeping her phone next to her for days, she'd almost given up on Tom contacting her and had no idea where it was. She looked around, feeling frantic. *Calm down*, she told herself, *it could be anyone*. She looked under cushions and newspapers and eventually went to the landline to phone her mobile.

There was a ring from the bookcase. She ran over and looked at the screen. *Thinking of you*. She didn't recognise the number but it could only be Tom.

Her heart gave a leap. He'd contacted her. *Thinking of you too. How are things? When are you coming back? Sarah x* As she sent the message off she saw her hand was shaking. Tom had sent her a text; he was thinking of her. She held the phone close to her breast.

She jumped as she heard the key in the lock and Rory came in. 'Come on, we're going out. We're filming HJ's poetry evening at the Canongate Centre and he wants you to come too.'

Sarah started guiltily as if he could read the phone messages. 'Now? I'm not dressed for going out.'

'You look fine. Come on, we'll be late.' Sarah grabbed her coat and fluffed up her hair in front of the hall mirror, before obediently following Rory down the worn stone stairs.

The Canongate Centre was a decommissioned church which had been converted into an Arts Centre. The pews were removed, but otherwise little had changed from when it was in use. A small film crew was standing in a corner, adjusting the lamps. The beams of light emphasised the gothic curves and pillars and cast deep shadows over the drafty interior.

Where the altar had stood there was a raised podium and a gaunt figure with dreadlocks was reading from a crumpled paper. As he read in a staccato, breathless voice, Sarah could feel the anguish in the psychedelic whirr of words and images. The poet finished with a muted flourish and raised his eyes for the first time to the circle of watchers.

HJ Kidd was standing at the rear. 'Danny, that's brilliant. It lays bare your feelings and we share your pain.' He paused and walked towards the bony frame of the poet, hunched over his paper, his dreadlocks falling over his face. 'Look up,

Danny. Your words have so much more impact when you raise your eyes and look into the faces of your listeners.'

Danny looked further down and muttered. 'I want my words to speak for themselves. I write these words for *me*. I don't care about the listener.' He looked round at the cameraman and sound engineer. 'And I can't read with these wankers here. We're not performing poodles. This isn't what I came to the poetry group for.'

HJ moved towards him. 'Your words are a wonderful gift. Share this with others. Other people can experience the release you felt when all your feelings were crystallised into words.' HJ looked directly into the eyes of the tortured young man. 'You have helped me. You inspired me to write again. What we have here is beautiful and we can share it with others through filming this programme.'

Danny shrugged his shoulders and went to join the small group sitting to the right of the podium. Rory leant over to Sarah. 'We've got it all on camera. This is great television, showing what an inspiration HJ is.'

Sarah looked over at Danny's hunched figure. Did Rory see everything in terms of great television?

After a moment's pause, an overweight young man, with a round, childish face and a too-tight AC/DC T-shirt, walked in a determined way, head down, onto the podium. He clutched an exercise book tightly. Lifting his head he turned directly to the cameras. 'Before I read my poem I want to say that it is HJ who's given me the confidence to stand up and read my poetry. I was bullied at school, I had no friends, I stayed in my bedroom nearly all the time. Now I can write, I feel the tightness released from my chest. I can create something.'

Sarah looked at his eyes shining in the arch lights and glanced at Rory. Was this a set up? Rory was grinning and rubbing his hands together. 'This is pure magic. I couldn't have scripted it better myself.'

The poet began to read in a low, even voice. Sarah listened carefully. To her surprise it was a short, beautifully-crafted poem about autumn. In the hushed pause after he had finished, the image of melancholy, stark bare branches, and leaves crisping in the first frost on the black streaked pavement, stayed in her mind.

HJ appeared at Sarah's side and put his arm round her shoulder. 'Now you can see why this project is so important to me. Poetry has given young people like Neil a focus in life, has even saved lives in some instances.'

Sarah nodded and turned to face her old teacher. He was looking at her with concern in his deep blue eyes. 'Sarah, I need your help. I agreed to this programme because of this project, because of the talent of these young people. I don't want it to be about me. Or my family.'

He cleared his throat. 'We're estranged and it would only cause hurt if old wounds were reopened. I've asked Rory to stop asking about my family, but he's a journalist; I'm not sure that he will do what I've asked.'

He paused again. 'You have more influence with him than I, and I'm pleading with you to persuade him to back off. You've heard the talent of these young people and you can see how important this project is. I want Rory to go ahead with the programme, but my family has never understood me and I'm afraid that his digging up the past could stir up some things that should better remain forgotten.'

He pulled Sarah nearer towards him and and moved his face very close to hers. 'Please, Sarah, do this for me.'

Sarah tried to move away. He was too close; she felt uncomfortable, but she nodded agreement and his mood immediately lightened.

'And now watch this. Lara is going to be the star of the show.'

Sarah looked back at the stage and saw a beautiful girl in a long Indian cotton dress sitting on the edge of the stage. She looked about fourteen, but Sarah guessed that she was probably quite a bit older. Her long blonde hair swung over her face as she bent over her guitar and strummed a few chords.

In a surprisingly low voice she started to speak. She didn't play as she recited a poignant story of love and rejection, and then finished with another haunting snatch of melody. The effect was electrifying. The girl looked up; there were tears glistening on her cheeks.

HJ moved over to her and embraced her, stroking her hair. 'Lara, that was amazing.' He held her at arm's length and turned to the audience. 'The power of words, ladies and gentlemen. You canna beat it!' As he lapsed into the local vernacular the group of listeners laughed, and the tension of the moment was broken.

Rory was literally rubbing his hands together with glee. 'Thank you all. This will make wonderful television.' There was a ripple of applause and the camera crew began to dismantle their equipment. Sarah glanced at Rory, who was talking to HJ, and wondered if he would be prepared just to concentrate on the poetry and give up on the family angle.

As HJ and Rory stood together, Danny, the poet with

117

dreadlocks, came towards them. He held out his hand to HJ and Sarah heard him muttering what sounded like an apology. As she moved closer she heard him more clearly. 'Shouldn't have burst out like that. You're the greatest, HJ.'

Rory snapped his fingers towards the cameraman. 'We have to get that on film. Danny can you say that again for us?'

Danny turned towards Rory and muttered vehemently. All Sarah could catch was '…you wanker.'

*

In Stornoway, Tom sat in a bar near the docks. After the bonfire he'd driven straight to the port, wanting to get off the island as quickly as possible. The next ferry was at six o'clock in the morning, so it was not worth paying for a hotel room. He parked in the queuing area behind a couple of vans and a German minibus and decided to sleep in the hire car. It was fortunate that the ferry operators had won the battle with the Kirk to be allowed to sail on the Sabbath, or he'd have been stuck on the island until Monday.

He walked towards the nearest bright light and found groups of fishermen and harbour workers sitting at formica tables in a plastic and laminate bar area. A huge television dominated one wall and a red-faced barman stood behind the long bar, gazing at the weather forecast. Tom ordered a beer and a whisky chaser and sat at a free table. The television and the voices of the other drinkers bounced round the spartan room, the strip lights on the ceiling accentuating the utilitarian atmosphere.

Tom drank quickly and ordered another round. The

shadow of the half-formed suspicions about his father clouded his mood, but he pushed them to the back of his mind and thought of Sarah. She'd sent a message and tomorrow he'd be back in Edinburgh. He smiled at the thought. As the alcohol took effect, he ordered another whisky and concentrated on the memory of her kiss and the shape of her breasts under the soft woollen sweater.

PART 6

'Be sure your sins will find you out.' My father's voice echoes through the gloom of the Free Presbyterian Church. I shiver uncomfortably on the hard wooden pew. His broad shoulders and huge leonine head loom over me from the pulpit, the outline made darker and more threatening by the light cast by the unstained window behind him. His eyes fix on me, his features distorted by rage.

'We are all sinners. God wrote the Bible to warn of the consequences of sin, and to bid you flee from the wrath to come. The only salvation from sin comes by grace through faith in Jesus Christ.' His voice rises for the final thundering verse. 'For the wrath of God is revealed from heaven against all ungodliness and unrighteousness of men, who by their unrighteousness suppress the truth.'

Sarah got up from bed and took her dressing gown from the back of the door, not wanting to disturb Rory. After getting home from the Canongate, Sarah had told Rory what HJ had said about not wanting his family involved in the programme. Rory had laughed and tousled her hair, telling her to leave the television to him and he wouldn't interfere with her housework.

Sarah knew it was no good arguing; she'd never been able to change his mind about anything. They'd gone to bed and Rory had turned to her. 'You know, you should come to the filming again. It was good having you there.' Sarah felt stupidly pleased by these few kind words and when she felt his hand moving to her breast their bodies moved together in the comforting rhythm perfected by their years together. But afterwards, she felt her father's eyes glaring down at her in disgust.

123

CHAPTER 11

Sarah sat in the kitchen with a cup of coffee, as the grey morning light began to shine through the shutters. She felt so confused; she should be happy, she had an attractive husband, a lovely family, a beautiful home… but she couldn't stop thinking about Tom.

Seeing him again made her remember how she'd fancied him when she was young. She'd been too shy to even admit the attraction to herself at the time and her parents had made it clear that anything to do with sex was dirty and unmentionable. But she had liked her best friend's older brother. Perhaps if things had been different they would have gone out together, maybe even have married.

She shook herself. She must pull herself together; she was acting like a teenager. These thoughts were pointless. She was married, had responsibilities and it was Sunday again, which meant lunch. She stood up and mechanically started to gather together the ingredients. Rory was still asleep. She hoped he'd stay for lunch; it always made the atmosphere easier because her mother hung on his every word.

The phone rang, interrupting her thoughts. It was Lottie. 'Mum, I just wanted to let you know that Liam and I aren't coming to lunch today.'

Sarah gripped the receiver more tightly. 'Oh, Lottie. You must.'

Lottie's voice was firm. 'No, we're not coming. Liam doesn't feel comfortable or welcome and I can understand why. We're going to do something different today, something for us.'

'Please come.' Sarah could hear the desperation in her own voice. 'Your dad'll be here. Don't pay too much attention to what Granny says. She doesn't mean anything. She just opens her mouth without thinking.'

'No, I don't want to be part of this charade any more. And don't worry. You'll have your beloved Nick there so everything'll be all right.'

Sarah gasped. Where had this come from? 'What do you mean? I want you both here, and I want Liam to come too. This is the day for the family, the only time we all spend together.'

'Playing happy families? Well, we're not and there's no use pretending we are every week.'

Sarah felt aghast. She'd always assumed that Sunday was a family tradition that everyone loved. All right, Rory often wasn't there and her mother was difficult, but she and the children…

Lottie took advantage of the pause to press her theme. 'And you've always favoured Nick, anyway.'

'Lottie, you know that isn't true. You two are the most important things in my life and I love you both equally. Please, please come. You can't phone up and throw this at me.' She gulped, holding back the sob that was threatening to break through. 'Look we'll go out together next week and you can talk about this, but *please* come today.' She felt her voice crack. 'It's so important to me.'

There was a pause. Lottie must have sensed how close

she was to the edge and spoke in a softer tone. 'OK Mum, we will come. But I'm warning you if Granny makes any of her remarks we're going. I'm not prepared to put myself and Liam through this ordeal every week.'

An ordeal? How could Lottie see the family lunch so differently from her? Sarah struggled to keep her voice calm. 'Thank you, Lottie. Thank you so much. I'm looking forward to seeing you both later.'

'See you later, Mum.'

The phone clicked down at the other end, but Sarah continued to clutch the handset. Lottie's words echoed through her mind. Was it true that she favoured Nick? He was more open, more affectionate, had always talked to her more. Lottie was composed, self-sufficient, liked to sit alone in her room. Sarah had always thought it was what she wanted. She realised she was shaking in her thin housecoat; the perfect world she'd tried so hard to keep intact seemed to be falling apart.

Rory came through to the kitchen, pulling his silk paisley dressing gown round him. 'Any chance of a coffee?' Sarah nodded and ground the beans, filling the kitchen with the tangy aroma. As she prepared the cafetière, Rory sat at the scrubbed wooden table and waited for his coffee.

'I've been thinking. That junkie guy was right. We don't need the big production team for this programme. What we need is intimate, investigative fly-on-the-wall television, and I'm going to do it. I'm going to ditch the crew and film it myself from now on.'

Sarah brought over his coffee. 'A more pared-down approach might suit HJ better too, concentrating on the poetry rather than the family.'

'Ah, I'm certainly not going to neglect the family angle. That's what gives the programme its USP. I know there's a mystery there and I'm going to find out what happened. This programme's going to be a cracker.'

'But HJ asked you to lay off the family aspect. And his sister didn't seem that keen,' Sarah started tentatively.

'Lay off the juiciest aspect of the story? No way, José. *Rory Dunbar's Special Report* is going to change the direction of Scottish Broadcasting.'

'But…' Sarah started and then decided to change tack. 'You will be here for lunch, won't you?'

'I've got so much to do with this programme. I need to be able to give them something concrete soon. Sorry, I just don't have the time.'

Sarah felt tears welling up behind her eyes. 'Please, Rory. I need you here today.' She told him about Lottie's phone call, her voice shaking.

'So mean old Granny was nasty to little milk-sop Liam?' he mocked. 'What a wimp.' Sarah felt her face crumple and suddenly Rory flashed his TV smile.

'Tell you what, I'll stay, but I want you to do something for me as well. Help me with the Kidd programme. He seems to like you. I mean he especially asked you to come last night, so perhaps you can find out something about the family secret.'

Sarah felt herself torn. Had she really sunk so low that she would join in with Rory's shabby journalistic tricks? Was it so important to have Rory there? She felt ashamed of herself as she realised the answer was *yes, it was.*

'OK, I'll give you all the help I can.' It was only after she'd spoken that she realised how ridiculous the situation was: having to plead and bargain with her husband to stay to Sunday lunch with his own family.

Rory drained his coffee cup and stood up yawning. 'OK, if I'm staying I think I'll just go back to bed. You'll have a lot to do with the preparations for lunch.'

*

After the early crossing, Tom docked at Ullapool and drove quickly through the mist-strewn Highlands, his mind racing. The images of his father's pictures appeared before his eyes; he also remembered the violence and heavy drinking of the last days of his life. Could he have done something to Shona? Tom tried everything in his power to blank these thoughts from his mind, but they kept bubbling back into his consciousness.

As he approached the Forth Road Bridge he felt a pulse of excitement. Beyond the silvery waters, the skyline of Edinburgh floated into view through the mists. Although he'd been in South Africa for so many years, it still felt as if he was coming home, and he was getting closer to Sarah. He so wanted to see her.

As he crept back into the Regent Guest House, hoping to avoid Mrs Ritchie and her requests for Rory's autograph, he felt a wave of sadness. Sarah would be serving Sunday lunch at Great King Street now. How he wished he could be there.

*

Rory opened the door to his mother-in-law and Nick. 'Flora,' he said, taking her hand and kissing it. 'How lovely to see you. And looking more beautiful than ever.' Flora simpered and allowed him to take her coat.

'Hi Dad,' Nick followed his grandmother through the door.

'Great to see you, son. Looking good.' Rory ran his eye over the pale blue cashmere pullover looped over his son's polo-shirt. 'Going to play golf?'

Sarah gave Rory a warning glance but Nick just grinned. 'If you want to be at the cutting edge of contemporary journalism, you'll need to keep your finger on the pulse of modern fashion.'

Flora looked puzzled while Sarah led them through to the dining room and offered drinks. They were just going to raise their glasses in a toast when Sarah heard the front door open. Rory leapt up and Sarah heard him welcoming Lottie and Liam effusively. He seemed to be overacting his role considerably.

Rory brought them through and poured drinks. He raised his glass. 'A toast to the family. Great that we're all here together,' he beamed at Sarah. 'And thanks, Sarah, for preparing this delicious meal.'

Sarah began to serve the soup, wondering if she might not prefer absent Rory to this pastiche of pater familias. Obviously thinking his main role was to make Liam feel welcome, Rory launched into chat show mode. 'I realise how little I know about you, Liam. You're from Fife, aren't you?'

Liam blushed at the unaccustomed attention. 'That's right. I was brought up in Newmills. My dad worked at the Valleyfield Colliery before they closed it down.'

'My dad was a miner too.'

Sarah smiled at this poetic licence. Rory's dad might have

been down the pit when he was very young, but he was certainly a retired milkman when they met.

'And are your family still there?'

Liam's face reddened again. 'My mum and dad have both passed away and I didn't have any brothers and sisters.'

Rory almost whooped. 'That's amazing, the same as me. I'm an orphan too. My parents waited a long time for me and then afterwards they realised they couldn't equal perfection.'

Sarah cringed.

'And Sarah's an only child too. You twins don't realise how lucky you are.'

The twins exchanged ironic looks.

'Of course Sarah's was a very difficult birth,' began Flora, who'd been anxiously looking for an opportunity to get into the conversation. 'She was such a big baby…'

'Can I take your plate, Mum?' Sarah cut in, but her mother pressed on undeterred as she carried the dishes into the kitchen. While arranging the roast beef on the plates she could hear her mother's penetrating voice detailing the length and pain of her labour. Sarah went back and saw the young ones nodding in an embarrassed manner with Rory interspersing encouraging remarks into Flora's monologue, like 'How brave.' Sarah even heard, 'Looking at Sarah, you must think it was all worth it.'

She clattered down the plates. 'How was the Bridge Club this week, Mum?'

'So exciting. We have a few new members and they are all such lovely people. Mona McLean, her husband was Lord McLean, the High Court judge, you know…' Having been set on a new track, her mother listed the pedigrees of all the members of the club. Sarah sat down and emptied her wine glass. She filled it up immediately and thought back to the week before. Tom had been there then. If only he were here again this week; then it would be more bearable. Oh Tom, when would she see him again?

Her musings were cut short as her mother mentioned Lady Antonia Moncrieff. Rory immediately interrupted.

'Do you know Lady Antonia?'

Flora stopped in mid-sentence and pursed her carefully rouged lips. 'Well, not exactly, but I do have it on very good authority that she will be joining our club very soon.'

Rory looked crestfallen. 'So you don't actually know her personally?' Flora shook her head reluctantly, and realising she'd disappointed Rory, continued brightly, 'So have you met any exciting people on your show recently? All my friends are very interested to hear about you.'

Rory got over his disappointment and launched into his favourite subject, himself, telling some entertaining tales. When Sarah brought in the tiramisu, she saw that Liam and Lottie were holding hands happily and her mother was nodding enthusiastically.

Sarah gulped another glass of wine and heaved a sigh of relief. Family problems averted for a while. The conversation drifted on amicably enough as she got the coffee and mint chocolates.

Then her mother started up again. 'You're such a good-looking boy, Nick. So like your father.' She gave a toothy simper in Rory's direction. Lottie looked sick.

'Any more coffee?' Sarah said desperately.

'I'm sure you must have a delightful girlfriend. Why don't you bring her along to Sunday lunch? We would love to meet her. And Lottie always brings her friend,' Flora carried on undeterred, giving the reference to Liam her usual sneering emphasis.

'Playing the field you know, Granny. So many beautiful girls–' Nick spoke quickly, trying to lighten the atmosphere, but it was too late.

'Yes, Nick. Why don't you? I'm sure Granny would love to meet your friend,' Lottie said, standing up and looking defiantly at Sarah. 'Well, it's all been lovely, but I'm afraid we really have to go now.'

Liam stood up next to Lottie. 'Thank you for the great food, Mrs Dunbar.'

Sarah followed them into the hall. 'Thanks for coming, both of you.' She gave Lottie a hug and whispered, 'We'll have that shopping expedition – very soon.' She turned to Liam. 'And you must call me Sarah.'

She was giving him an awkward hug as Rory joined them. 'Hurrying off already, you two young lovebirds? Well, have fun and don't do anything that I wouldn't do,' he paused. 'That gives you a wide range of options then.' He laughed at his own dinosaur joke, kissed Lottie and gave Liam a manly punch on the shoulder.

The door closed behind them and Rory turned back to Sarah with an *aren't I doing well?* grin that made her want to slap him. However, she smiled and went back to the drawing room where her mother was still giving Nick a lecture on the merits of settling down with a lovely girl and not leaving it too long. He was giving his normal sonny-boy smile, letting it all wash over him.

Sarah braced herself. Usually she would do anything to avoid conflict, but she had to speak. 'Mum, I know you don't mean to be unkind, but you really mustn't speak to Liam like that. Lottie gets upset.' She realised that she had drunk most of the wine and decided to say it all. 'You know, Lottie was thinking of not coming at all today.'

'She could really do so much better than that young man. He's not very prepossessing, is he?'

Instead of biting her tongue as she usually did, Sarah spoke out, the emotions of the last few days giving her courage.

'Liam is Lottie's choice and it's not up to us to judge. He seems a very pleasant, well-mannered young man, although it's difficult for him to get a word in edgeways sometimes.'

Flora turned her gimlet gaze to Nick. 'I think it's up to you, young man. If you brought someone along then Lottie's little friend wouldn't seem such an outsider.'

Nick gave a smile so like his father's. 'I'd sooner throw a friend of mine to the lions than bring them along to face you lot!' The lightness of his tone made it sound like a joke but Sarah knew he meant every word. He stood up from his chair. 'Anyway Granny, if I brought someone else along I wouldn't have so much time to devote to you. Come on now, your chariot awaits.'

He led his grandmother to the hall and gave his mother a wink. 'Thanks, Mum. The food was great.' A thought seemed to occur to him and he moved his head closer to his mother's. 'We must get together very soon, go up town, have a drink.'

'I'd like that.'

Nick gave her a hug and a kiss. 'See you soon, lovely Mummy.'

Rory came out of the dining room and and swept Flora into his arms. 'Goodbye, my favourite little flower,' he said, kissing her on the cheek. Flora beamed. Rory did the manly punch bit with Nick, who then took his grandmother's arm and led her down the stairs.

Sarah closed the door. She felt completely exhausted. Rory looked at her like a dog expecting a treat. 'Well, I think that went very well.'

Sarah sighed, 'Could have been worse.' She looked at the kitchen piled high with dirty dishes and at the white starched tablecloth stained with coffee rings.

'Right,' said Rory. 'I'm going to *have* to do some work now. I haven't read all of the poems in that folder and I need to write a full proposal for the programming meeting tomorrow.' So saying, he went into his study and closed the door firmly.

CHAPTER 12

Sarah was hoovering the dining room when the phone rang behind her. She gave a jump; she'd been thinking of Tom. Could it be him? She saw the number on the display – her mother.

'Hello, Mum.'

'Hello dear. I hope I'm not disturbing you when you're doing something important.' Sarah bit her lip. Her mother managed to imbue this simple sentence with a loud and clear sub-text: *of course I'm not disturbing you as you never do anything important.* Her mother, on the other hand, was always busy, the constant round of bridge games, hair appointments, lunches and coffee afternoons.

'No, Mum. Rory's just gone out.'

'He works so hard, dear boy. Well, if you've got nothing on perhaps you could do something for me. Mona McLean – a very dear friend of mine - has arranged a luncheon at the Waterfront Brasserie. You know the Brasserie? Very French, the in-place at the moment, and she asked me to join her and her friends. She's the widow of a high court judge, you know.'

Ah so that's why you've phoned, to let me know about this social coup, thought Sarah, but she just said gently, 'That's very nice.'

'I have a little favour to ask of you. It's so difficult to get to Leith by public transport. I thought you could just come over and pick me up and drop me off at the restaurant.'

'Mum, it's only half past nine. What time's your lunch?'

'We're meeting at twelve thirty, but I thought you could come and have coffee with me first. I've bought a new jacket and I'm just not sure which skirt would go with it best.'

'Of course. When would you like me to come round?'

'As soon as you like. And you could just pick up a couple of croissants from the French patisserie in Stockbridge on the way.'

Twenty minutes later Sarah drew up outside her mother's bungalow in Corstorphine, clutching the requested bag of croissants. Her mother had moved here from their gloomy Portobello house after her husband had died.

Her mother was waiting at the bay front window. 'Now, I was just wondering what had kept you. Was there a long queue at the patisserie?'

Sarah fixed a smile on her face. Why didn't her mother call it the baker's like everyone else? How did Flora expect her to get there in less than twenty minutes? Why did everything her mother said irritate her? *I must be patient,* she reminded herself.

'It's lovely that you're going out to lunch. Come and show me what you're going to wear.'

Sarah followed through to a bedroom where one entire wall was covered with mirror-fronted fitted wardrobes. Her mother opened one section where clothes were neatly arranged in blue-green tones. Some of the more precious items were protected in plastic covers. She began to give a detailed description of where every piece was purchased. Sarah hoped she was nodding at appropriate intervals as her mother pulled out different articles on padded silk hangers.

'Really, you should get some new clothes yourself. You

137

always seem to wear the same drab colours.' Flora selected a pretty powder-blue blouse and held it up in front of her daughter. 'Of course, being a larger size does make it difficult for you to carry off brighter colours,' she added, sliding the blouse back into the packed wardrobe. Sarah kept her face motionless. She was used to her mother's lack of sensitivity.

Eventually her mother found an outfit that satisfied her, dressed carefully, checked her perfect make-up and, spraying on some White Satin, led Sarah into the front room. She opened a polished mahogany cabinet and took out a bottle of sherry and two crystal glasses.

'I think we'll just have a little drink before we set off.'

'I've got to drive, Mum.' Sarah wondered what had happened to the idea of coffee and croissants.

'Just a little one will be all right, just to get myself in the mood for my lunch. Lady Antonia Moncrieff will be there, too. Her husband was a law lord. Rory seemed interested in her yesterday.'

Sarah remembered her promise to Rory. Perhaps her mother could find out something from HJ Kidd's sister. 'Oh yes, I've heard of her. Her brother was my English teacher when I was at Brunstane High.'

'I think you must be mistaken, my dear. She is a Lady. She wouldn't have a brother teaching at that dreadful school. I was so pleased when your father came to his senses and sent you to a decent school like St Margaret's.' She took a deep sip of her sherry. 'Just fill me up, will you dear? I did hope that you would meet some nice girls at St Margaret's. Do you never have lunch with any of them? With Rory being so busy you do seem to lead such a boring life.'

Sarah flinched and before she could stop herself found herself trying to prove that her life was not as uneventful as her mother suggested. 'Actually Rory is making a programme about Lady Antonia's brother and I went along to the filming on Saturday night.'

Flora looked interested. 'Rory's making a programme about him? That is exciting. I must mention it to Lady Antonia at lunch. I'm so proud that Rory's my son-in-law. They're all so interested in hearing about him. What did you say the brother's called?'

'HJ Kidd. He's a poet. He's published several books and a few poems have even been printed in the *Scotsman*. He taught at Brunstane High School for forty years and has just retired.'

It occurred to Sarah that Lady Antonia might not be all that keen to talk about her brother after Rory's experience, but she was sure her mother could get information out of her if anyone could.

She changed the subject. 'Actually, I thought Brunstane High was a good school. Why did you send me there if you thought it was so terrible?'

'It was your father. He was very much against anything that might smack of showing off. He said if he preached at the Free Church he should not be sending his own daughter up town to a fee-paying school. Of course, after what happened,' Flora glared at Sarah as if it had been her fault, 'I was able to get my way and send you to my old school.' Flora looked pensive. 'It was rarely enough I did get my way. We thought differently about almost everything.'

Sarah couldn't remember her father very clearly, a stern frightening man who seemed to have a grudge against the world. She wondered how her parents had ever got together.

As if she could read her thoughts, Flora continued. 'There were many people who wondered why I married him. Well, I'll tell you the reason, it was because he *asked* me. I should have married someone from my social circle, the brother of one of my school friends perhaps, but after the war there were so few eligible men and they were all so swiftly snapped up.' Flora took the bottle and refilled her glass. 'I had my admirers, of course, but somehow it never quite worked out, so I married your father. He'd had a very distinguished war career, of course, and a good job doing the books at Dysons.' She paused, 'I thought he was a good man. A man of the church.'

Flora looked over her glass. Her beautifully arranged white hair seemed slightly askew and her pale blue eyes glistened beneath her perfectly-pencilled brows.

Sarah wondered if she had been drinking before she arrived. Her mother suddenly seemed quite drunk. Flora leant forward in a confidential way. 'But he was a beast. You know there's an unpleasant side of marriage that all women have to put up with, but he was insatiable.' She took another large sip of her sherry. 'I tolerated it until I was pregnant, but then I told him it was over. And I never allowed him to touch me like that again.' Flora smiled, her lips pulled tightly over her prominent teeth.

Sarah squirmed uncomfortably. Her mother had never talked about anything remotely sexual before, had not even told Sarah about periods until she'd been frightened by the blood on her nightdress. And then it was something dirty and embarrassing. 'Mum, do you want a lie-down? Do you feel well enough to go out?'

'What are you talking about? There's nothing wrong with

me. I don't know what you're wasting time for. It's time for me to go out to lunch… you know, with Mona McLean and Antonia Moncrieff? They're the widows of prominent lawyers. Please hurry up. I don't want to be late.'

As Sarah drove her down to Leith, her mother slumped into a shallow sleep. They drove down Leith Walk, where many of the Georgian buildings had been cleaned up and glistened pale and dignified in the cool autumn sunlight. Leith was very much gentrified. Her mother would never have been seen dead there in the old days, but now the old warehouses had been converted into yuppie lofts and the docklands had glittering new apartments and smart restaurants.

They drew up outside the Waterfront, which looked suitably upmarket with black leaded windows, hanging baskets, and dark green paint with gold lettering.

Flora seemed to sense that they'd arrived. As she gathered her handbag and stepped out onto the pavement, her legs painfully thin above her smart court shoes, she pulled herself together. 'What was the name of that poet? HJ Kidd? I'll ask Lady Antonia about him.' She gave Sarah a faint smile and walked carefully towards the restaurant.

Sarah sat watching her and mulling over the events of the day. When had her mother started drinking in the morning? Or was it just the tension of this particular lunch date? She'd been trying for years to be accepted into the inner circle of the Bridge Club and this was certainly an important day for her.

Sarah thought back to what her mother had said about her father. Perhaps that was why he was so bad-tempered; it would explain the pent-up anger and tension that had always

141

seemed so close to the surface with him. Her mother was probably right that they should never have married: this bear of a man from a long line of farm labourers and his tiny snobbish wife with her love of clothes and the good life had always seemed an incongruous couple.

Sarah wondered if that was why her father had always seemed to regard her with distaste. She had heard of other fathers who treated their daughters like princesses, whereas she was never good enough, always the awkward, clumsy one. Both her parents had seemed disappointed that Sarah's height had been inherited from her father's side of the family.

Back in the sanctuary of her flat, Sarah put on a compilation CD of seventies hits and picked up the paper. As she listened to the familiar music, she laid the paper down beside her; she was reading the same headlines over and over again. So many things were happening, disturbing the normal equilibrium of her life: Logan Baird being released, her mother's bizarre behaviour, the tensions between the twins, coming into contact with Captain Kidd again, and, of course, Tom. He never seemed to be far away from her thoughts now.

The strains of Les McKeown's introduction to the Bay City Rollers' 'Bye Bye Baby' came on and she was overcome by a wave of nostalgia and regrets. That was a hit when Shona was killed. They danced to this together in her bedroom. The last time she could ever remember dancing to a pop song. After that it was all blank, lonely.

The music changed... *Woke up this morning half asleep.* The beginning of 'Flowers in the Rain'. Pop music had been banned in her house. All she could remember were stiff meals with stilted conversations and long, gloomy silences. Television was considered a sin and a copy of *Jackie* provoked a rant on the wickedness of the world. Her mother was always a shadowy figure in the background, never standing up to her husband, but spoilt in many ways, seemingly content as long as she was given her treats, new clothes and a weekly trip to the hairdresser.

On the other hand, anything Sarah had wanted was frivolous, a waste of money; like her clothes, for example: they had to be respectable, old-fashioned and drab, and never seemed to fit, bought to accommodate her long arms and legs, but hanging shapelessly round her undeveloped body.

No wonder she'd spent as much time as she could with Shona and her family. Shona had radiated joy, had brought light into Sarah's life. And she was daring: Sarah felt a tinge of guilt as she remembered the things they'd got up to together. They'd phoned people up, boys in the class, even once Captain Kidd. Shona had put on a different voice and said the most ridiculous things while Sarah stifled her giggles in the background.

And mixed with her memories of the past there was the image of Tom. Shona's cool big brother. And now he was back in Scotland. She looked at her phone again. She hadn't heard anything since the last text message. Was he back in Edinburgh?

Her mobile phone beeped. She looked at it, and felt a tremor of excitement. A message from Tom. *Are you at home? Can we talk?*

She texted back immediately. *Where are you? Do you want to come round now?*

The mobile rang almost immediately. Tom's voice. Still Scottish but with a slight overlay of a South African accent. 'I'm very close. Just outside actually. I was just going to call in but I didn't want to interrupt anything. Is this a good time?'

'Of course. Just come right up.'

Sarah could feel her heart beating faster with anticipation. She plumped up a few cushions and then looked in the mirror. Would it look too obvious if she put on some lipstick?

The door rang and she saw Tom standing there. His tanned face looked pale, his eyes dark and tired. They looked at each other slightly awkwardly and then bumped noses as they both went the same way attempting to kiss each other on the cheek.

CHAPTER 13

Sarah took a deep breath. 'Would you like something to drink? A coffee?' She led him into the front room. He accepted and sat down at the end of the Chesterfield.

As they drank, Sarah asked him about his visit to the Outer Hebrides. Tom told her about scattering the ashes, and the love and welcome he felt from his mother's family. He briefly mentioned going to Lewis and, seemingly emboldened by her look of intense interest, mentioned his half-brother. 'It was so strange finding out I had an older brother and then losing him within a few minutes. I was amazed by the sense of loss I felt.'

Tom looked up and his eyes met Sarah's. Sarah felt her stomach flip.

The phone rang, breaking the moment. Sarah wondered whether to answer it, but saw it was her mother. She picked up the receiver and her mother's cultured Edinburgh tones rang out clearly; she was of the generation who believed you had to shout into the phone. 'Not disturbing you, my dear, am I?'

Sarah raised her eyebrows at Tom. Without pausing for an answer, her mother hurried on.

'I just had to phone you because I had a most interesting conversation in the Brasserie.' She exaggerated the French pronunciation. 'You know I was there with Lady Antonia.

Well, I asked her about her brother and she didn't want to talk about him at all!'

'Yes, I don't think they have much contact,' said Sarah in a calming voice, because her mother sounded highly excitable.

'But you don't know why, do you?' Flora's voice dropped in a conspiratorial way. 'After lunch, Mona, you know Mona McLean – her husband was a law lord,' Sarah held the phone from her ear and glanced over at Tom, circling her hand in a 'get on with it' gesture, 'gave me a lift home, she has a driver, of course, and she told me the *whole* story. Apparently, Antonia and her brother were very close when they were young, but there was a terrible falling out. Something happened when he was about seventeen and he had to leave the family home and was told never to darken their door again.'

Sarah winced at her mother's melodramatic language.

'So he left there and then and the family have never had anything to do with each other since.'

Sarah waited, but when nothing more came she asked, 'So, what happened?'

'Nobody really knows but Mona thinks it's something to do with a young housemaid they had. I think they were found together.'

'Surely that wouldn't be enough to cause such a family rift? I thought that was par for the course at that time, rite of passage for young men of his class?'

'Sarah, I really don't know where you get these ideas from. Probably from one of those books you're always reading.' Her mother said *books* like Lady Bracknell intoning *handbag*.

'Anyway, Mum, I'm glad you had a good time. Thanks for ringing to let me know.'

'I thought Rory would be interested.'

'I'll tell him as soon as he gets in. Speak to you soon – and see you on Sunday.'

'Ah yes, Sunday. Please ask Nicholas if he could bring his young lady. I'm sure she must be a delightful person to have captured his heart.'

'I'll ask him.'

'Well, my dear, I have to go now. Give my love to Rory.' Sarah was left looking at the phone, quizzically.

She looked across at Tom. 'I did wonder if there was something strange about Kidd's family. He was very adamant that he didn't want them included in the programme.'

Her voice trailed off as there was a click at the front door and Rory came into the room, followed by Captain Kidd. Sarah blushed, hoping they hadn't caught her last sentence and hurried into the kitchen to put the coffee on.

'Hi Tom,' Rory put his arm round his shoulder. Tom and Kidd exchanged greetings and Rory pulled a paper out of his pocket. 'I've just seen Archie and he's given me this. It's tomorrow's paper. Logan Baird was released today.'

Rory handed the paper to Tom before heading for the kitchen. On the front page above the headlines were thumbnails from the featured articles. He saw a miniature version of the most famous photo of Shona, the one that had appeared on all the posters. The Insight Article was on page fourteen.

Tom's hand trembled as he found the page. A larger picture of Shona stared out at him, looking back over her shoulder, laughing. He remembered that photo being taken on the beach; such a happy day, everyone unaware of what was to happen so soon afterwards. He quickly skimmed the article.

Portobello murder case man freed after thirty-seven years in jail.

A man who has spent nearly forty years in prison was released last night, pending a fresh appeal against his conviction in the notorious Portobello murder case of 1976.

Rory came back from the kitchen with a bottle of Italian red and four glasses. He uncorked it and poured them all a glass. Tom closed the paper; he couldn't bear to read this now.

'Have you had a chance to speak to the police yet?' Rory asked.

Tom shook his head; he knew he was putting it off, but the shock discoveries about his father in Lewis had made him uncertain what to do next. Like everything in his life he hadn't wanted to confront, he tried to forget it, hoping it would go away.

Rory raised his glass to him. 'Now I know that you didn't exactly hit it off with Archie the other day, but I think it would be good if you met again. You see that he's been true to his word and he's kept you and Sarah out of his article.'

Tom took a deep breath of relief.

Rory sipped from his glass. 'I think you should speak to him. He's got a few good contacts in the force,' he tapped his nose, 'and he'll be able to give you a bit of background before you talk to the police. He's always in the Café Royal at lunchtime, so what about meeting for a drink tomorrow at about one?'

Tom nodded. It was a good idea.

Rory emptied his glass. 'So that's a date then.' He gestured towards his old teacher and lifted his camera case. 'I can't stay long, the Captain and I are off filming. We're concentrating on the animal poems at the moment so we're going out tonight to film him reading some of his poems outside – down to Portobello beach to do *Seagull* and then off into the woods for *Owl*.' He nodded at Kidd. 'The Captain's got great presence when he reads.'

Sarah, who'd come into the room during the last sentence, nodded. 'I wanted to ask you about the *Seagull*. When you read it at the reunion it sent shivers down my spine. What inspired that?'

Kidd looked pleased. 'Thank you, Sarah. What a lovely thing to say. Now how did this poem come about? I read an article that stated that DNA research shows that very close relatives of modern birds were already around about 100 million years ago. If you look closely at the seagull, especially the older ones, you can see that they really are living fossils. I'm also interested in theories that a species have a collective consciousness so there are shared memories.'

'Save all this for the film, HJ,' Rory interrupted. Then he paused and pointed as he saw Sultan stalk into the room with an arrogant swagger, his tail straight up. 'Here comes Sultan, right on cue. I told you about him. How about reading *Tibby the Cat* with him?'

HJ Kidd looked pained. 'I was eight when I wrote that. So embarrassing. I'm not altogether convinced that such a poem would add anything to the programme.'

Rory shook his head. 'Great human interest, great accessibility. And it's a lovely poem, *eyes like marbles and wire whiskers.*'

HJ Kidd still didn't seem convinced. 'We can discuss that later.'

Rory leapt up. 'Anyway, we'd better be going. We don't want to miss the evening light on the beach.'

Kidd smiled at Sarah. 'Always delightful to see you, my dear. I did so enjoy seeing you at our poetry evening at the centre, and I hope you will join us for some more of the filming.'

Sarah flushed under the intensity of his gaze. 'I'd like to do that. I really enjoyed watching the filming.'

Rory drained his glass and stood up quickly, turning to Sarah. 'Right, I'm off now. I'll be late so don't wait up.' He punched Tom on the shoulder. 'See you in the Café Royal.' He lowered his voice. 'And we're really going to have to have that night out together soon. Jennie's still in town, you know.' With a sly wink he picked up the camera and his coat and ushered HJ Kidd into the hall.

The door slammed behind him. Sarah and Tom looked at each other again. Tom felt anger welling up inside him. Rory talking like that in front of Sarah, ignoring her most of the time. 'Rory seems to go out a lot.'

'It's his job. I'm used to it.'

'But don't you get lonely sometimes?' Tom regretted saying it as soon as the words were out of his mouth. It sounded like a cheesy chat-up line.

Sarah smiled. 'I like being by myself. I like reading, listening to music.' She laid back and the cat leapt onto her lap and stretched out, flexing his claws and purring softly. 'And I've got Sultan for company.'

Tom wanted to shout: *you're a beautiful, sensual woman and your husband's a lying philandering bastard. You deserve so much more.* But he couldn't. She seemed so cool, so composed. Then he remembered the passion of her kiss at the door.

He raised his glass and looked across at the beauty of her face. She lowered her long lashes and then looked up at him, her lips slightly apart. A wave of passion passed between them that made his stomach lurch.

Tom reached out to her and drew her towards him. Sarah responded by moving towards him and moulding her body to his. Her lips so soft and yielding, her tongue tracing the outline of his mouth. He put his hand under her cashmere sweater and fumbled for her bra fastening.

Then nature took over. Hands, tongues, needy, reaching a frenzy of excitement as they pulled the rest of their clothes off and their bodies melded. It was irresistible. The rush of feeling coursed through his whole body.

Afterwards he held her close, and kissed her gently on her eyelids. During his encounters in South Africa he'd never felt anything like this. Then, he'd wanted to get away as quickly as possible afterwards, but with Sarah he felt he wanted to stay for ever. The heaviness of sleep overcame him and he fell asleep in her arms.

*

The room was dark and the street lights outside cast shadows on the ceiling when he woke up. Sarah was asleep with her head on his chest, her mouth moving slightly as if she was talking in her sleep. He looked at his clothes scattered on the floor and tried to reach them without

151

disturbing Sarah. He'd better get dressed – what if Rory came back?

As he moved Sarah opened her eyes, blinking as she looked round the room, then at him. She sat up straight and shook her head, her brown hair swaying gently. They dressed quickly and Sarah reached for the wine glass and took a sip. 'At least I can't blame it on drunkenness,' she said, looking at him with a mock-apologetic expression. Her eyes were sparkling.

Tom lifted his glass and clinked it against hers. He felt literally lost for words. He wanted to say, *that was the most wonderful thing that has ever happened to me*, but just murmured, 'That was lovely.'

Sarah smiled at him. 'Yes, it was.' Then a look of sadness crossed her face. 'Oh Tom, what are we going to do?'

Tom took another slug of wine. He wanted to tell her what Rory was really like but he couldn't. 'You seem to lead separate lives,' was as far as he felt he could go.

Sarah lowered her eyes. 'Tom, I feel so close to you. I feel… *right* with you. I wish we could have got together earlier, under different circumstances.' She bit her lip. 'But I have to stay with Rory. There's something I have to tell you. I hope you won't hate me when you hear it.'

Tom couldn't think of anything that Sarah could tell him that would change the way he felt. He held her hand more tightly trying to show this.

Sarah took a deep breath. 'Everyone thinks I'm so good.' Her voice rose and Tom stroked her arm.

'After my father died I met a boy, the brother of a girl at school. He was the kind of boy my mother had always dreamt of: good family, best school and university, training to be a lawyer. He said he loved me and I believed him. I went to bed with him. I knew it was wrong, I was not that kind of girl.'

She gulped a huge breath. 'And then I found out I was pregnant. I was so sick, so frightened. I thought when I told him we'd get married, that he'd make everything all right. But,' she looked round the room with a distracted stare, 'he told me to get rid of it, said I was just a silly little girl.'

Tom put his arm round her. He could feel the tension in her body. She took a tissue from her pocket and twisted it in her hands. 'And I did. I didn't tell anyone. I went to a clinic and had an abortion. Used all my savings. Then I stayed at home for weeks. I told my mother I was ill and she accepted it without any questions. Didn't really seem to notice. It was just the time when she was coming to life again, catching up with all her old school friends and going out to lunch.'

Tom stroked her hair, wanting to show support but not wanting to break the flow of words. After another pause Sarah seemed to calm herself.

'Then I went back to college and finished the course. I got a job at the *Scotsman* and met Rory. We worked together and one day he asked me to come for a coffee. I don't know how but I told him everything. He was so easy to talk to, so unshockable. He was the first person I could talk to and he understood. He made me feel that everything was all right. He listened to me. He was the only person I'd told and he didn't condemn me.'

Tom felt a twinge of jealousy as Sarah took a deep breath. 'I began to fall in love with him. I'd vowed I'd never go to bed with a man again until I was married, but I did. The first time we slept together must have been the night we conceived the twins. The nightmare came back – I was pregnant.' Tom held her closer. Poor Sarah, from what he knew of her and her background, he could imagine how terrified she must have been.

Sarah raised her eyes and looked at him. 'I was so scared when I told Rory. I was sure he'd tell me to have another abortion.' She faltered over the last words and Tom saw tears welling up in her eyes.

'I didn't know then that he was already married. I felt even more terrible when I found out. But he told me he loved me. He left his wife and let me have my babies. He gave up everything for me. Tom, how could I ever leave him?'

Tom watched her, his heart aching. He murmured platitudes about everyone making mistakes, being able to put the past behind. He thought, but he didn't say, that Rory had probably wanted an escape from that early marriage, judging by what he'd said in the pub, and he had certainly not been faithful to her since then.

Tom felt so confused. He'd been attracted to Sarah the moment he met her again and now – seeing the vulnerability beneath her composed exterior – he felt more. They were linked through Shona, but there was a deeper connection. He wanted to protect her, to kiss her eyelids for ever, to hold her safe. She deserved so much better than Rory. But what did he have to offer? He was a homeless South African bum, with no home, no qualifications, no prospects.

PART 7

Portobello prom. The sky is bright and the sun sparkles on the water and the wet sand. Shona and I are walking arm in arm. The breeze off the sea is warm as it gently ruffles our long hair. I hear the ebb and flow of the waves, the laughter of children digging in the sand and the barking of a dog as it leaps to catch a ball in the shallow waves. Couples walking hand in hand and the distant cry of a baby.

A gaze bores into me. I look back and see the small dark eyes of Logan Baird fixed on us. He is standing in the gloom of the shadow of the Free Presbyterian Church. His ankle-length dark coat is hanging open, his narrow white face framed by long lank black hair, his eyes small and close together. Despite 1976 being the hottest summer on record, a chill passes through me.

CHAPTER 14

Tom splashed through the shallow waves as he pounded along Portobello beach. He was alone apart from a few early dog walkers and a flock of seagulls squawking and squabbling over the rubbish bins. The air was cool as the sun rose palely over the distant Lothian coast. As he reached an effortless rhythm, his thoughts returned to Sarah.

He remembered last night. The torrent of passion Sarah had unleashed had triggered a reverberation in him that seemed to make his body take flight. Sarah, so beautiful, so sensual, so vulnerable. He wanted to kiss her, to hold her, protect her for ever.

This was ridiculous – he felt like a seventeen-year-old. He'd only ever felt anything remotely resembling this once before. His heart caught as he remembered Layla. He was a lonely seventeen-year-old with nothing in common with the stocky Boers in his class, who mocked his Scottish accent and his interest in football. When he met up with the community who lived on a farm high up over the rocky coast along from the Plettenberg Bay, he'd felt accepted. They were an international group, living in the big farmhouse or in tents scattered amongst the exotic shrubs and colourful flowers of the 'fine bush'.

Layla was beautiful with long straw-coloured hair, an intriguing Scandinavian accent and an enigmatic smile. She had sensed the trouble in him as she massaged his shoulders. He could remember her low voice as her supple hands ran over his back, locating the knots and easing the pain away.

'You need to release the pain and feel the sorrow flow out of your body. Relax your mind and let the bitterness drain out.'

Over and over, like a mantra. He'd felt the pain easing, replaced by a wonderful buoyancy, as if he was floating. 'Breathe in sparkling shiny air. It will give you energy and strength. It will flow into every part of your body. Let go of the past and breathe in new life.'

As she turned him over and ran her fingers down his legs he felt himself stiffen. He tried to think it away but it quivered and grew, and then Layla moved closer. Tom felt a stirring at the memory as he ran. How strange that the memory of Layla was coming back so strongly now. Being with Sarah was the first time that lovemaking had meant anything since Layla.

After that day he'd spent every moment he could at the farm, learning to make the beautiful drift-wood sculptures the community made to order or to sell at the market in Knysna, smoking joints and exploring Layla's golden body. His father was drowning his sorrows in the Moby Dick Bar and his mother was absorbed by the One World Church, so they didn't seem to notice their son was skipping school, running wild.

One hot day, he went up the dusty red road to the farm earlier than usual. The day was hot and airless and the only sound that broke the silence of the afternoon air was the rhythmic rasp of the crickets. As he approached the house it was quiet, only the hum of low voices could be heard from some of the tents. He went up to Layla's room and opened the door.

He stood frozen in the doorway; brown buttocks were moving up and down into Layla's golden body. As his eyes became accustomed to the shadows of the darkened room, the curtains drawn against the afternoon sun, he recognised John, the 'leader' of the community. Realising there was someone else in the room, his handsome face with its chiselled Zapata moustache looked round and Layla gave an enigmatic smile.

Tom ran to the edge of the bush and watched the waves crash against the honey-coloured rocks below. His body heaved with sobs. He loved Layla. He'd never dared to say it, but he'd felt it.

Some time later he sensed a presence behind him. Layla laid her hands on his shoulders and began to massage the tension in his neck. Tom turned round angrily and brushed her hands away.

'Tom, you knew you were not the only one.'

'I didn't. I love you. I thought you were my girlfriend.'

'Love is not possession. Our community is built on love, we must share it. We must love everyone.'

Tom could still feel the hurt, the open raw gaping wound of his disappointment. Soon after that, the community had moved away along the coast, Tom had dropped out of school completely and the place in his heart where love should be became hard. The succession of superficial relationships had made this place more brittle. Now he felt it melting, the feelings he'd forgotten for so long coming back. He loved Sarah.

Despite her loyalty to Rory, he felt it in her, too. He wanted to help her shake off the feelings of guilt and

161

responsibility that were shackling her to Rory, wanted to share his own reawakening with her. He was going to win her. Rory didn't deserve her. She should be loved, sharing the wonders of life instead of keeping up the lonely façade of her sterile existence. And bound up with his thoughts of Sarah were his memories of Shona, the brilliant whirlwind of energy she'd been and the woman she could have become.

He ran further along the beach, leaving the dogwalkers behind, his thoughts in tune with the steady rhythm of his footsteps. He was meeting Rory and the journalist at lunchtime. Sarah would have seen the newspaper by now. He felt a coward for not showing it to her last night, but their emotions had taken over.

As he approached the west end of Portbello beach, the image of Logan Baird came into his mind. To him, Logan was still the creepy teenager he'd been in 1976, but Tom realised he would now be in his late fifties; a man who'd been locked up for the whole of his adult life, a man to be pitied. Tom had spent so many years hating Baird, but now there was the nagging question always just below his consciousness – who *had* killed his little sister?

He remembered that awful box and the pictures there. Could his father have murdered his own daughter? Tom couldn't bear to contemplate it; surely no man could do anything like that to his own flesh and blood. But, on the other hand, he'd read about so many cases of unthinkable things happening within families.

Forcing these thoughts away, Tom increased his pace as he ran along the beach, wanting to push himself to the limit, cleanse his body of these suspicions and lose himself in the thump of his heart and the relentless pounding of his feet.

*

Sarah sat at her desk in the cramped Charinet office in Johnstone Terrace. Through the grime of the small window she could see the castle from its less familiar rear-view. She looked at leaflets for the Christmas appeals piled up on the desk. They were to be sent off to volunteers for distribution and her mind-numbing job today was to pack them in envelopes and take them down to the post office at the end of the day.

She looked at the silent phone. She'd been here for three hours and it hadn't rung once. The group of charities she worked for seemed to be dying of apathy. Once again she wondered how long she could put up with the boredom of this job. It was poorly paid, but she'd wanted to do something when the children left home and had imagined that in this job, for an umbrella organisation handling the administration for small charities, she'd be doing something good, making a difference. She'd quickly realised that working for charities didn't necessarily mean doing anything to help people.

She yawned. A mixture of lust and embarrassment ran through her body; it had been so wonderful with Tom. She wanted to be with him again, losing herself in his long-limbed body, releasing herself into his arms. But it was impossible; she was a wife and mother.

But what kind of mother? She'd thought everything was fine in her family, but had she been blind to problems right under her nose? She remembered that awful phone call from Lottie. You should love your children equally and Sarah was sure that she did, despite what Lottie had said.

She hesitated; it was true that she'd always found Nick easier to talk to. Lottie seemed so self-contained, content with the way she organised her own life, happy with her job in HR, and happy with Liam. Had she neglected her, missed something important? Sarah resolved to contact her and go out with her one day soon.

But Nick? He'd sounded so intense when he'd said they must have a drink together. She wondered what he wanted to say. Was it about a girlfriend? He seemed to play the field, never seeming to settle long with one girl. What was behind Lottie's barbed remarks? Did she really know what was going on with her children at all?

Sarah sat up straight; she was going to be a better mother, talk to her children, find out what they really thought. Who should she contact first? Lottie, or Nick?

Nick answered almost immediately. 'Hi Mum. Is everything all right?' He sounded slightly worried; she didn't usually phone him at work.

'Yes, fine. Is this a bad time? Can you talk now?'

'I have a conference call in about fifteen minutes but it's OK to talk now. What is it?'

'Nothing really. I'm just a bit bored at work and I was thinking about lunch next Sunday. You know that Lottie always brings Liam along and I wondered if you'd like to bring someone?'

There was a pause at the end of the phone. 'There's something I've been wanting to talk to you about for a while, but I don't want to do it in front of the family.'

Another pause. Sarah answered carefully, trying to keep the concern out of her voice. 'You mentioned meeting up for a drink? What about after work today? Just let me know when and where and I'll be there.'

'Yeah… that could work if we make it early. I tell you what. I'll come into town after work and we can meet in the Dome in George Street. They make a good gin and tonic. Can you be there at quarter past five?'

'That'll be fine. Looking forward to seeing you then.'

Nick's voice was suddenly hurried. 'Got to go now. See you later. Bye.'

Sarah put down the phone thoughtfully. What was all that about? She shrugged her shoulders and went back to the piles of leaflets. She'd find out soon enough and meanwhile she had plenty of other things to worry about. She remembered Tom's kiss, and her stomach gave a lurch. She tried to put it to the back of her mind. She was a wife, mother and daughter, and she was going to be a good mother today.

*

The sound of the one o'clock gun was echoing from the castle ramparts over Princes Street as Tom turned into the narrow cobbled lane leading past Register House. He pushed open the heavy revolving door of the Cafe Royal, and blinked as his eyes adjusted to the darkness after the bright sunshine of the September day. The light shone through the stained glass windows into the high room, dominated by the huge circular bar. Along the far wall were tiled murals of some of the many Scotsmen who'd made this small country the centre of so many inventions and technological developments.

'Tom,' Rory's voice came from one of the semi-circular niches on the near side of the room. 'Mine's a pint of 80 shilling, and Archie'll have a pint and a dram.'

Tom bought the order and a pint for himself and carried them over to the wooden table, scored by years of use. Rory was sitting next to Archie, who was watching Tom with ironic drooping eyes.

Rory raised his arm in greeting, 'Hi Tom, I can't stay long but I think you two are going to have a lot to say to each other. Archie, tell the boy what you've found out.'

Archie took a long draw from his pint and laid it on the table, ignoring the foam moustache on the upper lip of his leathery smoker's face. 'Hi Tom, have you been to the police yet?'

'Not yet. I'm hoping you'll be able to give me a bit of background info and then I'll give them a call.'

'They can't be aware yet that you're in the country or they'd already have contacted you. They have to re-interview everyone associated with the original case, and I guess they'd like to start with the family.'

'Do you know who's leading the investigation?'

'DI Fergus Chisholm, a decent enough chap. He should do a good solid job. He has to go carefully, though, because whatever they find is going to put the original investigating team in a very bad light.'

Tom took a slow sup of his pint. 'What do you know about the original investigation?'

Archie took a battered notebook out of his pocket. 'It was run by Detective Inspector Charlie Sinclair. The first time he'd been put in charge of a murder probe, and mistakes were definitely made. I say that charitably. Someone uncharitable might say that he made up his mind pretty quickly that Logan Baird was the perpetrator and decided to ignore or withhold any evidence that didn't back up his case.'

Rory, who'd been leaning back and taking no part in the conversation, broke in. 'I remember him. Young, flared trousers, long hair, a bit flash… fancied himself as a bit of a star.'

'He had quite a meteoric career after that, ended up as Assistant Chief Constable. Died in Spain about five years ago, so unfortunately we're not going to be able to get him for the shortcomings of the investigation.'

Tom wanted the conversation back on track. 'So what was the arresting evidence, exactly? And why did they set Baird free?'

Archie downed half of his pint and put his glass on the table. 'After Baird was picked up, he was questioned for hours on end – about eleven without a break. There was no offer of a lawyer, no proper recording of evidence. At the end, he signed an admission of guilt–'

Rory leant forward. 'I was sure he'd admitted it.'

Archie shook his head. '–which he withdrew before the trial. It would never be allowed nowadays and was not good practice even in the wild seventies. But the defending lawyer didn't make as much of that as he should. In fact, he seemed to be certain of Baird's guilt as well.'

Tom gasped. He'd hated Baird for so long, but this injustice was staggering.

'There was also eyewitness evidence which placed him in the park that night, and they found a footprint which they claimed was his near the bank of the burn leading to the culvert where…' Archie saw the expression on Tom's face, and changed direction. 'The footprint was a size 7-9 Chelsea boot from Freeman Hardy Willis. Baird always wore these boots, which also happened to be one of the top-selling styles of the year. The clincher, as far as the police were concerned, was Shona's pink cardigan found in the churchyard next door to Baird's house. There were semen stains on it, which were a match for Baird's blood group – O+. More exact means of testing wasn't available at that time and although 24% of the adult male population share this blood group, it was seen as conclusive, combined with the other evidence.' Archie leafed through his notebook.

Tom was aghast. 'But this evidence is all circumstantial.'

Archie nodded. 'Baird was definitely odd, which made it easier to pin it on him. He always wore black clothes and spent a lot of time hanging around the churchyard. His bedroom was apparently painted black and he slept in a sort of box, which the press reported as a coffin.'

Rory leant forward. 'It's true – I know someone who actually saw it. He was a total nutter – scared all the girls.'

'Of course, as soon as suspicion fell on him plenty of people came forward to say they'd seen him acting suspiciously. Some teenage girls said he'd exposed himself to them, but all withdrew the allegations later and wouldn't go to court to testify. However, the damage was done and the police were certain they'd got the right man. Only someone with local knowledge would have known about the culvert, and the fact that the grating could be removed, so he fitted the bill. The press and the public were baying for a conviction and the police had found an easy target.'

Archie paused, but neither Tom nor Rory said anything. 'So, he's been mouldering in Carstairs for the last thirty-five years, ineligible for parole because he would never admit his guilt, and because he was considered to be in denial, he couldn't even get on any courses or training.'

Tom gasped again, astonished at the Catch 22 situation.

'The only visitor he ever had was his mother – and even she'd helped the police in the original investigation because she thought he was guilty. After she died in 1980 he had no visitors at all and just withdrew more and more into religious mania. No one bothered with him over the years until the Reverend Hamish Mackay, a prison visitor, started to take an interest in his case.

'He was convinced of Baird's innocence and persuaded the SCCRC to look into the original case. When the forensic evidence was reinvestigated, DNA tests showed that the semen sample was definitely not Baird's. Hence the appeal and his release, pending the review court case.'

Tom leant forward. 'But if they have DNA, can't they find out who the killer is?'

Archie took another long draw from his pint. 'You'd think so, but from what I've heard, they've run the sample through all the databases and haven't found a match. That means the murderer wasn't a convicted criminal, and nor is any member of his family. Even if the murderer is dead, they should be able to find out who it was through family matching. A lot of people get found out like this – someone in the family commits a minor offence, DNA is taken and, bingo! The murderer, who thinks he's got away with it, is traced.'

'So at the moment the police have no idea who the killer is?' Tom thought of his father, and his suspicions. He shuddered. The murderer couldn't be anyone with a criminal record so that disposed of the serial killer theory. He was going to have to go to the police.

Rory put his arm round Tom's shoulder. 'It's bad, Tommy. But with DI Chisholm and ace reporter Archie Kilbride on the case we'll find the bastard that did this.' He glanced at his watch and leapt out of seat. 'Got to go! Sorry boys, I'm late!' He picked up his camel coat and swept out of the bar with a wave in their direction.

Archie gave a lop-sided grin. 'Wonder which lady he's keeping waiting today?'

Tom started to feel an automatic reflex of anger at Rory's behaviour, but then remembered his night with Sarah, and realised he was in no position to take the moral high ground. But he still couldn't believe that everyone seemed to know about Rory and just accepted the way he acted.

'How does he get away with it?' he asked. 'I'd have thought the papers would've been filled with kiss and tell stories.'

Archie shrugged his shoulders. 'I don't know how Rory manages it, but he seems to keep all his women sweet. We don't have spurned lovers queueing up to sell their stories – as we do with Premier League footballers, for example.'

Tom noticed the glasses were empty and collected them up to take to the bar for a refill. Archie signalled that he was going outside for a cigarette and by the time he came back Tom had lined up the drinks.

'Bloody stupid law,' Archie said as he sat down, scattering ash from his jacket and breathing smoke over the table, 'sending honest tax-collectors out into the cold and the rain.'

Tom took a sip of his pint and looked round the bar. It

was strange; he'd never been in the Cafe Royal before but he felt at home, he felt right here. The years in South Africa, drifting from one boring dead-end job to another, through quickly-forgotten relationships, it all seemed so very far away. He drank his whisky quickly and felt a glow of wellbeing. He was even beginning to like Archie.

The image of Sarah's breasts in her soft woollen jumper sprang into his mind. Archie looked at him. 'Saw you down at the school with the lovely Sarah. She was a friend of your sister's, wasn't she?'

Tom started. Archie was obviously a good investigative journalist if he could read minds. 'Yes, they were always together, you know, those joined-at-the-hip teenage girls.' In his mind's eye he saw them, arm in arm, giggling together. 'Looking at Sarah makes me realise just what was taken away from Shona. She never had the chance to grow up, get married, have children, a husband.'

He swallowed hard; the alcohol seemed to be affecting him strongly. He awkwardly changed the subject. 'How come you know so much about the Baird case? You seem to be very well-informed about the investigation.'

'Contacts, my son.' Archie tapped the side of his nose. 'Years of hard graft in the pubs where coppers drink. I've lost count of the number of pints I've had to buy in the course of duty. It's hard work but someone has to do it.' Archie took another slug of his whisky, watching Tom carefully.

Archie seemed to sense his mood and changed the subject to football and the financial woes of the Heart of Midlothian Football Club. Tom leant back and listened gratefully. Archie was an entertaining companion. As he finished his whisky and grimaced at the tales of ineptitude and corruption in the boardroom, Tom found his thoughts drifting back to Sarah. He felt in his pocket for his mobile phone and wondered if she'd sent anything. He'd sent a message saying *wonderful* on his way home last night but there'd been no reply. Still, he knew she was working this morning.

The bar began to fill up with after-work drinkers and Tom realised they'd been there the whole afternoon. Archie stood up. 'Time for me to go, Tommy, when the drones come in. We'll be in touch.' He gave Tom an affectionate punch on the shoulder and, taking a cigarette from his pocket, shambled from the bar.

Tom, who still had a third of a pint in his glass, took out his phone. No message from Sarah. *In town. Fancy a drink?* he typed in. He sat looking at the screen expectantly, disappointed that there was not an immediate reply.

.

CHAPTER 15

After battling her way through crowds of shoppers on windy George Street, Sarah turned into the impressive bar of the Dome. She found an empty table in the corner of the converted bank, surrounded by pillars and palms, and immediately a waiter came to take her order, lighting a candle on the table. Evening light shone through the huge glass dome above her, casting shadows on the tables, which were filled with business men in sharp suits and well-dressed women with shopping bags. She sipped her gin and tonic and wondered what Nick wanted to talk about.

About ten minutes later Nick arrived, looking smart in a pin-striped suit and spotted tie. He bought a G&T at the wooden central bar and sat down next to his mother. 'Thanks for coming up to town, Mum. I wanted to talk to you alone.'

'Nobody has much chance to get a word in edgeways when Granny's around,' Sarah smiled.

'That's certainly true – but also I wanted to speak to you without Dad being there.'

Not much danger of that recently, thought Sarah.

'Well, fire ahead. What is it you want to say?' Sarah looked at Nick – his fine-boned beauty, his immaculate clothes, his wit and easy charm, the succession of short-lived romances with beautiful, well-bred girls and suddenly she

173

knew what he was going to say. She saw him hesitate; she'd help him out here. 'Nick, you know there's nothing you can say that would shock me. Nothing that would ever make me love you less.'

Nick raised his eyes and looked directly into hers. 'I've fallen in love.'

Sarah put her hand over his. 'That's wonderful news. Tell me about it,' she added, thinking carefully about the pronoun.

'Olly is the most wonderful person I've ever met. He makes me so happy. I can't think of anything else. I've wanted to tell you about him but you know Dad, and Granny...'

'That's wonderful news. Don't worry about them. It may take a bit of getting used to but they love you and they'll be happy if you're happy.' As she said it, Sarah hoped this was true.

'Actually, you don't seem very surprised, Mum.' Nick took a sip from his glass and looked at her in a quizzical way.

'I can't say that I'd *guessed,* but now you've told me it all makes sense. I've always had the feeling you were looking for something. I just wanted you to be happy, to find the right one for you.' She took another sip of her gin. 'And I'm pleased you trust me enough to tell me now. Tell me more about Olly. I want to know all about him.'

Nick took the opportunity gratefully and in the way of lovers everywhere, eyes sparkling, he described the details; how they'd met, through an old school friend of his, about the small art gallery Olly helped to run on Dundas Street, what a good cook he was, the theatre and the films they went to, his kindness and thoughtfulness. 'I just love being with him. I miss him every minute we're apart.' He looked at his watch. 'In fact, I'm supposed to be meeting him in the Witchery quite soon.'

'What are you doing this evening?' Sarah asked.

'I don't know. That's one of the fantastic things about him. He arranges everything – and it's always just exactly what I'd most like to be doing.' He smiled as if he was remembering something extra special. 'You've been fantastic, the way you've taken it. Actually I didn't worry about telling you but, well, would you tell Dad? I don't know how to.'

'No, it's much better if you tell him yourself. He'll respect you for that.'

Nick raised an eyebrow. 'Really? He's always making jokes about queers and poofters.'

'He meets lots of different people at work and you know he jokes about everything. He doesn't really think like that.' Sarah hoped she sounded reassuring enough.

'Doesn't he? He certainly gives that impression. But I really have no idea what he thinks. I can't remember when we last had a conversation, when he ever showed the slightest interest in what I was doing or thinking. He's hardly ever around and, when he is, he's just talking this showbiz crap. *Oh I'm such a big star.*'

Sarah was amazed at the bitterness in his voice. Nick had always seemed so easy-going. Had she really been so blind to everything, so worried about keeping up the façade of the perfect family life that she didn't know what was going on with her own children? She felt herself flush. 'Does Lottie know, about Olly?'

'Yes, she's cool with it. Likes him better than any of my girlfriends.' He smiled at the thought. 'Anyway, can't you tell Dad? And what about Granny? Shall we just keep quiet about Olly with her? I think I'd like to spare him the ritual of the Sunday lunch, if you don't mind?'

Sarah thought about it. It was tempting just to keep her mother in the dark, but she didn't want Nick to withdraw from family events because he couldn't bring his partner with him. Anyway, it was difficult to know how her mother would react. 'Leave it to me just now. I'm sure there must be one of her Bridge Club friends who has a gay son. You never know it may be the very latest thing in Edinburgh ladies-who-lunch society.'

Nick laughed and put on a mock-Morningside accent, 'Absolutely, darling, all the very best people have a gay in the family. It might just be the thing to get her full membership.'

They laughed together. Nick looked at his watch and began to shrug on his coat. 'Sorry, really have to go.'

Sarah heard her phone beep. Another message. She looked down surreptitiously and saw there were now four messages from TM. She looked up and saw Nick watching her.

'Hadn't you better answer it?'

'I will.' Sarah tried to keep her face straight but she must have had a smile that gave something away.

Nick shot her a knowing look and bent down to kiss her. 'Have fun, Mum. You deserve it.' And with that, he waved and hurried towards the door. Sarah's eyes followed him, pondering what he'd just said. Was she really so transparent? Was her son somehow giving her permission?

She looked at her phone. Tom's messages started casually enough but became increasingly worried. The last one read, *You OK? Where are you? X*

She texted back quickly, her hand shaking with excitement. *In the Dome Bar in George Street. Where are you?*

The answer flashed up within seconds. *Five minutes away. Can we meet?*

I'll be here. See you soon x. She put her phone down, her heart beating with anticipation.

A familiar voice interrupted her reverie. 'Sarah! What are you doing here all by yourself?' She looked up to see Patsy bearing down on her, swathed in carrier bags and topped by a purple cloche hat. 'What a lovely surprise! I was just thinking of you and that we must have that drink together. And now you're here. It's fate!'

Patsy sat down in the seat recently vacated by Nick and carried on speaking without waiting for Sarah to answer. 'I've just been shopping and I've got the most wonderful new underwear. It's true what they say about it spicing up your love life.' She giggled as she began rustling in one of the bags.

Sarah interrupted quickly before Patsy could pull anything embarrassing out. 'Oh Patsy, I'm sorry. I'm just going. I had a drink with Nick and now I have to get back home.'

Sarah looked towards the door, willing Tom not to come in and stood up quickly. 'We'll do it another time soon. I'll give you a call.'

Patsy's face fell. 'Can't you just stay for one? Surely it's not so important that you get home now. After all,' she added with a sly smile, 'Rory's often late, isn't he?'

Sarah moved towards the door quickly, feeling a little guilty as she saw the disappointment on Patsy's face. Patsy meant well, but she wanted to get too close. Since Shona, Sarah had never allowed anyone near her, not wanting anyone to see beneath the surface of the perfect family life she'd constructed so carefully.

Sarah gave a final wave and mouthed something that could be interpreted as 'I'll call you', accompanied by the 'phone' hand signal. She reached the front door safely, relieved that Tom was not quite as close as he had suggested.

Pulling her coat collar up against the bitter wind which was always channeled down George Street, she looked anxiously in both directions. She had no idea where Tom would be coming from. Almost immediately she felt his presence behind her and he leant over to give her a kiss. She turned her cheek and smelt the beer on his breath. She indicated her head towards the door of the bar and muttered 'Patsy alert!' before guiding him along towards Hanover Street.

The dusk was falling quickly, but looking towards the Royal Mile she saw the silhouette of the castle, spectacularly back-lit by a shaft of azure sky beneath the gathering clouds. She turned towards Tom and their eyes met. A look passed between them, full of desire.

They hurried towards Frederick Street, their bodies often touching, in the way of couples who want to be closer but are afraid to hold hands. As they walked down the hill, past the darkening shadows of the Queen Street Gardens, Tom brought her up to date with what Archie Kilbride had told him and Sarah gave an account of Nick's revelation. They were listening to each other, but beneath the words there was the unspoken subtext of lust and need. Their pace quickened as they turned the corner into Great King Street, and up the steps to the front door at 95. Once in the sanctuary of the stairwell, they stopped and kissed and, holding hands, ran up the stone steps.

Sarah put her key in the flat door and realised it wasn't locked. She widened her eyes and turned to Tom with a warning look. As she opened the door, Rory was standing in the brightly-lit hall.

'Oh, hello, you two. I wondered where you were, Sarah.' He looked towards Tom. 'I expect you've been bringing Sarah up to speed with what Archie said. He's a good man and he won't be too intrusive.' Tom nodded, not trusting himself to speak.

'Sarah, the police have been on the phone. They want to interview both of us about the Shona McIver case. I said you'd go down to Fettes Police Headquarters tomorrow morning.'

Sarah nodded but seethed inside. Why did Rory assume that everything she did was so unimportant that he could make arrangements for her?

Rory looked towards Tom. 'I did wonder whether I should mention your name but I think it's better if you contact them. It makes you seem a bit suspicious if you don't.'

Tom's mouth fell open, but Rory turned away without seeming to notice the effect of what he'd said. He took his coat from the hook and pulled it on. 'I said I'd go and see the police when I had time. I've got so much to do with *Kidd down with the Kids* at the moment.' He gave a wide smile. 'I got some terrific footage last night.'

'Great.' Sarah managed to find her voice.

'I'm going out with the Captain again tonight. I've had this fantastic idea to film *Eagle Rising* on Salisbury Crags at sunrise. Having the Captain reading it, sitting on the red stone of the cliffs with the back-drop of the sun rising over Arthur's Seat will be magic. The weather forecast is good for tomorrow, but it may be the last chance we have for a while so I want to *carpe diem* while I can.'

Sarah nodded, realising that Tom hadn't said anything

since they came in. Rory didn't seem to notice. He grabbed up his camera case. 'I'll be out all night so I'll see you tomorrow then.'

'Bye,' said Sarah in a weak voice, which disappeared into the back of the slammed door.

She turned round to look at Tom and they moved together without a word. Their bodies came together and their lips met. Sarah felt her mouth fall open as she pressed her body against Tom's. He held her head, his fingers spreading through her hair as he kissed her deeply.

'Oh Sarah,' he breathed.

They pulled off their coats and Sarah led him towards the bedroom. They stumbled into the room, pulling off their clothes and fell onto the bed, releasing the suppressed lust that had been simmering since they had met outside the Dome.

As their breathing reached a normal level again, Sarah whispered, 'Which side do you like to sleep on?' She felt alive, energised, as if she'd been sleepwalking for her whole life so far, as Tom fell asleep, breathing gently, a smile on his face.

Sarah watched him sleeping, his beautiful features calm, his breathing even. She knew now what she wanted in life. She wanted to be with Tom. She was only fifty, she had many years ahead of her and she was going to take control of her life. She'd spent her whole life doing what was expected of her, keeping other people happy. Remembering something she'd seen on a philosophy programme on TV once, she decided she was going to stop being a tram, she was going to be a bus and decide her own destiny.

Looking at Tom sleeping so peacefully next to her, a

momentary shadow of fear passed over her. What if he went back to South Africa? No, he couldn't. She knew he felt the same way she did. They belonged together. She laid her head on his chest and drifted into a dreamless sleep.

Sometime in the night they woke up and made love again, with slow dream-like movements, the feeling intensified by the hours they had lain with their limbs entwined together.

*

The doorbell rang. Sarah sat upright in bed and blinked in the early morning sunlight shafting through the gap in the velvet curtains. Tom leapt out of bed and started to dress.

'Rory?' he mouthed in panic.

Sarah pulled on her housecoat and shook her head. 'He wouldn't ring. I'll go and see who it is.'

Still half asleep she stumbled to the front door and used the entryphone system to ask who was there.

'Police.'

Sarah felt confused; wasn't she supposed to go to them this morning? She pulled her housecoat tighter round her and automatically pressed the buzzer to open the front door. She looked at her watch. Five to eight. What was going on?

The footsteps came closer, and she saw two policewomen come round the corner and approach the front door. 'Mrs Dunbar? May we come in, please?'

Sarah automatically led the police officers into the drawing room.

'Mrs. Dunbar, would you like to sit down? I'm afraid we have some bad news for you.'

The words burst into her head and echoed through her

brain. The words she'd heard on countless police dramas on TV. Her legs went weak and she sank into the corner of the sofa. 'Who?' she breathed.

'I'm very sorry to have to tell you that your husband has been involved in an accident.'

CHAPTER 16

The Edinburgh Royal Infirmary was a shiny concrete new-build, which had replaced the gothic red-stone building in the city centre. Sarah had phoned the twins while the police were driving her to the hospital. The officers had asked a few gentle questions on the way, about why Rory was up on Salisbury Crags, the ridge of jutting red cliffs on Arthur's Seat, at six thirty in the morning. Sarah was amazed at her own composure; she told them about the programme he was making and the filming with HJ Kidd. It hadn't really sunk in; all she kept thinking was, thank goodness they didn't find Tom. Remembering the passion of the night before, she felt herself blushing.

When they arrived at the hospital, Sarah saw Nick and Lottie huddled together by the automatic doors at the entrance. Together they went up to the intensive care ward and the enormity of what had happened hit her for the first time. The over-bright neon light bounced off the shiny white walls onto an array of machines, screens and tubes.

Rory was lying on a pure white pillow, with a sheet pulled smoothly up to his chin under the tunnel of a ventilator. His head emerged like a marble statue, his face calm, eyes closed, his lips with a slight smile. A white cap of bandage hid most of his hair. A small Filipina nurse was standing next to him, adjusting one of the monitors.

'How is he?' Sarah's voice felt cracked. Unnatural.

'The doctor will come and speak to you in a moment.' The nurse turned away, avoiding eye contact.

Sarah sensed Nick and Lottie next to her. She reached out and tentatively touched Rory's cheek; it was warm and waxy to the touch. 'Rory, can you hear me?' Sarah realised she was whispering.

There was no reaction. Sarah heard a muffled sob and saw Lottie's shoulders shaking; Nick was staring at his father's face, his features so similar, so finely engraved.

There was a cough behind her. Sarah looked round and saw a tall figure in a white coat. 'Mrs Dunbar? I'm Doctor Blair.' The doctor reached out his hand to shake hers. His floppy hair and tired, youthful face made him look too young to be qualified.

'How is he?'

'We'd like to run a few more tests before we can give a definitive answer. Would you and your family like to go to the café and I'll speak to you as soon as I have the results?'

Sarah felt a lump in her throat. The policewoman had said Rory was alive but critical and she'd felt hope; the young doctor's measured tones filled her with a sense of dread. Nick put his arm round her, gently guiding her out of the room and into the long corridor. Sarah walked, her limbs moving robotically. All her senses seemed heightened: the green linoleum squeaking under the brisk white shoes of hospital staff, the click of the shiny lift doors, lights reflecting off the glass of the smiling staff photos on the white walls.

Turning a corner, they saw an alcove with racks of magazines and a large plastic potted plant. HJ Kidd was sitting on one of the burnt orange chairs, his head in his hands. As they approached, he lifted his head, then got up and put his arms round Sarah.

'Sarah.' His handsome face was grey and drawn, the skin around his eyes in deep baggy folds. He looked much older than the last time she'd seen him. 'Is there any news?'

Nick stepped forward and introduced himself and Lottie. He explained what the doctor had said and led them all towards the cafe. It was filled with patients in dressing gowns, some of them attached to drips, visitors, staff on their breaks, all chattering loudly, but they managed to find an empty table in the corner near a window looking out over the carpark. Lottie took orders and moved the remains of the previous occupants' meals onto a tray.

Sarah looked at her old teacher's stricken face. 'What happened?'

HJ reached across the table and took her hand, looking directly into her eyes. 'It was all going so wonderfully. The sky was perfect and the first rays of the sun were appearing in the east. Rory had taken a few trial pictures and had seated me on the edge of a rock with my book. He was so excited about the project and this particular sequence. We'd done a sound-check and he was giving me the countdown for when I should begin reading. I was looking at the book when suddenly his voice changed...' HJ's voice faltered. 'It became a scream. I looked up and saw him falling backwards over the cliffs. He must have stepped back to get a better angle.' He held Sarah's hand more tightly, struggling to speak. 'I rushed to the edge and looked down. I saw his body lying on the rocks at the bottom of the cliff.'

Sarah saw the image before her eyes.

HJ regained some composure and carried on. 'I immediately dialled 999 and tried to get down to the bottom of the cliff. I went as quickly as I could but the police and paramedics were there before I arrived. I tried to get close to Rory, but they kept me away and wouldn't let me travel to the hospital with them.' He gulped again and looked up at Sarah. 'The police took me to the station and interviewed me. I gave them my statement and came here as quickly as I could. How is he?'

Sarah tried to speak but no words came out. Lottie took over. 'He's unconscious or in a coma, but he looks very peaceful.'

'The doctor asked us to wait here while they do some tests,' Nick added. 'I think there'll be more news later.'

Sarah looked down at a dry-looking scone on her plate. She didn't know how to act, she didn't know what to feel. Her hand shook as she reached for a pale coffee, slopping some of the liquid out of the cup, before putting it back on the saucer with a clatter.

'Mum, try to drink something.' Lottie was reaching out for her mother's cup when there was a scream behind her. Sarah looked up and saw her mother, candy-floss hair askew, designer coat open, bearing down to the table.

'They won't let me in to see him!' she wailed. Nick stood up and gently lowered his grandmother into a chair, but she continued in a high-pitched squawk. 'Poor dear Rory. They won't let me see him. My own son-in-law. I love him so much, the son I never had.' Her voice trailed off in an extravagant sob. She took a lace-trimmed hanky from her pocket and dabbed her eyes.

'Excuse me, Mrs Dunbar?' The Filipina nurse was

standing behind Sarah's chair. 'Dr Blair would like to speak to you now. If you'd like to come up to his office…'

Mrs Campbell stood up. 'Can I go up and see my son-in-law now?'

HJ Kidd laid his arm gently on her shoulder. 'I'm sure we'll be able to go up to the ward after the doctor has spoken to your daughter. What can I get you? A cup of tea? A cake?'

Flora simpered. 'That would be very nice. I don't think we've been introduced.' Sarah looked round gratefully as HJ explained who he was and heard her mother trill with delight. 'How nice to meet you. I had the pleasure of meeting your sister at luncheon just the other day…'

Sarah nodded to the twins to come with her and they followed the nurse along the corridor to the doctor's office.

Dr Blair was waiting for them and indicated three chairs. Standing next to him was a kindly-faced mixed-race woman in her forties. Sarah looked at the doctor, trying to guess from his expression what he was going to say.

'Mrs Dunbar. We've completed all our tests now. Your husband suffered a severe trauma to the brain as a result of his fall. We've done everything we can for him, but our tests show that there is no brain activity.'

He paused. Sarah felt as if she'd turned to ice. She stared at the doctor.

Nick leant forward. 'What does this mean? Is he in a coma?'

Dr Blair moved uncomfortably in his chair. 'There was such severe internal bleeding in the brain that there has been complete loss of brain stem function. I'm afraid he is brain dead.'

There was a sharp intake of breath from Lottie. 'But he's breathing, he's warm.'

Dr Blair gave a tired sigh, his eyes filled with pain. *He hasn't had to do this many times before*, thought Sarah. She was surprised to notice that she felt sorry for him.

'At the moment his breathing is being maintained by the ventilator. The law requires corroboration from a second doctor to make completely certain but, as I said, there was no brain activity detectable from the tests we have done so far. We've also tested for any other conditions that could produce these results, but there is no sign of drugs and only moderate alcohol in his system.' The doctor cleared his throat again and indicated the woman standing next to him. 'This is Mrs Brown. She would also like to have a word with you.'

Mrs Brown stepped forward and shook hands with the family. 'You have my deepest sympathy. You may think it insensitive of me at this time, but I am a transplant co-ordinator. In a case like this there is the possibility for a great deal of good to come from a tragedy. Do you know Mr Dunbar's attitude to organ donation?'

Sarah's mouth fell open and she could not suppress a gasp. This was so final. She couldn't believe it – Rory dead?

Mrs Brown continued in a gentle tone. 'Many families find comfort in the fact that their loved one can save many other lives through the donation of organs.'

Once again, Sarah tried to speak but no words came. To her relief, Nick spoke. 'Didn't he have a donor card on him? My dad was really in favour of organ donations, he did a programme on it once.'

Sarah nodded in agreement and Mrs Brown reached

forward and touched her hand. 'With your permission, we'd like to test his vital organs. After the results are through we would put the transplantation programme into action as soon as possible. We have a long list of people on standby for heart, lungs, kidneys, livers, corneas and many other organs.'

Dr Blair added, 'One person can make so much difference to so many lives.'

He stopped abruptly, seeming to regret the interruption, thought Sarah. Mrs Brown was obviously a professional, used to this, but Sarah felt strangely that she had to make the young doctor's difficult job easier. She found her voice again. 'I understand. He's not in any pain, is he?'

'He can't feel anything. He is at peace. Even if he had survived, the amount of brain damage would have meant that he would have been profoundly disabled.'

Sarah imagined Rory in a wheelchair. 'He would have hated that.'

Mrs Brown nodded. 'We will prepare the paperwork. You can go and spend time with your husband, say your farewells.'

The young doctor hesitated and then added. 'Please don't be too shocked if you see one of his limbs move. There may still be vestiginal reflex actions, but this does not come from the brain. There is no brain activity at all.'

He stood up; he and Mrs Brown shook hands with all of them before leading them out of the small office. Dr Blair indicated towards the ICU. 'I am so sorry I was not able give you a more positive diagnosis, but I promise to keep you informed of any developments.' Sarah felt he really meant it.

The rest of the day passed in a blur. Sarah sat by the bed, seeing Rory's handsome face still and peaceful, as if sculpted from marble. He was still connected to a wall of machines and she watched as lines rose and fell, beeping regularly. She realised she was holding her breath, waiting for a flat-line, waiting for the warning screech of countless hospital dramas she'd seen on television.

Doctors and nurses came in and out of the room, nodding respectfully, doing tests and holding charts. HJ Kidd and her mother came into the room, the poet standing silently, his face etched with shock and Rory's mother-in-law interrupting the calm with hystrionic wails.

After a few hours a nurse came and told them to go for something to eat. Nothing would happen for a while. The others went but Sarah stayed by the bed. She couldn't eat anything; she was in suspended animation, not sure of what she felt, what she should do.

Nick and Lottie came back and stared at their father. Nothing had changed. Rory lay as still and peaceful as before, the machines clicking and whirring in the background. Then Sarah felt a presence behind her. A more senior doctor, whose name she didn't catch, approached them and stated regretfully that at 18.08 Rory Dunbar was pronounced dead and, in accordance with the family's wishes, the organ transplant programme was being set in motion.

PART 8

Young Rory, his long hair blowing back from his face, a denim jacket over his T-shirt, collar up, scarf flapping loosely in the wind. He is standing on the tussocky grass slopes of Arthur's Seat, Edinburgh spread out beneath him, the blue waters of the Forth sparkling in the distance.

The sun is shining warm on us, the breeze soft. I feel the stirring in my stomach, feel two pairs of legs kicking under my lace-trimmed smock. Rory stands warm and strong next to me, holding my hand, his arm round my shoulder. I feel so safe, so happy. Rory pats my tummy and kisses me tenderly. He steps back and beams at me, his arms stretching towards me.

Then he falls back.

I can't catch him, he's slipping away from my outstretched hands. He melts away from me.

CHAPTER 17

Sarah woke and reached across the empty bed, which seemed to be swaying in the darkness. A dull ache blocked her thoughts, creating a dense fog she couldn't penetrate. There was something terrible, just below the surface. Then she remembered – Rory was dead.

The door opened and light shafted in. A figure was silhouetted in the hall light. 'Mum?' Lottie's voice. 'It's me. Can I get you anything? A drink?'

'What are you doing here?' Sarah sat up and looked around, everything disjointed, everything wrong.

Lottie sat down beside her and patted her arm. 'Dr Meldrum left something to help you sleep. Would you like some more to take you through to morning?'

Sarah put her arms out to her daughter. 'Oh, Lottie. What are we going to do?'

Lottes's voice was calm. 'You don't have to do anything. Just rest. Nick is dealing with the arrangements at the moment and I'll be here with you. Would you like anything to eat?'

Sarah sat up. 'I have to get dressed. There is so much to do. What about the funeral?' Her voice caught on the word.

'Don't worry about that.' Lottie's voice was solicitous. 'As it is an accidental death, it has to be reported to the Procurator Fiscal, but the police say the body will be released soon as there is no indication that it was anything other than a terrible accident.'

Sarah lay back in the pillows, glad that she didn't have to think, aware of the irony in the role-reversal as Lottie took charge.

*

Tom pounded along the side of the road leading from Duddingston over to Dunsapie Loch. He'd run on this side of Arthur's Seat before, but now it almost seemed prurient. He'd intended to keep well away from the Salisbury Crags, but his feet seemed to lead an involuntary path towards the foot of the rocks.

As ever, running helped him to sort things out in his head. The events of yesterday raced round and round in his thoughts. Being with Sarah, making love, their closeness, and then the knock at the door. The police voices describing the accident…

The rest of the day he'd spent pacing round his small bedroom in the Regent Guest House, thinking about Sarah and wondering what was happening. He longed to phone her or send her a message, but he didn't want to intrude, didn't know who else might be with her.

After a claustrophobic day in the B&B, he'd spent the evening in a seedy Portobello pub, nursing a few lukewarm pints and looking expectantly at his phone. How was Rory? He wished Sarah would contact him, wished he could do something to help her.

The next morning, after a restless night, he'd been eating his full Scottish breakfast in the cramped breakfast room of the B&B when a brief announcement came on the radio. Rory Dunbar, BBC Scotland's journalist and chat show host, had died in hospital as the result of injuries sustained in an accident on Arthur's Seat. Mrs Ritchie had swayed and collapsed on a chair, tears coursing down her plump cheeks.

Tom's feet pounded the tussocky ground and his thoughts raced round his head in the same relentless rhythm. What should he do now? Should he contact Sarah? Offer his condolences? She needed time to grieve, she'd be surrounded by her family, she'd not be thinking of him.

Sarah. Her name pulsed through his head with every step. *Sarah – I wish I could help you, hold you safe.*

*

Sarah lay in bed, aware of the movements in the house. The phone seemed to be ringing constantly and she could hear Lottie answering briefly. Unable to lie there any longer, she got up and walked through to the en-suite bathroom. Rory's shaving stuff was lying on the shelf below the mirror and she smelt the distinctive scent of the Hugo Boss aftershave he liked so much. He was never going to use them again.

Making a huge effort, she forced her limbs to function as she showered and dressed, hearing more rings of the phone and the doorbell. She thought she heard a man's voice.

'Mum's resting at the moment and she really can't see anyone,' she heard Lottie's competent voice insist.

As Sarah walked gingerly into the hall, Lottie was talking to a tall figure in a crumpled trench coat. Archie Kilbride – Rory's journalist friend.

Archie spotted her and moved towards her, embracing

her with a gesture of unexpected tenderness. 'Sarah. I can't believe it. Rory gone. I thought he'd go on forever, he was so full of life.' He paused. 'He was a great journalist, and a great mate.'

Sarah smiled at the obvious sincerity in Archie's voice. The journalist seemed to collect himself and then carried on. 'I hope I'm not intruding now, Sarah, but it's important that I talk to you before any other journos arrive. There's going to be a lot of press interest. Rory's a Scottish celebrity.'

Lottie nodded. 'The phone's never stopped ringing all day, all the Scottish papers and nationals as well.'

Archie told Lottie to take the phone off the hook and turned towards Sarah. 'Can we sit down somewhere? There are a couple of things I want to say before these journalists are all over you.'

'Take a seat in the front room. I'll make some coffee,' Lottie said, moving towards the kitchen. 'Is that OK, Mum?'

Sarah nodded and went to sit on the leather Chesterfield while Archie slouched on the wing-backed chair opposite her. He looked straight at her, took a deep breath and spoke in a serious tone. 'Now, when celebrities die, one of two things happens. They're either beatified by the press – or the press look for all the dirt they can.' Archie looked awkward. 'Now we know that Rory was a great guy, but he certainly wasn't a saint.'

Sarah held her breath, and wondered what was coming next.

Archie leant forward. 'Rory had great personal charm, people loved him, but there are a couple of indiscretions in his life which could raise their ugly heads now.'

Sarah sat up straight and widened her eyes. 'Isn't there

such a thing as respect for the dead? Surely the gutter press won't go raking up all kinds of rumours when he isn't here to defend himself?'

Archie raised his hands in a defensive gesture. 'Sarah, Sarah. We're both on the same side here. I just wanted to make you aware of what might happen – and warn you against journalists. They're a slimy bunch and you have to be careful of people trying to worm their way into your confidence.'

Sarah gave a bitter smile. 'Like you are, you mean. What are you getting at?'

Archie looked at her, sadness in his drooping eyes. 'Sarah, you know I loved Rory and he was a great guy. But, you must know that he was not always…' he coughed with uncharacteristic sensibility, 'totally faithful.'

There a sound from at the doorway where Lottie stood, holding a tray of coffee. She stormed into the room and stood in front of the journalist, her eyes blazing. 'You're upsetting my mother. I'd like you to leave.'

Archie looked up at her. 'I'm sorry, you weren't supposed to hear that.'

'Evidently not, but I'm glad I did. My father died yesterday. How dare you speak to my mother like that? How can you be so insensitive as to come here today and slander his memory like that?'

Archie stood up. 'I'm truly sorry, but I really *do* have your mother's best interests at heart.' He turned to Sarah. 'I just wanted you to be forewarned and on your guard. I'll go now, but remember that I will do anything I can to help you.'

Sarah felt numb inside. She'd always avoided this kind of conversation. Rory had always come back to her, always reassured her that she was the one, so she'd pushed any unspoken suspicions away. And now Archie had put her subconscious fears into words and she realised that it wasn't a surprise.

'Archie, sit down, please.' She turned to her daughter. 'Lottie, thank you for standing up for your father like that. He'd be very proud of you, as he always was. Your father was a very charming man, a very loving man, but we have to face up to the fact that there may be some truth in what Archie is saying.'

As Lottie gasped, Archie said, 'But your mother was always the most important person to him. She was the one that he really loved and respected.'

Lottie gave a mirthless laugh. 'Not so much that he'd remain faithful to her, it seems.'

Sarah held out her arms to her daughter and held her close, somehow gaining strength from the return to her role of mother and protector. 'Lottie, he loved us, we were his family. He was just a very attractive man in a business where he was surrounded by beautiful women.'

Lottie looked up at her mother and kissed her cheek. She turned to Archie. 'But they won't print any of this, will they?'

Archie looked down. 'I'll do my best to keep it quiet, certainly in the *Scotsman Publications*, but there are lots of sensational rags and your father's big news.'

The sound of the doorbell interrupted him. Sarah looked up from Lottie's hair as Archie moved towards the door. 'I'll get rid of them.' He pressed the button and spoke into the entry phone. He turned to Sarah. 'HJ Kidd? Can I let him in?'

Sarah hesitated, then nodded. Archie opened the door

and Sarah heard footsteps hurrying up the stone stairs. Captain Kidd burst into the hall, carrying a huge bouquet of flowers. 'Sarah, my dear. How are you today?'

He stopped with an embarrassed grimace, realising what he'd said. 'I don't want to disturb you at this time, but I just wanted to give you these,' he indicated the flowers, 'and let you know that if there is anything at all I can do to help, you only need ask. Really. Anything.' He stood looking awkward, all his usual assurance gone.

Sarah took the bouquet. 'It's so kind of you, HJ. Really I don't think there's anything we need at the moment, but I'll let you know.' Then something did strike her. 'We don't know when the funeral will be yet, but perhaps you would be willing to read something then? A poem? I know that Rory would have liked that.'

HJ's face lit up. 'Of course, I would be delighted, honoured to do that.' He coughed and shuffled, clearly uncomfortable. 'Actually, as you mention it, and as I'm here, I wonder if I could take back the papers I gave Rory? My childhood poems. Would they be here?'

Sarah indicated towards the closed door of Rory's study. 'He was working on them in here, so I'm sure they'll be on his desk.'

HJ hurried towards the room. Archie raised his eyebrows. 'A bit odd, him coming round for papers now?'

Sarah whispered back. 'He was with Rory when it happened. He's bound to be upset.'

Archie shrugged his shoulders. 'Still weird in my book.'

After a few minutes, HJ reappeared with the manila folder. 'Do you think this is everything? Could Rory have taken any things to his office?'

Sarah shook her head. 'No, he was working on this alone and always at home. That's why he was even doing the camera work himself.' Her voice caught but she carried on calmly. 'I think Rory would have kept everything together, but if I find anything else I'll let you know.'

'Yes. Right. Thank you. Thanks very much. Look, I won't take up any more of your time… Nice to see you again, Mr Kilbride.' With that HJ gave Sarah a perfunctory hug and hurried out of the door.

Lottie reappeared with the flowers beautifully arranged and put them on the polished mahogany coffee table. 'Has he gone already?'

The doorbell rang again and there was the sound of footsteps and muttering right outside the flat door. A voice called through the letterbox. 'Mrs Dunbar, would you like to make a statement about your husband's death?'

Sarah started. 'How did they get inside?'

Archie moved towards the door. 'That plonker must've let them in. Never mind, I'll get rid of them. And I'll ask your neighbours not to open the stair door to anyone they don't know.' He patted Sarah on the shoulder and handed her a card. 'Just give me a call if you need me. Remember, I'm on your side.'

*

Sarah breathed deeply after Archie left. What he'd said about Rory hadn't really shocked her. It was something she'd always known deep down, but hadn't wanted to admit to herself. In a way, having to acknowledge the truth made her feel strangely empowered. And she surprised herself by finding she didn't blame Rory; that was just the way he was and, remembering last night with Tom, she wasn't really in a position to take the moral high ground. She wished Tom could be here with her now, but that was impossible.

She put the phone back on the hook. There were calls from so many people. With some of them, like her mother and Patsy, she felt she was doing the comforting. Other calls gave her a sense of purpose. The Head of BBC Scotland rang personally, offering condolences, which even sounded sincere. He said that the corporation would, of course, be organising a memorial service and to leave everything in his hands. The hospital phoned to say that Rory's organs had been given to seven people, seven lives saved. They promised to forward further details as soon as possible.

Nick came round, saying he'd spoken to the police and hospital authorities and also to John Coltrane, the family solicitor. Sarah felt the composure of the day before returning, as she and Nick sat down with Lottie to make lists of who they should inform. She was pleased that they were all working so well together; the family tensions of the last few weeks seemed forgotten as they were united by the tragedy.

Towards late afternoon, the phone rang again. Lottie answered and looked over to her mother. 'Police,' she mouthed. Sarah took the phone and explained that she would have to reschedule her appointment with the team investigating Shona McIver's death and that her husband, Rory Dunbar would not now be able to attend.

Archie phoned to say they should watch the Scottish news programme, *Reporting Scotland*. After a few small items of local news, there was a long feature on the death of Rory

Dunbar; it included clips from his earliest programmes, showing him as a long-haired roving reporter, and also a couple of his most famous interviews from *Chats with Rory*. The item ended with the trademark conclusion of his chat show. Rory turned round and looked directly into the camera with his dazzling smile: 'It's good night from me, Rory Dunbar, and keep safe until we meet again next week.'

Sarah snapped the television off. The tears, which had refused to flow over the last two days, flooded from her.

CHAPTER 18

Tom sat in his claustrophobic room in the Regent Guest House, watching *Reporting Scotland* on the tiny box television. As the report on Rory's death finished, he slammed down the remote control. 'What a cheap trick. Not a dry eye in the house I'm sure.' He wasn't certain what he felt about Rory. He had been his best friend when he was young, charming and charismatic, but the way he had treated Sarah appalled him.

After the local news programme there was a trailer for a programme later that evening. A reporter was shown standing in front of Carstairs State Hospital, where criminals in need of psychiatric care are imprisoned in Scotland. The strong wind inflated the reporter's jacket and made his hair stand on end. Fighting against the sound of the gale, he shouted into his microphone. 'After nearly forty years in prison Logan Baird has just been released, pending his case being heard by the Court of Appeal. Our special report investigates the circumstances which led to this greatest miscarriage of justice in the history of the Scottish penal system, tonight at 9pm on BBC Scotland.'

Tom groaned. After speaking to Archie Kilbride he'd got the impression there wouldn't be any programmes or reports until after the appeal, but it seemed that the BBC had jumped the gun. He reached for the bottle of whisky on his cheap chest of drawers and took a hefty slug from his tooth-glass. He wouldn't be going to the pub tonight.

He put the sound down on the television and let the images flicker in the background as he waited for nine o'clock. He filled up his glass and looked around the room; the single bed with the uncomfortable dip in the centre, the pink cabbage-rose wallpaper, the frills round the edge of the kidney-shaped dressing table, clashing with the 70s swirls on the carpet. He hated this room.

He poured another drink. Here he was, fifty-three years old, without a home or a job, without any real friends, and – he gulped another swig of whisky – in love with the widow of his best friend.

The *Scottish Special Report* logo came up on the screen and he flicked on the sound. The prat in the wind-inflated suit was still fighting to make himself heard. 'For thirty-six years, this grim building has been home to Logan Baird. He came here in 1976 as a nineteen-year-old. Earlier this month he was released after new DNA evidence showed he could not have been the murderer of little Shona McIver, whose body was found in a culvert just yards from her home in Portobello, Edinburgh's seaside suburb. This evening we are going to investigate what went wrong during Baird's conviction, and how he must feel, back in a world very different from the one he left in 1976.'

A montage of images from the mid-70s appeared on the screen to the background of Rod Stewart singing 'We are Sailing'. How gloomy the photos made the time seem – bombings, strikes, dark streets. Tom couldn't remember any of that – he remembered the sun shining on the sands, football in the park, laughs at school, Shona and Sarah dancing to the Bay City Rollers. Then pictures came of houses for sale for £10,000, Bagpuss and Kojak, flared trousers and platform soles, Turkish Delight and Caramac. That was more familiar, all technicolour until…

The scene cut to the reporter on Portobello prom, in front of the low wall round Abercorn Park. Tom wondered if he could even bear to watch as the reporter used his serious voice to describe the night in September 1976 when Shona McIver disappeared after being seen playing in this park. The familiar photo of Shona smiling on the beach flashed up on the screen. Tom took another drink of whisky and reached for the remote control. His hand shook. No, he wouldn't switch it off. He had to watch this. It would be worse to lie there, wondering what was being broadcast.

The camera panned to the bushes beside the culvert 'where little Shona's sexually-molested body was found' and then moved on to the arrest of Logan Baird. They showed a school photo of him in his uniform, unsmiling and with staring eyes, but relatively normal compared to the way he'd looked after he'd left school. Tom remembered him in his ankle-length black coat, his long dark hair falling over his face, standing hunched in corners, never looking up.

Weren't there any more recent pictures of him? Perhaps he thought the devil would take his soul if he was photographed. Tom gave an involuntary giggle. He blinked to focus on the screen; the whisky was blurring his brain. He felt tears very close behind his eyes but he refused to let them fall as he concentrated on the rest of the programme.

Actually, the rest of it wasn't that bad, because the focus of the programme was definitely Baird. There was a description of the trial and some contemporary footage of

Baird being bundled from courtroom to van under a blanket. Then there was a long interview with Rev. Hamish Mackay, a square-jawed teuchter with a manic gleam in his eye. He described his first meeting with Baird during his prison visits and spoke movingly of Baird's love of religion, and his protestations of innocence.

The interviewer dared to ask why Baird had confessed to the crime at first, but Mackay was ready for that one. 'Logan wasn't able to talk about it for a long time, but after we built up a relationship he opened up about that night. First he said that he had seen the devil with a little girl in the bushes. The police questioned him for eleven hours. He was confused and began to feel guilty, somehow feeling that the presence of the devil was part of him. He was a vulnerable teenager who had words put into his mouth by the police at the time. They made him sign a statement without allowing an adult or legal representation to be present.'

'Why did he never make any kind of appeal in all the years he was in Carstairs?' The reporter asked and Tom began to think that the interviewer wasn't perhaps as big an idiot as he looked.

Once again Mackay was ready. 'This poor young man was incarcerated and forgotten by all save his mother, and after her death, he had no visitors until I came in contact with him. Because he wouldn't admit his guilt, he was abandoned by the system. He was prejudged and pigeon-holed by the psychiatric mafia, who deemed him psychotic and pumped him full of inappropriate medication. In fact, he's now been diagnosed as bipolar. He would have been released a long time ago if he had been put on the correct medication programme and people had listened to him.'

'Where is he now? Is he now being treated?'

'He is living in supervised accommodation, organised for him by some of his supporters. It is very difficult for him, as he has come out into a world that has changed so much, like Rip Van Winkle waking up after so many years. The technology, traffic, shopping is all very new to him, but with the support of the Lord and his friends, he's making good progress.'

The rest of the programme was padded out with some background information on the work of the Scottish Criminal Cases Review Commision, which since its establishment in the nineties has resulted in twenty-five successful appeals. It also mentioned the DNA testing which proved that Baird was not the killer, and the fact that the case had been reopened by the Lothian and Borders Police. But there were no further details about this except that the investigation was on-going and no new suspects had yet been announced.

Tom thought again about his father's pictures. He had to go to the police; he'd ring them tomorrow. He pushed the memory of the images from his mind again. The whisky made this easier to do.

Portentous music announced that the programme was coming to an end. The reporter turned to the screen and made a few final remarks, sure that, after this terrible miscarriage of justice, all viewers would wish Logan Baird well for his continued adjustment to twenty-first century life.

Tom put the television off. He was relieved they hadn't delved too deeply into Shona's life and there was no speculation about any other possible perpetrators. Tom looked at the whisky bottle. It was almost empty. What the hell, he would finish it off. He drained the bottle into his glass and knocked it back, before falling into a troubled sleep.

*

Lottie gently removed the wine glass from her mother's grasp. Sarah's head had fallen to one side in the corner of the Chesterfield when she'd slipped into an exhausted sleep.

*

Tom woke up the next morning with his mouth furred and his head pounding. Why had he drunk that whisky last night? After seeing what drink had done to his father he tried not to lose control, but last night... a wave of self-pity washed over him. The programme about Baird and Shona, Rory dying, Sarah seeming so close and now so far away, his lack of home, plans, direction...

He got up and showered. He didn't think he could face Mrs Ritchie's grief or a full Scottish breakfast so he pulled on his running shoes and, shouting a vague, 'No breakfast for me today, thanks,' slid out of the front door.

The haar was down and the air was like damp grey cottonwool. He turned down towards the prom and began to run along the wet sand at the water's edge. The beach was almost deserted, all sound muffled except for the gentle lap of the receding tide. Occasionally the ghostly figure of an early-morning walker and his dog loomed out of the mist but no greetings were exchanged.

His head throbbed and the damp cold air seemed to scratch his lungs like a Christmas tree. At first he had to force his legs forward but when he got into his rhythm, his mind came into gear, too. He wasn't just going to sit around and do nothing until his mother's meagre inheritance ran out. He had to be proactive; he was going to stay in Edinburgh, look for somewhere to live and find a job.

He stumbled as he missed his step. This thought seemed to have jumped fully-formed into his mind without any warning. He *wasn't* going back to South Africa. Already Plettenberg Bay seemed so far away and the years he'd spent there melted into a blur of nothingness. Scotland was where he belonged.

The sun was shining above the mist, casting a shimmering sheen over the damp sand. Tom stopped and looked at the sky as the sun broke through the clouds. Taking his mobile phone from his back pocket, he found Sarah's number. *Thinking of you. Anything at all I can do to help, just let me know. Hope to see you soon, Tom.* It was very bland but he guessed there would be lots of family around Sarah at this time. He hoped his message would show he was thinking of her, but not cause any problem if anyone else read it. He hesitated for a moment and then pressed send.

He turned round and made his way back along the beach. Looking up at the row of Victorian houses, the red-stone tenements, the baths, his school and the Free Presbyterian Church lining the shore, he was taken back to the life he'd lived here – before Shona was taken from them.

Next to the church were the tenements where Logan Baird had lived. Where was he now? Had he come back to the only place that he'd ever known, apart from Carstairs? Hatred welled up in him like a wave of nausea. Years of anger had their own power, which he struggled to quell: Logan Baird was innocent, the DNA tests had proved this, so Logan Baird was a victim, losing so many years of his life locked up in that institution.

Tom walked towards the prom, almost feeling that Baird would appear like a ghost before him at any moment. Would he even recognise him now? He must be getting on for sixty, so very different from the spooky teenager he vaguely remembered.

He stepped up onto the prom. In the front garden of Captain Kidd's house he saw his old teacher, bent over some rose bushes, dead-heading the shrivelled blooms. He was wondering whether to speak or just pass by when HJ Kidd raised his head.

'Tom,' HJ stood up and approached the low granite wall. He held out his hand.

Tom shook it. 'Have you seen Sarah? How is she?'

'I went round to visit her briefly. She seems to be bearing up remarkably well, considering...' His handsome features twisted in pain. 'You know I was there when it happened? After we saw you at Rory's house, we did some filming and then climbed up the Salisbury Crags to catch the sunrise. I was just about to read, Rory was getting the right angle, he stepped back and...' his voice cracked in pain.

Tom felt sympathy for the older man. He hadn't really thought about how the accident had happened until that moment. He realised he'd only been thinking about Sarah and himself. 'I haven't seen many news bulletins. They just said it was an accident. I didn't know you were there – it must have been awful.' He shuddered, his body cooling down in the chill morning air.

HJ noticed. 'I do apologise, you must be freezing. Please come in for a cup of coffee.'

Tom hesitated, then accepted. He wanted to find out more about Sarah.

They went through the hall into the large kitchen at the back of the house. There was a range along one wall and a long scrubbed wooden table in the middle of the room. Hannah Kidd came in from the scullery, drying her hands on a cloth. The room was warm and welcoming with the smell of coffee and fresh washing.

Hannah made some coffee as HJ described going round to Sarah's, and seeing Lottie and Archie with her. Tom was pleased to hear that – it made it seem more normal for him to contact her, too. He felt the shape of his phone in his back pocket. Had Sarah replied? He hadn't heard it beep, but sometimes the sound was masked by the roar of the sea and wind when he was jogging. He resisted the temptation to sneak a look.

HJ finished speaking and then looked over the table at Tom. 'And how are you, Tom? You're still staying in Portobello, I see.'

Tom began to explain what he had decided on his run, his ideas hardening as he formulated them into words. He explained that he'd decided to stay in Scotland and was looking for a job and a place to stay.

HJ looked thoughtful. 'You said you did odd jobs in South Africa?' He hesitated. 'Now, I don't know if you would consider working as a janitor/handyman, but I have an idea that might help you.' Tom sat up straighter, eager to hear what he had to say next. 'Have you heard of the Canongate Centre? It's an old church near the Grassmarket, which is used as an arts centre, and for community groups. There's a playgroup and a youth club, for example. It's where my poetry group meet and there's also an amateur theatre group that puts on small experimental productions. We've had a resident caretaker there for as long as I can remember, but he's well past retirement age and wants to go and live nearer his daughter and grandchildren in Forfar.'

Tom felt a glimmer of hope. HJ looked up at him as if to gauge the reaction on his face. 'I'm on the Board of Governors and we thought it would be quite easy to find a successor for Jimmy, but it's been proving surprisingly difficult. There's many a person with the practical skills who can deal with small repairs, but we need someone who can satisfy the background checks, as there will be children and vulnerable adults there. The hours can be long and we need someone prepared to take responsibility for the day-to-day management of the centre. Also the accommodation's very small, only suitable for a single person.'

Tom tried not to show too much enthusiasm. It sounded ideal, although he was a bit worried about the long hours. 'How long would I actually have to be on duty?'

'There has to be someone there, for security reasons, whenever the centre's open, but it wouldn't always have to be you. You would be in charge of a small team of hourly-paid workers, including cleaners, and it would be up to you to draw up a rota so that there was always a responsible person there. We have an established team, as we pay above minimum wage and want to be fair employers, but they're mostly part-timers and none of them are interested in the responsibility of the full-time job.'

Tom's mind was already racing. This could solve all his

problems, the chance to find a home and a job in one go. 'I'd certainly be very interested.'

HJ looked encouraged by his enthusiasm. 'I'll have to contact the other board members about an interview, but if you'd like to have a look round, there's our poetry group meeting this evening and you could come along with me to talk to Jimmy and see the accommodation. If you like what you see, you'll have to submit your CV and references and we could start the vetting process. You are still British, aren't you?'

'Yes, no problem there.' Tom grasped HJ's hands. 'Thank you so much. You've got no idea what this means to me.'

HJ smiled again. 'I'm happy to help you in any way I can.'

Tom stood up. He was eager to get back to the B&B and start getting things organised, tweaking his CV and collecting references. He would also have to see the police before any kind of background check was set in progress.

He arranged to meet HJ that evening and jogged back along the prom. Looking round the saccharine room he fantasised about sleeping in the gothic gloom of a decommissioned church. He looked at his phone: a message from Sarah. *Missing you x*.

*

Sarah bustled around in her kitchen, putting coffee cups on a tray. Her mother had come round early 'to help' and had got in her way. Patsy arrived with a cake, which was thoughtful of her, but dissolved into such floods of tears that Sarah ended up comforting her. Now Flora and Patsy were sitting in the drawing room, swapping reminiscences, in competition with each other about how upset they were.

Sarah wished she could be anywhere else; she was tired of being strong and brave. She wished Tom were with her; she wanted his arms round her, keeping her safe.

Flora was dabbing her eyes with a lace-edged hankie as Sarah came into the room. 'We were very close, the dear boy.'

'It was only the other week we had our reunion and the dedication at the school,' added Patsy. 'He was so charismatic, he lit up the room.'

Flora could trump that one. 'I shall so miss our Sunday lunches. He was so charming, so attentive. Only last Sunday he called me his little flower.' She let out another sob and then looked up at Patsy, 'Because of my name, you know.' Patsy patted the older woman gently on the arm, acknowledging defeat.

Sarah clattered the tray down on the coffee table. She distributed the cups and Patsy's chocolate cake was duly admired.

'Do we know when the funeral is?' asked Patsy, wiping the crumbs from her mouth.

Sarah shook her head. 'We've decided we're going to have a very small private family funeral as soon as the body is released and then there'll be a bigger memorial service arranged by BBC Scotland. Nick phoned today. He's been doing the liaison with the Procurator Fiscal. The post-mortem's been carried out, and a fatal accident inquiry isn't necessary. I think the fact that HJ Kidd witnessed the whole thing and was able to make a full statement has helped. I'd like the funeral to take place as soon as possible.'

'If there's anything I can do to help, just let me know,' Patsy said.

Flora nodded morosely. 'That poor dear boy.'

Sarah was overcome with a wave of total weariness. It was so hard keeping up the pretence of normality, when underneath her brain was whirred with the maelstrom of feelings about Rory, about Tom, about her family, about Shona… about Tom. She couldn't help it, her thoughts were always returning to him.

She stood up. Her limbs seemed so heavy, she felt she could hardly move. 'Thank you so much for coming, both of you. But I'm feeling really rather tired now, so I think I'll have a lie down before Nick and Lottie come round.'

Patsy leapt up, gathering the dishes, and carrying the tray into the kitchen, calling back over her shoulder. 'Just leave these to me! Anything I can do to help!' Flora stood up and carefully placed her Liberty scarf around her neck. She pecked Sarah on the cheek and made her way to the hall, collecting her coat. 'I'll see myself out. And I'll come again tomorrow to give you some more help.'

Sarah stifled the groan she felt. Her mother meant well but her 'help' consisted of sitting around saying how wonderful Rory was, and how much she missed him. Sarah briefly wondered how she'd react when the inevitable 'Rory the philanderer' stories got into the papers. A small mean part of her wanted her to find out what her beloved Rory was really like.

Patsy followed the older woman into the hall. 'Let me know if there's anything I can do for the funeral. I've let all the old schoolfriends know and I'm sure there'll be a good turn-out from them. And if you need anyone to give a reading, or say anything…' She smiled expectantly.

Sarah muttered something about the memorial service

being the place for that, and waved them off as quickly as she could. When the door slammed behind them she mouthed a silent scream and took a bottle of wine from the rack in the kitchen. She poured out a large glass and sat down with it in the drawing room, feeling her heart rate return to normal.

Nick and Lottie weren't coming round this evening. She wanted to have a little time to herself. She looked at the phone. She really ought to contact the police to reschedule the meeting, but that could wait until tomorrow.

She looked hopefully at her mobile phone and saw there was a message from Tom. She hadn't heard it coming in. She read it with a tingle of excitement. *Up in town this evening. OK to pop in for a short visit?*

She sent one back quickly. *Great – looking forward to seeing you. X*

CHAPTER 19

Sarah sat back in the Chesterfield listening to Pachelbel and sipping her wine. She relished the peace and beauty of the Georgian room, lit only by the standard lamp behind her head. Despite all the conflicting emotions in her, she felt a strange glow of contentment. Tom was coming round.

The phone rang. She looked at it wondering if she should just let it ring out. *Oh, what the hell.* If it was a journalist, she'd just tell him where to go. Feeling a kind of recklessness, she picked up the receiver.

'Hello, Sarah, it's Barbara.'

Sarah hesitated. The voice sounded vaguely familiar, but she couldn't place the name, although the caller obviously expected to be recognised. 'Hello?'

'It's Barbara, Barbara Barrowfield, Rory's first wife,' the voice said firmly, obviously detecting her hesitation. 'We need to meet to discuss the funeral arrangements. Would this evening be convenient?'

Sarah's jaw literally dropped. She'd never thought of consulting Rory's ex-wife. In fact, because Rory never mentioned her, she'd almost forgotten her existence. Of course, there was Rory's daughter. She would want to come to the funeral, although Sarah didn't think she and Rory had much contact.

'Hello, are you there?' Barbara's brisk tones made Sarah realise she hadn't answered.

'Sorry, I was just thinking. We don't actually have a date for the funeral yet.'

'I think the sooner we discuss this the better,' the efficient voice rapped back.

Now Sarah remembered why the voice was so familiar. After being the Drama teacher at Brunstane High, Babs had gone on to achieve minor fame in a TV police soap, playing the aptly-named Sergeant Mone. She'd developed something of a cult following, partly for her Rottweiler tones, but mainly for her prominent breasts encased in her police uniform. Listening to her now, Sarah realised the character she played was not that different from herself in real life.

Sarah hesitated. 'Well, I am free in the early evening…' Better that Babs came round now than when the twins – or worse, her mother – were around.

'Very well, I'll be round in twenty minutes.' Sarah heard the click that signified the end of the conversation and was left staring at the handset. Oh well, might as well get it over with. At least she'd have Tom to unwind with later.

She took another swig of wine and looked out at the traffic driving down Howe Street. Cars and buses were waiting at the traffic lights, a taxi was picking up a man in a pin-striped suit and shoppers were scurrying across the street laden with shopping bags. It seemed unbelievable that everything was carrying on as normal and her life, once so quiet and dull even, had been turned upside down in the last few weeks. Meeting Tom again, the news about Logan Baird, Nick's revelation, Rory gone… so much had happened.

She felt the wine going to her head. She looked at the

bottle and shrugged her shoulders – she was a widow, and her husband's ex-wife was coming round. She deserved a drink. She poured another glass.

*

The Canongate Centre was on the Cowgate, the gloomy street running under the elevated sections of the South Bridge and George IVth Bridge. It led from Holyrood to the Grassmarket and got its name from the fact that cattle were herded to market there in the old days. Tom remembered that it was considered a dangerous place when he was young, where the homeless gathered with their cheap drinks, waiting for the hostels to open. It was still dark there, but the Grassmarket had been gentrified and even the Cowgate seemed cleaner.

On the way, HJ had explained the set-up. When the church became surplus to requirements, Edinburgh District Council had taken it over and had funded the Arts Centre over the years. Unfortunately, it had fallen victim to the cuts. One reason why HJ had agreed to Rory's programme was that he hoped to raise the profile and maybe secure funding from elsewhere.

'I don't want to be too negative but I can't honestly say how long the centre will be able to stay open,' HJ said sadly, 'so I can't guarantee the job will last for ever. But Edinburgh is proud of being the Festival City and has a commitment to the Arts, and also to the community groups. To be brutally honest, if we say we can't fill the post that will be another nail in the coffin. That's why Jimmy's stayed on until now, actually, because he didn't want to let us down. So, I hope you will take the job. I want to help you, but it will also be good for the centre.'

The church was a dark Gothic building, almost overshadowed by the arch of George IVth bridge and the unlit tenements on each side. Tom went through the side door with Kidd into what must once have been the vestry. They were greeted by a gnomic man with random tufts of hair on his head and deep inquisitive eyes.

'Jimmy, this is Tom McIver. We may have found your successor.'

Jimmy's wizened face lit up. 'Good to see you, Tom. Here's a great wee job. I've been doing it for twenty-three years, since my wife passed, but now it's time I was away to my girl and her weans up in Forfar.'

Tom smiled at him and HJ suggested that Jimmy show them the accommodation. It was not quite the romantic monk's cell that Tom had imagined but it was serviceable. There was a small sitting room with an old-fashioned gas fire, a G-plan type sofa and an ancient box television. With its swirling carpet and geometric wallpaper it looked like something out of a seventies sit-com, but seemed cosy enough, especially with the long mustard-coloured velvet curtains drawn. To the left there was a windowless bedroom, almost completely filled with a double bed, and to the right a small kitchenette. Even though it was not the Gothic cell he'd imagined, Tom wanted to live here; a base where he could escape the pinkness of the Regent Guest House.

As they walked into the main part of the church, Jimmy explained the different aspects of the job, and reassured him about the hours and responsibilities. The lights flickered over the huge arched vaults, throwing long shadows and reflecting from the simple stained-glass windows. Tom felt comfortable in the stark empty space and had the renewed feeling that this was the place for him, if they'd have him.

'I'll be thinking you're no the nervous type,' Jimmy added. 'Some people dinnae want to live alone here. We're near the Grassmarket and the hostels and that, but it's no like it was in the old days. We dinnae have trouble with the boys, if you just tell them this is no the place for them. We dinnae have alcohol here so they're no interested really.'

The front door creaked open and an overweight young man shuffled into the church, avoiding eye contact and sat down on one of the chairs. HJ greeted him and sat down next to him. 'Hi Neil, how are you today? Have you written anything this week?' Neil mumbled and pulled some papers out of his bag.

Kidd looked over at Tom. 'As you can see the group is beginning to assemble. You're very welcome to stay…' He broke off as a pretty girl with long blonde hair and a shaggy Afghan coat came in and gave Kidd an enthusiastic hug. HJ shrugged with a *what can I do?* look and Tom looked at his watch.

'Actually, I said I'd go round and see Sarah.'

'Of course, the dear girl. I think she needs all the support we can give her at the moment. Please do give her my love.' He came over to Tom and shook his hand. 'I hope you will consider the job. Think about it and come round to see me when you've got your CV and references. We'll go through the application process together.' He smiled hopefully. 'I don't think I'm giving too much away when I tell you that the job is yours if you'll take it. You're just the sort of person the centre needs.'

Tom smiled and said he'd contact him very soon. The small sum of money his mother had left him was nearly gone. Living and working at the centre would solve those problems and he'd be doing something useful at last.

The thought buoyed him up as he went out into the damp evening air, the mist swirling round the silent dark corners of the Cowgate. As he walked towards the brighter lights of the Grassmarket, he slowed down. It was perhaps a bit too soon to go Sarah's. He saw the friendly glow of the lights shining through the leaded windows of The Last Drop and popped in for a quiet pint.

*

The bell rang and Sarah opened the door, hearing brisk steps clacking up the stairs. Babs was shorter than she seemed on television and had put on some weight round her middle since her hey-day as Sergeant Mone, but she held herself well, emphasising her huge jutting bosom. She was well into her fifties, with a strong-featured face, thick black brows and startling spiky magenta hair.

As Sarah muttered a few welcoming platitudes, Babs interrupted. She evidently didn't want to waste any time on social niceties. 'I haven't got long, but there are a few things I think we should discuss before the funeral is arranged.'

Sarah nodded and indicated the drawing room where she had arranged the wine glasses and some olives on the table. Babs sat down but brushed aside the offered wine with an impatient gesture. Sarah helped herself to another glass.

'I don't suppose Rory kept you informed, but he used to see me regularly. In fact, he came round just last week.'

Sarah tried to remain impassive, but she was sure surprise registered on her face.

Babs gave a smug smile. 'He needed someone to talk to, someone who really understood him.'

Sarah didn't trust herself to say anything.

'I didn't let him see Abigail at all when she was young, didn't want her corrupted, but more recently they've been seeing more of each other and got on really well. She's a lawyer now, deals with women's rights. So now that Rory's gone, she's fighting the case for the children.'

Sarah frowned. 'Children? I thought you only had the one.'

'I only have Abigail, but there are the others.'

'Others?' Sarah gasped. The enormity of the word reverberated round her brain.

'So he never told you about them. He really did keep you in a glass cage of ignorance.'

Sarah took another gulp of wine. 'What others?'

'Four, as far as I know, all boys. There is Daniel and the twins, Simon and Sean, and then little Jamie; he's only about ten. These boys all know that Rory's their father, although he's never publicly acknowledged them. It's important that they can be included in the funeral, to give them closure, and also to make sure that they get their legacy.'

Sarah hadn't even thought of Rory's will and her mind was still trying to catch up. 'Four children? Who's the mother?'

'There are three. Daniel's mother is Judy Johnstone, the journalist who used to work with Rory at the *Scotsman*. She's married now and lives up north, but Dan's always kept contact with Rory. The twins' mother is Mental Miranda. I don't know what surname she's using at the moment. She had a rich husband and passed the twins off as his until the relationship broke down. There was a messy divorce, he got suspicious about the twins, and had a DNA test. That's when the truth came out. Those twins have just started uni now. Then there's Jamie. His mother is Rosie, one of the researchers on *Chats with Rory*.'

Sarah, whose mind had been flailing as she tried to follow the list, gasped again. She knew Rosie. She remembered when her baby was born. She'd even asked Rory who the father was, as Rosie seemed determined to bring her son up on her own. Rory had said it was a married man. At least he'd told the truth about that.

'Anyway, the children should all have their rightful place at the funeral. Abigail has contacted them all and as soon as the funeral details are known she'll let them know. And she'll make sure they all get their rightful settlement from the will. Rory has always supported his children, and assured them and their mothers that they would be provided for in the future. Have you seen the will yet?'

Sarah's brain felt numb. 'I think it's at the lawyer's. Nick's dealing with that side of things.'

A new worry hit her. She'd always left the finances to Rory. They'd never seemed to have much money, and now she understood why. But they'd had enough and she loved their flat. Surely she'd be able to stay there? She couldn't bear it if she had to leave.

Babs stood up, thrusting her imposing chest out. 'There's no point staying any longer. I've said all I have to say. I just wanted you to be aware of the situation.' She handed Sarah a card. 'Contact me as soon as you have a date.'

As she was strutting into the hall, the doorbell rang. Sarah pressed the button to open the main door and heard footsteps coming quickly up the stairs. It must be Tom. She hoped Babs would make a move before he reached the top, but she was still at the doorway when Tom appeared round the corner, his long legs taking the steps two by two.

Babs looked at him, and turned to Sarah with a knowing smirk, 'You'll be hearing from me.' With that she gave Tom a nod and set off down the stairs, clacking in her high-heeled boots.

Tom raised his eyebrows questioningly. Sarah pulled him into the hall and closed the door before putting her head on his chest, 'Oh Tom.' He put his arms round her and rested his head on the top of her tousled hair, holding her very close.

PART 9

Lying in the darkness. Stale damp air. A weight on my chest, bearing down, crushing me. I struggle to get up, I must escape. In the distance there's a thin sliver of light. I want to run but my feet won't move. They are being sucked down. I know I must run, must escape. Behind me there's something unthinkable, so terrible I can't put a form to it. I just know I must escape. My limbs won't move, the walls are closing in on me. Suffocation. Claustrophobia.

CHAPTER 20

Tom felt Sarah moving beside him, her arms and body thrashing wildly. He put his arm round her, trying to calm her. He stroked her cheek as she threw her head from side to side, her face contorted with fear. 'Sarah, it's all right. Don't worry. Everything's all right.'

He thought back to the evening before. As he'd walked down from the Grassmarket, dodging the taxis on the Mound, across the silent emptiness of Princes Street still in the throes of the great tram-line fiasco, he'd wondered how Sarah would react to seeing him.

He was sorry that Rory was dead on an intellectual level, he was his oldest mate, but Sarah was his main concern. How would it affect them, their relationship? Would she be so caught up in the death that she pushed him away? Or – he hardly dared to express the hope – would it make it easier for them to get closer?

He'd planned what he was going to say. Condolences, of course, and then he'd tell her about the job and HJ Kidd. He hadn't had the chance. As he came in the door, passing a short forceful woman just leaving, Sarah threw herself into his arms. She clung to him as she told him what had happened since they were last together. Tom was confused by her story – death and transplants, unfaithfulness and children, the funeral and journalists. She'd been drinking, he could tell, as the words tumbled out, but he managed to calm her, holding her close.

There was a pain in his chest where he imagined his heart must be. Was this what love felt like? It had never been difficult for him to find sex – there were always lots of fun girls in Plett. He had the reputation of being a loner, which attracted some women, especially the bored housewives and the ever-younger girls who tried to convert him. The relationships never lasted long; after the thrill of the chase he'd felt claustrophobic as soon as they were bedded. He'd thought he was incapable of love.

With Sarah it was different. Their lovemaking was wonderful but the difference was afterwards. He wanted to stay with her; he wanted to walk with her, cook with her, sit in silence with her.

Sarah stirred. Tom stroked her hair, feeling emotion swelling inside.

'Tom…' Sarah opened her eyes. 'Oh, my head, I feel so bad.'

'It's all right, Sarah, it's all right.'

'Oh Tom. I'm sorry.'

Tom held her close. 'Sarah, you don't have to apologise. There's nothing to worry about. You've just gone through the most traumatic few days – you're entitled to a few drinks.' He kissed the top of her head. 'Whatever happens, I'll always be here to help you.'

Sarah looked up at him. 'Everything seems better when you're here.'

'What about the funeral? Do you want me there?'

Sarah lowered her eyes. 'You know there's nothing I'd love more, but it's going to be as private as possible –

strictly family only.' She held him closer. 'But I'll need you afterwards. I think it's going to be hell.' She straightened up and shook her head. 'Sorry, this has all been about me. How are things going with you? Have you been to the police?'

Tom hesitated. He was going – and he'd tell the police everything. But first of all he had to tell Sarah about his suspicions, about the chest and his father's pictures. He hated keeping things from her.

He told the whole story, ending up by saying, 'So I'm really afraid that my father might have been the killer.' He hoped that Sarah wouldn't hate him.

She put her arms round him. 'You've been carrying this suspicion round with you ever since you were in Lewis?'

Tom nodded.

'I'm glad you've told me now, but I wish you'd told me sooner. Because I think you're worrying needlessly; your suspicions are based on very little really. I think those kind of drawings are not unusual in adolescent boys.'

Tom shook his head. 'But he impregnated a fourteen-year-old girl and ran away, leaving her to face the consequences alone. He had a child he never saw. He was a monster.'

'He was a frightened teenager.' Sarah spoke calmly.

'But the way he was with Shona, and the way he turned to drink after she died. This is the only explanation.'

Sarah stroked his hair. 'He loved Shona, and isn't it understandable that he would be upset after her death? He was her father. I'm sure he must have felt guilty afterwards, feeling he should have been able to look after her, save her from what happened.'

Tom stared at Sarah. Everything he found out about her

made him love her more. She was so empathetic, so positive, always seeing the best in everybody. But, he wasn't comforted by what she said. In fact, having put his suspicions into words he became more convinced that he was right. He didn't want to think about it.

Changing the subject, he told Sarah about the Canongate job. When he'd finished telling her, she held him tight, her eyes sparkling. 'Are you really going to stay in Scotland?' Her face lit up. 'I was afraid you'd go back to South Africa. I wanted you to stay but I didn't dare to hope too much. I couldn't bear the thought of you going away again.' She seemed to be about to say more but she just took his face in her hands and kissed him tenderly.

*

Seafield Crematorium stood on the coast road between Leith and Portobello. The day of Rory Dunbar's private family funeral was one of those crisp autumn mornings, when the sky glowed uniform blue and the leaves on the trees shone red, orange and gold. Sarah arrived by taxi with Nick, Lottie and Liam, and Flora. As they were dropped outside the grey-harled chapel, Sarah looked around and breathed a sigh of relief; the courtyard was deserted.

After Babs Barrowfield's visit she'd dreaded the thought of the funeral, but Nick had calmed her down. He hadn't been surprised when Sarah had told him about Babs' revelations because the lawyer had told him that the will contained bequests to other children too. He said Abigail had contacted him and they'd had a good chat. Sarah couldn't get over his coolness and maturity. He'd been unfazed by everything that had happened, dealing with the police, hospital, lawyers and funeral directors.

As soon as the body was released for burial they began to organise this private family event. Sarah had told Archie about Babs' visit and the other children, but he too seemed totally unsurprised. Sarah wondered if everyone had known apart from her; it still hurt her to think that Babs had known about everything and Rory had always kept her in the dark.

Archie had recommended Seafield for the cremation, quieter and less fashionable than Warriston or Mortonhall, and fortunately the earliest morning slot was available just a few days later. The funeral directors were sworn to secrecy and any enquiries were directed to the memorial service that was being organised in St Giles Cathedral at the beginning of December.

She hoped that this occasion would satisfy Babs and Abigail and the 'family' and that they would not insist on too much prominence at the memorial service, which was being organised by BBC Scotland, and which would concentrate on Rory's professional achievements.

Sarah was just reflecting on the bizarre quality of the day when her mother's voice interrupted her thoughts. 'You really should have worn a hat, you know. And your hair… it looks far too informal hanging down like that. I made a special appointment with Ricki yesterday.'

Sarah looked at her mother. She'd tried to tactfully broach the subject of the other children, but she knew her mother hadn't really been listening, just fretting about what she should wear. She usually favoured pastels, but for this occasion was wearing a voluminous black coat with an astrakhan collar and a matching hat, which totally dwarfed her tiny frame and rendered any visit to the hairdresser's totally superfluous.

'The twins look appropriate, but that boy…' Mrs Campbell glared at the young ones who were standing on the other side of the courtyard. Nick and Lottie were smart in dark suits and white shirts, but Liam had obviously incurred Flora's disapproval with his black shirt.

There had been some discussion about whether Liam should come, as it was strictly family only, but Lottie had put her foot down, claiming that he was more family to her than the rest of them. Sarah had quietly asked Nick if he wanted to bring Olly, but was relieved when Nick said he didn't really think this was the occasion for a public outing.

A shiny grey saloon slid into the courtyard and stopped in front of the door. Babs Barrowfield stepped out of the front seat wearing a fitted black costume carefully emphasising her most famous asset and a black pill-box hat with a veil over her face.

From the back seat a squat younger version of Babs stepped out. This must be Abigail. Sarah looked to see any sign of Rory in her, but she was almost a clone of her mother. She had short cropped hair and was wearing a shapeless black tunic but, despite her lack of height, she exuded confident determination. She was followed by a very tall, dark-haired youth with a long narrow face and close-set eyes. This must be Daniel, looking like an elongated version of a young Rory.

Babs strode towards Sarah, her high-heeled boots clacking on the cobbles. 'Good morning, Sarah. What an ungodly hour to organise a funeral.' She turned towards Abigail and Daniel and introduced them. Abigail looked up at Sarah through fierce eyes and greeted her briefly in a deep voice. Daniel stood in the background, looking self-conscious and mumbling a few unintelligeable words.

Sarah introduced her mother and indicated the group of young ones, who were on the other side of the courtyard under a weather-beaten statue of an angel with wide-spread mossy wings. Abigail led Daniel across the courtyard, while Babs stayed with Sarah and her mother.

Moments later, a black Daimler swept in through the gates and purred to a halt. Like something out of an old Hollywood film, a striking figure in a long black fur coat, a broad-brimmed black hat and dark glasses swept out of the car, followed by two very handsome boys in dark suits, who oozed self-confidence.

'Oh God, Mental Miranda,' whispered Babs. 'I told her not to come. Family only.'

Miranda approached Sarah, holding out her slim black-leather gloved hand. 'My condolences, Sarah. We have suffered a very sad loss. Rory was a very special man.'

Sarah took her hand and murmured agreement. The twins nodded briefly in her direction and then strolled over towards the rest of the young ones, pulling cigarettes and lighters from their pockets in mirror movements. Abigail, who was at least nine inches shorter than any of the others, stood in the centre of the group and appeared to be dominating the conversation.

Babs looked at her watch. 'Jamie should be here by now. I told Rosie he had to come. I even offered to bring him with me.'

A few moments later a taxi drove up and Rosie stepped out holding the hand of an attractive-looking boy with shaggy dark hair hanging into huge brown eyes. Rosie was dressed in a striped sweater and jeans, with large gypsy earrings, her long dark hair in soft curls. Jamie was wearing black jeans and a black polo-necked sweater and was impatiently trying to wrest his hand from his mother's grip.

Rosie hurried over to Sarah. 'Look, I'm really sorry. I'm not staying – I didn't want to bring Jamie along, but Babs insisted. Poor Jamie doesn't have a clue what's going on, and neither do I, to be honest.'

She stopped the breathless rush of words and stood in front Sarah, her head hanging, unable to look her in the eye. 'Sarah, I'm so sorry. I can't believe Rory is dead. He was so alive, the most vibrant person I know.' She raised her head; her eyes glistened with tears.

Sarah reached out and gave her a hug. Rosie was the first person who seemed genuinely upset about Rory. 'Do stay. I think it's better for Jamie if you're here with him.'

Rosie looked down at her clothes. 'But I'm not suitably dressed.'

'Don't worry about that. This is a very small private occasion and nobody worries about what we're wearing.' Sarah looked round as she said this and saw her mother standing on the edge of the group, her mouth hanging open with astonishment as she watched the scene unfold before her. Sarah found herself stifling a giggle; the day was taking on the quality of farce.

Miranda lowered her glasses and looked round the crematorium courtyard. 'Where is everybody? I was sure there would be crowds of people here, the press.'

Babs broke in. 'I told you that today is strictly private, family only.' She put great emphasis on the word family. 'You can save the outfit for the memorial service. The press will be there, all right. But you know the deal. Your money was always dependent on this story staying out of the papers, and that still applies. So just keep your head down and your mouth shut, if that's possible.'

'But it's my boys' rightful inheritance,' Miranda said in a sulky tone.

'Don't give me that. You never even admitted Rory was the father until that stupid pillock you married did the DNA test.'

'But Rory always knew. He told me to keep it quiet but he always supported me.'

Sarah stared in amazement as they carried on as if she, the widow, was totally irrelevant to the entire proceedings. She could see outrage building up in her mother's face and the giggle threatened to break free again.

There was a gentle cough behind them. While they'd been talking, a hearse had glided up and the coffin was being lifted out of the back. The dark-suited funeral director greeted them solemnly and ushered them into the side chapel. It had been agreed that the service would be brief and non-religious, conducted by Melanie, a humanist celebrant recommended by Babs. She had provided Melanie with details of Rory's life and Melanie delivered the address in a heartfelt tone, full of emotion, even though she had never met Rory.

The service passed in a blur for Sarah. After about ten minutes the coffin slid behind the curtains to the accompaniment of Elgar's Nimrod. Sarah idly wondered who'd chosen the music, or if it was the crematorium's default setting.

She heard loud sobs behind her, but she felt stony, numb, totally detached from what was going on. Lottie took her hand and gave it a squeeze and Nick put his arm round her as the coffin slid behind the curtains. Sitting between Nick and Lottie she was overcome with love for them. Rory had done something right.

As they emerged from the gloom of the chapel into the bright autumn sunlight, she felt overcome with tiredness. She would have liked to go straight home and lie down, but Babs had insisted that everyone go somewhere after the ceremony. In the end it had been decided – by whom, Sarah wasn't sure – that they would go back to her Great King Street flat.

The young ones had gathered under the angel's moss-covered sightless eyes again and Miranda's twins had lit up cigarettes. Abigail came over to her mother with her phone in her hand. Babs shook her head.

'Look, Mum. I've discussed it with the others and we want a record of this occasion,' said Abigail firmly.

Babs pursed her lips. 'We've gone to so much trouble to keep this secret. The funeral directors won't say anything and I'd trust Melanie with my life. We don't want photos floating around.'

'Mum, I'll only share it with the others. I'm not putting it on Facebook, for heaven's sake. We've all lost our dad, but we've found each other, and we'll keep in touch. We want this photo.'

She thrust the phone at her mother, who took it and began squinting into the viewer as Abigail arranged the family in age order. Sarah was amazed there was anyone who could get the better of Babs, but obviously Abigail could.

The camera clicked. Sarah had to admit there was

something impressive about the scene. Abigail stood on the left, then Lottie and Nick, up to Daniel towering over the others, down to the handsome twins, Simon and Sean, and then a long way down to Jamie standing on the edge. They were all dressed in black and smiling, except for Jamie who just looked puzzled. With the sun shining down on them and the trees in the background, they looked for all the world like a group of the groom's drinking friends at a wedding.

CHAPTER 21

Detective Inspector Fergus Chisholm was sitting behind his desk at Police Headquarters in Fettes Avenue peering into a computer screen when Tom was shown in. He had broad shoulders, a large head with a high shiny forehead and intelligent eyes behind rimless glasses. Tom immediately felt he could trust him.

The detective stood up and shook hands and then indicated that Tom should sit down. 'Thank you for contacting us. Our information was that your family had emigrated to South Africa. We would have caught up with you eventually, of course, but you've saved us a lot of time and trouble.' He pushed his glasses up and looked at him keenly. 'Are you in Scotland because of the news about Logan Baird?'

Tom shook his head. The coincidence of the timing had struck him too. 'No, my mother died recently and I came to scatter her ashes at her birthplace on Eriskay. But I'm glad I am here at this time, and I'll do anything I can to help find Shona's murderer.' Tom hoped this was true; he was still uncertain about whether he should implicate his father. 'I'm the only one of the family left now.'

'I'm sorry for your loss and I realise how distressing it must be for you to have to go through all this again now. The death of your sister must have been a terrible thing. But we have to do this. We know that Logan Baird is innocent. It isn't one of those cases where a long-term prisoner has been released on a technicality. Undoubtedly there were errors made in Baird's arrest and conviction, which may have been enough to secure release, but the subsequent investigation has shown that Baird could not possibly have been the murderer. That means that the real killer has never been found.' Tom nodded. Archie Kilbride had been right.

Chisholm took off his glasses and continued. 'Semen left on the victim's cardigan was of his blood group O+, but the more advanced tests available to us today have proved that he could not have been the killer. At the moment we have no leads. We have run the sample through the National DNA Database, which at present has over five million samples, without finding a match. Therefore, we have reopened the case and will leave no stone unturned to find the real killer.'

Tom nodded again as Chisholm shrugged his shoulders. 'Of course, with such a very old case, it is exceptionally difficult. Witnesses have died or moved on, or have simply forgotten. There is, of course, the possibility that the perpetrator is also deceased.'

Tom hesitated. Should he bring up his suspicions about his father or was this a case where it really was better to let the proverbial dogs lie. No, he had to know the truth. He took a deep breath. 'I think I may know who the murderer was. I went up to my father's birthplace in Lewis and there I found some very,' he searched for the right word, 'disturbing images which made me see my father in a different light. I know that in most cases of murder a family member is responsible. And also his behaviour afterwards—'

Chisholm waved his hand, cutting Tom short. He had an air of authority and, although he was probably younger than Tom, made him feel like a schoolboy. 'Let me stop you there, Mr McIver. You have no need to worry about your father, as that possiblilty was already excluded at the time of the original investigation. The family is always the first place a good investigator looks. We checked your family's blood and your father, and you, are both blood type A+. The perpetrator was type O+.'

He looked up at Tom with a weary smile. 'So you and your father are absolutely out of the picture. We are looking for someone who has not been caught in our DNA net, and what's more no member of whose family has ever been involved in a crime as far as we can see.'

Tom felt the most enormous sense of relief. He hadn't realised until that moment how much the suspicions about his father had been weighing on his mind. He experienced a momentary sense of outrage that he had also been considered a suspect, it was his sister after all, but then he felt a lightness come over him.

'So what's the next step?'

'We're going to reinterview all the original witnesses we can still trace. This is a very difficult case and we have to face up to the fact that we may never find out who did it.'

'But you must.'

Chisholm rubbed his eyes. 'We'll do our best. There are only limited resources and, because the appeal will be granted anyway, it is not one of our major priorities. We are going to invite as many of those who gave an original statement as possible for another interview. However, many are deceased and it's difficult to trace women especially, as their names change on marriage. I can assure you, though, that we will do our utmost to find out who was responsible for this terrible crime.'

Tom nodded. It seemed that was the most he could hope for.

'Well, as you're here now, Mr McIver, perhaps we can use this opportunity to go over the events of that night.'

Tom described what had happened as accurately as he could, and this time he did admit that he'd been at the bandstand with Jennie. He didn't tell Chisholm exactly what had happened, though.

Chisholm picked up a pencil and wrote a couple of notes. 'Jennie Howie, you say. She was one of the young ladies who originally accused Logan Baird of exposing himself to her. She withdrew the statement and would not give evidence in court, none of them would, actually.' He scratched his head with his pencil. 'So she was also on the prom that night. Do you know where we could contact her? Her married name or address?'

Tom shook his head and explained she lived in Singapore, but had been in Scotland recently, staying in a hotel. Chisholm nodded. 'We may be able to trace her through hotel records. It's a long shot but we have so few leads we have to follow them all up. Tell me, were you in the park that night after your,' he coughed, 'encounter with Miss Howie?'

Tom shook his head. He should have been there to look after Shona. His Mum had asked him to look out for her, but he hadn't. Instead he had been with Jennie. Afterwards he'd felt so ashamed he'd gone straight home and hidden his head under his covers. The old feeling of guilt welled up in him again. He should have been able to protect his sister. He hadn't been there and it was his fault.

He answered the rest of the questions about Shona's friends and habits as best he could, his mind whirling with a mixture of emotions: the guilt he felt about not protecting his sister but also relief – his father was not a murderer.

*

Back at Sarah's flat, everyone quickly made themselves at home. Lottie had organised sandwiches and was preparing coffee for everyone, but the whisky bottle was quickly opened and the young ones settled down in the front room with something approaching a party atmosphere.

Sarah noticed that Babs quickly moved over to the whisky group in the front room. Flora reached into the cupboard for a sherry glass and helped herself from the drinks cabinet.

'Do you have a gin and tonic?' Miranda asked Sarah, removing her dark glasses.

Sarah was gratified to see the wrinkled skin round her eyes and her red lipstick seeping into the lines around her mouth. *No wonder she had to wear dark glasses,* Sarah thought, relishing her bitchiness. She automatically reached into the freezer for ice and served the gin and tonic. 'Sorry, no lemon,' she said but any irony was totally lost on Miranda, who took it without thanks and joined the others in the drawing room.

Rosie and Jamie hovered awkwardly at the doorway of the kitchen and gladly accepted orange juice. Rosie seemed to be about to say something, but then thought better of it and moved away, holding Jamie's hand tightly. Her barmaid duties over, Sarah put her hands on the kitchen table and let her head drop. Her limbs were aching and she just wanted to go to bed. She just wanted them all to go.

A roar of laughter showed that the young ones were bonding well. As the voices got louder the doorbell rang. Nick moved to answer it, followed closely by Abigail. He opened the door and John Coltrane, Rory's lawyer, came in.

He moved over to Sarah, muttering words of condolence. Nick stood at his shoulder.

'Mum, we thought it would be best if John came and read the will now, when everyone's together. I didn't tell you before because I didn't want to worry you with details like this.'

Sarah felt numb. Everything seemed to be taken out of her hands. She just wanted this day to be over and everyone out of her flat. A scintilla of fear ran through her: *her* flat. Please let it still be hers after the will was read.

Nick led her by the elbow into the front room and chased one of Miranda's twins from the high wing-backed chair. John Coltrane, looking like an overgrown schoolboy with his pink cheeks and slicked-back hair, coughed to get everyone's attention, opened his briefcase and began to read through some formalities.

Sarah's attention was wandering until he got onto the bequests. 'To my dear wife, Sarah, I leave the property at 95 Great King Street and all of the contents, with the exception of items chosen in clause nine.' Sarah's heart pounded with relief.

Coltrane drawled on in his typical Edinburgh lawyer whine. Sarah wasn't listening properly, just so relieved that she could stay in her flat, but she did hear that the trust fund established for his offspring was to be equally divided between his dear children, Abigail, Nicholas, Charlotte, Daniel, Simon, Sean and Jamie and that they and his dear mother-in-law, Flora Campbell, could each choose one personal item from the flat in his memory. All bequests were conditional on their maintaining the same level of personal discretion as had been previously agreed. The remainder of his assets were to go completely to Sarah Dunbar. Sarah bit her lip. Rory did love her; he made sure she was going to be all right.

When Coltrane mentioned the personal items, Miranda's eyes began flicking around the room. The lawyer finished and was offered a glass of whisky by Nick, but he refused, before sidling out of the front door, muttering something about important appointments.

Miranda stood up and said, 'We don't have to choose the items today, do we? I mean we don't know what he has and I would like to have a valuation of the worth of the items before I come to any decision.'

Abigail stood in front of her, her eyes blazing. 'It appears that you have not understood the significance of the bequests, which he made to his *children*.' She emphasised the word, glaring at Miranda. 'It is so they can have something personal to remember him by, not to make the most monetary gain from his estate.' Sarah looked at Abigail with new respect. She may be dumpy with no neck, but she had a powerful magnetism.

Sarah cleared her throat, emboldened by Abigail's forcefulness. 'Actually, I would prefer you to make your choice today. This has all been difficult for me and I don't wish to prolong it.'

Nick shot her a guilty look and raised his voice above the others. 'Please make your choice within the hour, and you should all check the objects with my mother before taking them away.'

Sarah looked at him gratefully, her head throbbing, 'I think I'm just going to have a lie down now.' She went into the cool darkness of her room and lay down on top of the covers. She let out a deep breath; it was as if she'd been holding it all morning and could finally breathe again.

Outside she heard the sounds of activity. She tried to block it out but she knew she could not relax until they had all gone. There was a tap at the door. Lottie opened it gently. 'Mum, are you awake?'

Sarah raised her head. 'Come in, darling. I can't sleep with all these people milling about but I just wanted to get away.'

'I can understand that. God, that Miranda's a cow, isn't she?'

Sarah pretended to look shocked. But then she laughed. 'You can say that again!'

Lottie sat down on the bed next to her. 'Mum, Nick got Dad's things from the hospital and he'd like to keep his watch, the one he got from his father.'

'That's perfect. I'm glad he's got it.'

Lottie hesitated. 'And I've got his wedding ring. Is that all right?'

Sarah paused. Rory's wedding ring. She wondered if he'd taken it off when he was with all those other women. What had it meant to him? She was surprised Lottie had chosen this, when they were all surrounded by evidence that it had not meant much to him.

Lottie seemed to sense her mother's hesitation. 'It's a lovely heavy ring, eighteen-carat gold – seems a pity to waste it!' She laughed.

Sarah felt confused by the levity in her daughter's voice. Lottie leant over and kissed the top of her mother's head. 'And is it all right if I give it to Liam?'

Sarah saw Lottie's eyes were shining. She put her arms round her daughter. 'Lottie, is there something I should know?'

Lottie hugged her. 'It's all unofficial, but we do want to get married. Everything that's happened has made me realise what's important in life. And I've also realised that everything's better, everything's bearable when I'm with Liam.'

Sarah felt a surge of emotion, a wave of love for Lottie, tempered by a tinge of sadness. Rory had never made her feel like that – not even at his most understanding – but Tom… How she wished he could be here with her now.

She pushed Lottie's beautiful curtain of hair back from her face and kissed her cheek. 'You're lucky to have found each other. I'm so happy for you.'

Lottie's face lit up into a smile and she kissed her mother. 'Thanks, Mum. But it's a secret mind, not a word to anyone at the moment – especially not Granny!' Mother and daughter exchanged a look and Sarah laughed out loud, feeling better than she had all day.

The sound of voices outside the bedroom grew louder and Lottie stood up. 'We'd better go and see what's going on out there.'

They went out to where Liam was standing awkwardly in the hall. Lottie ran over to him and his face relaxed in relief as she whispered something to him. Sarah smiled as she left them kissing tenderly.

She turned towards the kitchen and saw Miranda's twins, slouched against the marble-topped work surface, drinking large tumblers of whisky and blowing smoke from their cigarettes towards the ceiling.

'Excuse me,' Sarah said, trying to keep her voice steady. 'I'd prefer you not to smoke in my home.' The boys turned their heads towards her like two meerkats, raised their eyebrows in unison and gave her a 'what are you making such a fuss about?' look.

'No problem, we'll blow the smoke out of the window,' drawled Simon, or maybe Sean, while the other smirked.

Sarah felt loathing swelling up in her. She looked at them closely – she had thought them good-looking but now she saw the weakness in their mouths, the arrogance in their eyes and saw that they were ugly. 'I want you to leave now.'

'Don't worry, we're going. Mum's just seeing if there's anything else worth taking.'

Sarah stepped out of the kitchen, determined to see what Miranda was up to. A movement in Rory's office caught her eye and she saw Miranda rifling through some files on his desk. Rory, who could be messy in other respects, was meticulously tidy in his office. Sarah knew the folders hadn't been on the desk before. When she saw the papers in Miranda's hands she felt anger exploding in her. The thought of that woman pawing through Rory's things seemed the final indignity.

'Get away from those papers.'

Miranda looked up and sneered. 'I was just checking that

there was nothing of value here, and there isn't. We'll just stick with the paintings, the McTaggart and the Neil.'

She swept out of the room and signalled to her sons, each of whom was carrying a large framed painting. They left the flat without saying goodbye, slamming the door behind them.

A hush had descended over the flat and Sarah saw the rest of them standing at the door of the drawing room, watching in shocked embarrassment. Babs spoke first. 'Appalling woman, and those boys are turning out to be just as bad.' Sarah nodded in heartfelt agreement.

Rosie stepped towards her and took her hand. 'Thank you, Sarah. I know it's been a very hard day for you.' She paused and lowered her eyes. 'And I'm so sorry for…'

Her eyes moved to her son, who was holding a blue hard-back book of Scottish poetry. 'Mummy said I should ask if I can have this book. Can I?'

Sarah looked at it. She didn't remember ever having seen it before. She opened it up and saw an engraved plate on the front page. *Presented to Rory Dunbar. Dux of Towerbank Primary School. June 1971.* So Rory won that prize at his primary school. He may have been boastful, but he'd kept that quiet.

'What's a Dux, Mummy?' Jamie looked up at his mother, a questioning expression in his large dark eyes.

'That means he was best pupil in his school. Your daddy was very clever.' Rosie smiled down at her son and turned to Sarah. 'He goes to the Rudolf Steiner School. Being Dux is a bit of a foreign concept to him.'

Sarah smiled. 'Of course, you can have it, Jamie. And I'm sure you'll do just as well as your clever father.'

Rosie looked at her gratefully and gave her a

spontaneous hug. 'I so admire your strength and dignity. I don't think I could have faced a day like today.' She lowered her eyes again and blushed slightly. 'We'll be going now, but I hope to see you again.'

'You will,' Sarah said grimly. 'Remember we've still got the memorial service to get through!'

Rosie took Jamie by the hand and they waved goodbye as they closed the door quietly behind them.

Sarah caught sight of Daniel hovering awkwardly in a corner, his long limbs seeming even more uncoordinated than before. He blushed as he held out a box of cufflinks. 'Is it all right if I take these?'

'Of course. I'm sure your father would be pleased for you to have them.' She smiled encouragingly as the blush deepened and spread over Daniel's face and onto his neck.

Sarah felt as if she was in the reception line at a gruesome wedding as Abigail stepped forward, holding a small framed photo in her hand. Sarah recognised it; it always stood on Rory's desk, showing him aged about six, standing with his father and his grandfather in his grandfather's allotment. Rory had never been family-minded, saying university had separated him from the rest of his family, made him 'disenfranchised working class,' so it was strange that he had always kept this photo by him. It was the only photo Sarah had seen of Rory's grandfather, a small bent man with a flat cap and a large white moustache. Rory's father also looked old and stooping, with his trousers pulled up under his armpits and elastic round his shirt sleeves to shorten them. Sarah remembered that Rory's parents had already been well into their forties when he was born, the long-awaited menopausal miracle.

Abigail glanced at the photo again, looking unexpectedly anxious. 'I know that this means a lot to all of us and I'll have copies made,' she said her deep voice sounding even lower.

Sarah was filled with a strange feeling of gratitude. 'That's really thoughtful of you, Abigail. But you can keep this one, in the original frame. It shows your grandfather and great-grandfather too.'

Abigail looked up at her and Sarah saw that she had very beautiful eyes, Rory's eyes.

Sarah gave her a hug. 'Thank you,' she said, not quite sure what for. The emotion of the day was overwhelming her.

Babs stepped forward and even she seemed to have mellowed. 'Apart from that bitch I think it was all very satisfactory. Well done, Sarah.'

Sarah felt oddly pleased by her praise as she watched Abigail and Babs strut down the stairs, followed by the ungainly Daniel.

Nick put his arm round his mother. 'God, that was awful. But at least that's it over with now. Come and sit down, Mum. What can I get you?'

Sarah shook her head. She felt numb with exhaustion and just wanted the day to be over. 'Nothing thanks, Nick. Thank you. All of you. I couldn't have got through this day without you, but now I just want to be alone.' She paused as a thought struck her. 'Where's Granny?'

Nick indicated his head towards the 'snug', the little room with the television where the twins had retreated when they were young. Sarah looked in and saw her mother in an armchair with her head on her chest, fast asleep, still clutching her sherry glass.

'How did she manage to sleep through all that?' The

twins shrugged their shoulders and Sarah smiled. 'Actually, I think I could too. I'm shattered.'

'I'm not surprised,' Lottie held her mother tight. 'We'll just clear up and you can have a lie down.'

Sarah nodded and hugged both of her children. She saw Liam hanging back a little self-consciously and beckoned him over. 'Come on, group hug. Welcome to the family.'

*

Sarah woke up a few hours later on top of the covers with Sultan lying close to her. She stroked his silky black fur and felt comforted by his purr. She took off her funeral clothes and wandered through to the front room. Everything had been cleared away and there was a note on the table. '*Didn't want to disturb you. Just ring if there is ANYTHING we can do. Mum, you're the best! Love you Nick, Lottie and Liam x x x P.S. We've taken Granny!*'

Her heart literally swelled with love. She was so lucky with her children. She picked up the note and held it close to her chest. Then she looked up and saw the pale rectangle above the fireplace where the William McTaggart landscape had hung. It had been a present to Rory from his first editor, the autocratic press baron who'd recognised his potential and taken him under his wing. Miranda was right. It was the most valuable thing in the house.

Thinking of Miranda going through Rory's papers, the anger rose in her chest again. It was suddenly very important for Sarah to leave Rory's office in the state he liked. She went through to his study and began sorting through the folders on his desk.

As she put the papers into piles one of Rory's yellow post-its with his neat handwriting caught her eye. It seemed to be another of HJ's poems. So they weren't all in the folder he had collected. Then she saw what Rory had written. *So he liked young girls! Link with family scandal? Find out more!*

Her eyes scanned quickly down the lines of poetry and then she began to read the words more carefully.

Bright-eyed, they sit in rows,
Sleek hair shining,
Short blue skirts
Slender brown legs
In sparkling white ankle socks
And well-brushed sandals.
Minds like flowers
Drinking in knowledge
Like the morning dew.
Heaven would be
To be licked all over
By their tiny pink tongues

Sarah put the paper down. A shudder of revulsion passed through her. She remembered HJ coming round just after Rory died, searching in Rory's office. She'd thought it so odd. Was this what he was looking for?

She looked over the words again. HJ? A paedophile?

She heard the ping from her phone and saw the light was flashing. A message. Her hand trembling, she picked it up and saw TM had sent two messages. *How did it go? Thinking of you x* sent in the afternoon. A more recent message read *You OK? Want company? X*

Decisively she stabbed into the keyboard, *Am alone. PLEASE come NOW x*

PART 10

Through the fish-eye of memory the room comes slowly into focus. I sit squashed between two of my classmates on a long sofa, our legs stretched out, white ankle socks and shiny Clarks sandals, below blue school skirts, yellow and blue striped ties. About a dozen girls squeezed onto different pieces of furniture arranged in a circle. The heavy scent of roses from a large bowl on the polished mahogany table hangs in the air.

On a high-backed chair at the side of the tiled Victorian fireplace sits HJ Kidd, his black hair curling over the collar of his green velvet jacket. The After-School Writing Club has been invited to his house.

Through the high bay window the sun shafts into the room, and I catch a glimpse of the wide sky and the sparkling sea stretching towards Fife. HJ's wife, shoulder-length brown hair pushed behind her ears, brings in a tray of orange squash and butterfly buns. She lays them on the table and goes out, her lips pursed in disapproval. Glasses and cakes are passed round but all eyes are on our teacher.

'Your short stories were wonderful, all of them. I'm so proud of you and you should all be proud of yourselves. However, there was one that was especially good.' HJ pauses, and twelve pairs of eyes look at him expectantly. I feel a surge of hope.

'Shona, your story is exceptional. The imagery, the poetry of your words conjures up such a vivid picture. Come forward. I'd like to read it to our group.'

Shona goes forward and I feel disappointment bitter in my mouth. With his arm round her waist, he holds up her jotter and reads the story. Shona looks proudly round the room. The envy hangs in the air heavy like the scent of roses. Every single girl wishes she could be in

Shona's place, standing close to Captain Kidd with his arm round our waist.

He finishes the reading and the words fade. Shona stands up, eyes sparkling with delight. I see Kidd bend down and whisper something in her ear that makes her smile even wider.

CHAPTER 22

Sarah opened her eyes, for a moment not knowing where she was. The picture of her teacher's room on the Portobello seafront, where they'd all been sitting just a few weeks before, remained imprinted on the darkness of the bedroom. The memory hung over her like a toxic cloud; her feeling of disappointment, jealousy of her friend, and a strange disquiet as she recalled the smug expression on HJ's face as Shona had stood close to him. Shona's face had been triumphant, loving the attention and the praise.

Sarah sat up in bed, suddenly wide awake. Times were very different in the seventies but had none of them thought that a young teacher in his twenties being so close to a thirteen-year-old girl was inappropriate behaviour? They were so naïve. If a teacher had done that when Lottie was at school… Sarah shuddered.

The After School Writing Club at Mr Kidd's house. It all came back so clearly; that was the day Shona died. Like every Tuesday, they'd all gone down to Captain Kidd's house after school and he'd talked about the stories they'd written.

Afterwards Sarah had gone home for her tea before going round to Shona's house, as she did every evening. Shona had been in a funny mood, restless, and said they should go out. They'd hung about the park, Shona making remarks to the boys as they had passed by, and then she'd run off, saying she had a secret. Once again the image of Shona looking back and laughing was imprinted on her eyes.

She turned and saw Tom sleeping next to her, the cover thrown off, his long limbs spread over his side of the bed. His face looked beautiful, moulded in peaceful sleep.

He'd come immediately last night, almost as if he'd been waiting. He was in a good mood, obviously wanting to tell her something, but he listened to her recounting all the day's events, massaging her shoulders and easing the knots of tension away. It had all seemed unimportant as she spoke to him. She had felt safe, cocooned from the unpleasantness of the day.

Only when she was calm had she asked him about his day. Tom's face had lit up as he told her the good news, that he'd plucked up courage to go to see Chisholm and that his father was in the clear. His joy and relief were clear to see.

Sarah wanted to share his happiness, but she felt perturbed. Tom's father being out of the frame meant that they still had no idea who the murderer could be. A seed of suspicion started to grow in her mind: HJ Kidd had been acting very strangely and there was *that* poem.

Sarah showed it to Tom. As he was reading it, he raised his eyebrows in surprise, but at the end he laughed. Sarah felt a surge of annoyance.

'Don't worry about it. It's only a poem.' Tom kissed the top of her head. She put her arms round him, and not wanting to break the moment, put her suspicions to the back of her mind.

But in the night the memory of that day at Kidd's house came back to her, as clear and sharp as a film. She got her housecoat and moved quietly into the kitchen, but as she was making the coffee the scene kept replaying in her mind.

She poured the coffee and was just about to take Tom a cup when he came through from the bedroom in his boxers, stretching and yawning. 'Good morning, beautiful.' He bent over to kiss her. She looked up and smiled as their lips met.

'I'm just going to have a quick shower and get round to the Cowgate. I'm meeting HJ.'

As she heard Tom humming through the splashing of the shower, memories started melding together with recent events: HJ holding her a bit too close at the poetry reading; the unease she'd felt when HJ had his arms round the young girl poet that evening – and worst of all, the poem. She couldn't forget about the poem.

Tom came through, his hair damp from his shower. As he sat down at the scrubbed wooden table and took the mug of coffee, Sarah knew she had to tell him all about it.

He listened carefully as Sarah told him about what she'd remembered, looking thoughtful. 'So you were all at HJ Kidd's on that last afternoon. How was Shona after you left his place?'

Sarah sat very still and looked up at Tom. 'She was in a very strange mood. Said she had a secret. Could she…?' A thought struck her, so vividly and clearly that she couldn't believe that it hadn't occurred to her before. 'I know where she was going when she ran away. She was going to see Kidd.'

Tom shook his head. 'I can't believe he could have anything to do with it. He's a straight guy, he was a teacher for forty years and he's married.' He paused and added. 'And he's being so good to me, with the job and everything.'

Sarah felt a surge of irritation. 'Have you asked yourself why he's being so good to you? Has it occurred to you that he might want you onside?'

Tom reached out and pulled her closer. 'Sarah, don't begin to see evil everywhere. I wasted so much emotional energy suspecting my father and it was nothing.'

Sarah smiled doubtfully. 'It's everything that's happened, everything I've remembered. I'm beginning to get suspicious of everyone.' She wanted to share Tom's pleasure about the job, but couldn't.

Tom looked at his watch. 'Anyway, I'd better get going. HJ said he'd be waiting at ten and no doubt you'll have family coming round soon.'

'Oh yes, Mum will be coming round 'to help', I expect.' She sighed and cleared the coffee cups.

Tom had his hand on the door handle when the bell rang. Sarah answered the intercom, puzzled. 'It's a bit early for Mum.' She turned round and mouthed 'Archie Kilbride' to Tom as she pushed the buzzer to let him in.

Tom stood up. 'Should I hide?'

'Archie's no problem. You're just an early caller.'

Archie's footsteps could be heard coming slowly up the stairs before he arrived at the front door panting. 'These Georgian flats are all very well but why did they no install lifts?' He gave an ironic grin and kissed Sarah on the cheek. 'Hi Tom,' he said, not seeming to find it strange that he was there. 'Have you seen any papers this morning, Sarah?'

Sarah shook her head and led him towards the kitchen. 'Coffee?'

'I'll take one in a minute but I think you ought to see this first.' Archie took a folded newspaper out of his pocket. '*The*

266

Daily Recorder is not usually my reading of choice but this was drawn to my attention this morning.'

He opened it up and revealed the headline: *Rory Dunbar's secret funeral* over a picture of the children standing in a line in front of the spreading wings of the granite angel at the Seafield Crematorium.

Sarah's mouth dropped open. 'That picture was taken on Abigail's phone. How could she have…?' She was stuttering, her mouth seeming incapable of forming words.

Archie shook his head. 'Look at the picture quality and the shadows. This has been taken from a long way away, with a telephoto lens.'

'But how could they have found out? We were so careful.'

'There are always people willing to sell a bit of information. Or maybe they just followed you there.'

'What! People are watching us and following us?' Sarah was aghast.

Archie patted her arm. 'Don't worry. It's not MI5, just some small-time pap wanting to earn a quick buck. But you'd better take your phone off the hook and don't let anyone you don't know into the stair because the sharks will be on your trail. Actually it's quite surprising they haven't already been onto you. *The Recorder* must have got the photos at the last minute before the printing deadline.'

Sarah picked up the paper and began to read. '*Early yesterday morning at a secret ceremony at Seafield Crematorium, the body of Rory Dunbar, who died in a tragic fall at Arthur's Seat last week, was laid to rest. The popular television personality was accompanied on his last journey by his wife Sarah, first wife TV star Babs Barrowfield of Sergeant Mone fame and several other women. We show the picture of the seven young people gathered there, children who all bear a remarkable resemblance to the charismatic chat show host. Was this the last gathering of his secret family?'*

Underneath there was an even more blurred photo of the women standing at the chapel door. Rosie had her back to the camera but Sarah, her mother and Miranda could be seen very clearly. The strapline read. *Rory Dunbar's Wives Club?* A second fuzzy photo showed Babs and Abigail with the strapline: *Babs 'Sergeant Mone' Barrowfield with her daughter Abigail Dunbar, Rory Dunbar's child from his early first marriage.*

Sarah felt breathless with shock. They'd been so careful and this was exactly what she'd wanted to avoid.

The doorbell rang again. Archie raised his eyebrows warningly as Tom moved over to the intercom and said, 'Your mother.'

Sarah shrugged and nodded her head. How was her mother going to take this? Tom buzzed her up and the click of high-heeled shoes could be heard coming up the stairs. Flora arrived at the door, beautifully dressed in a lilac two-piece with matching shoes and handbag. She was holding the newspaper.

Sarah's heart sank.

'Have you seen this?' Flora waved the article in Sarah's direction. 'We're in the newspaper, not one of the quality ones, of course, but nevertheless. And have you seen the photo? They think that I'm one of Rory's wives!' She patted her hair. 'It isn't a very clear photo, of course, but it's quite a good one of me and it's really quite flattering that they should think I'm young enough to be his wife.'

Sarah's mouth fell open, shocked at her mother's self-absorption. To think she'd been worried about how she'd take the revelations about Rory's other children. To her amazement she'd accepted it with total equanimity, excusing Rory everything and acting as if it were all Sarah's fault.

Archie watched Flora with an amused smile, before turning back to Sarah. 'Seriously, perhaps you should think about making a statement, just to fend off any questions. Something to the effect *Sarah Dunbar and Rory's immediate family laid his body to rest in a private ceremony at the Seafield Crematorium. They now ask that their privacy be respected and they are left to grieve in peace.'*

Sarah breathed a sigh of relief. 'Could you do this for me? You could also add that a memorial service to celebrate his life and achievements will be held at St Giles Cathedral.'

'Do you know the date?' Archie took out a notebook and was scribbling some notes with a stubby pencil.

'Not yet, it's being organised by BBC Scotland, but I'll let you know.'

'And otherwise, no comment. What about the rest of the family? Do you think they'll say anything?'

'Their legacy seems to be dependent on them adhering to some kind of confidentiality agreement that was in operation while Rory was alive. I don't think we need to worry about them. And anyway now it's all out in the open it isn't that much of a story.'

Archie looked up from his notebook. 'There might be some slappers trying to cash in on the story, but just ignore them. A dignified silence is the way to deal with them.' Sarah nodded, relieved that Archie was on her team with his practical, unsensational take on things.

After everyone had gone, her mother to the Bridge Club, clutching her photo, Tom to meet HJ, and Archie to his usual Café Royal lunchtime drink, the phone started ringing. Nick and Lottie were both back at work, but had phoned when the photo had been brought to their attention. Neither of them seemed very upset about it, amused rather. Sarah was surprised that Nick immediately sprang to the defence of Abigail, insisting that the photo couldn't have come from her, even though Sarah had not even suggested it.

'It couldn't have been Abigail. She's a great girl, very loyal.'

Sarah was puzzled that he could have formed this judgement after only one meeting. Or perhaps the children really did have more contact with each other.

After a series of calls from journalists Sarah took Archie's advice and left the phone off the hook. She wanted peace to think about everything that had happened. She was so confused: she didn't know how she felt about Rory anymore. In some ways she was angry with him for all the lies and deceit, but at the same time they'd been together for nearly thirty years and there had been some good times.

Then she remembered Tom. She'd almost made up her mind to leave Rory before he died and now the relationship with Tom might be easier. But what would her mother say about that?

Rory! She slapped her forehead. Why was everyone so sure his death was an accident? She had a sudden vision of Rory and Kidd on Salisbury Crags. Kidd was the only person who'd been there, and because he was so charming, so public school, so old Edinburgh law lord family, everyone had believed his version of events without question. But Rory had suspected the teacher of being a paedophile; he'd also found out about the family scandal with the young housemaid. What if he'd found out that Kidd was guilty of Shona's death and challenged him about it? How very convenient his death would then be for Kidd…

CHAPTER 23

The doorbell rang. At first she ignored it but when it became more insistent Sarah's patience snapped. She answered the intercom prepared to vent her anger on whoever was there. 'Hiya, Sarah. It's me, Patsy. I tried to get through on the phone but it was always engaged. Are you all right?'

Sarah hesitated. 'Is there anyone else out there, Patsy? Reporters or photographers?'

'I can't see anyone.'

'All right, come up, but please don't let anyone slip into the stairwell.'

Patsy hurried up the stairs and came dramatically through the door, stretching her arms out towards Sarah. 'My poor dear girl, are you all right? As soon as I saw that dreadful story in the newspaper, I just had to come. How are you?'

Sarah looked at the concern in Patsy's small pointed features and wondered how genuine it was. Then she was annoyed with herself – she mustn't see evil everywhere. Patsy was good-hearted and, awful thought, her 'best' friend. 'I'm fine, really.'

Patsy went into the drawing room and sat on the Chesterfield. She patted the space next to her and Sarah obediently sat down. Patsy's voice oozed empathy. 'It must have been terrible. You said the funeral was for family only, but I didn't realise that his family was quite so large.' Patsy stifled a giggle and then put on her serious concerned expression. 'I knew about Babs Barrowfield, of course. We used to have quite a laugh at school, saying that she would have to sign Rory's absence notes! But all those others! How could you have borne it? How could you have stayed with Rory when he was having children all over the place?'

'I didn't know,' Sarah said and instantly regretted it as horror spread over Patsy's face.

'You didn't... know? Did they all just turn up at the funeral?'

Sarah decided as she'd gone so far she might as well explain. 'I did get a little warning. Babs seems to have been very well-informed and her daughter, who's a lawyer, acts as a sort of shop steward for the young ones.'

'Unbelievable,' Patsy lowered her voice confidentially, 'I mean, I did suspect Rory might play away a little, but I never dreamed... I thought you must know and just accept it.'

Sarah sighed. 'I was happy when the children were at home and I did accept that Rory had to work long hours. I thought that it was just part of his job. But anyway, none of that seems very important now, compared to the fact that Rory is...' Sarah hesitated. She couldn't bring herself to say dead. But she would have to get used to saying it, to telling people. She changed tack to avoid the word. 'All this, and Logan Baird getting out, has made me think of Shona so much.'

'And Tom coming back?' said Patsy with an inquisitive look.

Sarah ignored the remark and tried to find out if Patsy had any useful information about Kidd. 'I've been thinking alot about Shona. Were you in the After School Writing Club?'

'Oh yes,' Patsy's face lit up. 'We all were – it was with Captain Kidd after all.'

'Do you remember meeting round at his house the day Shona disappeared?'

'I do remember being in his house, very vividly. Was it the same day?'

'What can you remember about that meeting? What was said?'

'Sarah, it's nearly forty years ago. I can remember being there, but I can't think of anything that happened. Why are you asking? Is it something important?'

Sarah sighed. 'Not really. I've been thinking about that day and some memories are coming back. I keep going over things, wondering what happened to Shona.'

Patsy glanced at her watch, and stretched over to give Sarah an awkward hug. 'I think you should try and move on. We'll never find out what happened now. It's so long ago. It really doesn't do any good mulling over things that can't be changed.' She pursed her thin lips reflectively. 'You're really very strong. I don't think I'd ever be able to cope if anything like that happened to me.' She paused. 'Not that anything like that would happen to me, not with Gavin…' Sarah arranged her face in a deliberate grim smile and Patsy stood up hurriedly. 'Well, I just wanted to know that you are all right.'

'As you can see, I'm fine.'

Patsy pulled her jacket round her shoulders. 'Yes, well, just let me know if there's anything, anything at all that I can do.'

Sarah thanked her for visiting with as much politeness as she could muster and watched Patsy beetling down the stairs. Sarah was certain that the story would very quickly be doing the rounds on the jungle drums of Patsy's school reunion pals.

As she closed the door, her mobile rang. It was Tom. 'Listen, Sarah. I'm with HJ, he wants to talk to you. Can we come round and speak to you now?'

Sarah hesitated. She didn't want HJ Kidd in her house. 'Are you at the centre? I'll come over and talk to you there.'

'That's fine, and you can look round my new home. I've got the job.'

Sarah put the phone down, feeling annoyed with Tom. He was totally taken in by HJ. Could he not see that he was being used by him? She collected her coat and car keys and set off for the Cowgate, her mind racing with the thought that was gathering ever more substance in her mind – that HJ Kidd was responsible for two deaths.

*

Although the sky was bright, the sun did not penetrate the Cowgate where the gloomy hulk of the Canongate Centre loomed in the shadows far beneath the George 1Vth Bridge. HJ and Tom were waiting as Sarah went into the interior of the church, still shadowy despite the pale daylight struggling though the grimy windows.

Tom came towards her and they looked at each other, wondering whether to embrace. In the end they didn't and turned towards HJ. He was sitting on the edge of the makeshift podium.

He stood up and smiled. 'Sarah, I wanted to talk to you because I feel I owe you an explanation.'

Sarah steeled herself inside. She wasn't going to be won over by his charm, even if Tom seemed to be unable to resist it. She nodded her head and they all sat down at a dusty table.

'Firstly, Tom told me that you found that silly poem.'

Sarah nodded. 'That's what you came round to collect in such a hurry, the day after Rory died.' She emphasised the final word, imbuing it with some of the revulsion that she'd begun to feel towards him.

HJ looked sheepish. 'I must admit I did. I'd forgotten all about it until Rory mentioned it to me.' He cleared his throat. 'I wrote it forty years ago. It was a joke. It doesn't seem like a very good one now, but at the time it was just to tease a young colleague of mine. Once when we were out having a pint he admitted that he had this fantasy of being licked all over by the girls in his first year class.' His face clouded. 'It's hard to imagine now, but things were so different then. We all thought it was funny. I wrote him that poem to make fun of him. Nothing more.'

Sarah couldn't imagine on which parallel universe a poem like that could be a 'joke' and pressed on further. 'But there are other things. Rory found out something about your family, why you fell out with them. Something about a young maid.'

HJ laughed. 'Rory mentioned that too – he'd heard this garbled story and leapt to the wrong conclusions. There was indeed a falling out, but it wasn't because of a young girl. On the contrary, the old mater and pater were upset when they found out that my nanny, their faithful old family retainer, had been giving me a rather special kind of care and attention. She had to leave – after twenty years.'

HJ cleared his throat, his eyes far away in memory. 'I tried to defend her, saying it was the best thing that could happen to a young boy, but they took it as a breach of trust. The fact that it had started when I was fourteen and had gone on for years particularly annoyed them, I recall. Anyway, I stood there and said, 'If she goes, I go.'

'In the end we both went. Nanny got another position up north somewhere, I met dear Hannah, but the family never forgave me for the things that had been said. And I didn't want anything more to do with them – their values and attitudes were not mine.'

Sarah and Tom exchanged glances as Kidd carried on.

'I told Rory that and we had a good laugh about it, actually, especially after I admitted to still having a thing for large knickers and white flannel nighties.'

Sarah looked into his blue eyes and felt his charm. She hardened herself against it. 'But, at the After School Writing Club, you picked Shona out particularly.'

HJ's eyes saddened. 'It's true, I did see something special in Shona. As a teacher you want to develop all your pupils, to enable them to do the best they can. But there are some that touch you especially, with that extra spark of creativity, that freshness of perception, that indication of genius that makes you think this is someone who will outstrip you.' His eyes moistened. 'Rory was another one.'

'But Shona said she had a secret that night she ran away from me.' Sarah decided to say everything. 'She came to *you*, didn't she?'

HJ's face drooped. 'The police have contacted me

about the reopened case and when they interview me again I'm going to tell them the truth. There was something I kept hidden from them at the time of the original investigation. Shona *did* come round. I had submitted some stories from the writing group to an international competition. Shona received a certificate 'Highly Commended'. I wanted to give it to her, but I didn't want to make a big thing of it. She hadn't won a prize, after all, and none of the others had been mentioned, but I wanted to encourage her. She came round, she collected it, and I never saw her again.'

Sarah looked at him and saw that his eyes were glassy with tears. It was so easy to believe his version of events but she still couldn't forget that poem.

'I should have told the police then. I didn't mention it the first time they interviewed me, before she was found, and after that I couldn't. Not after failing to mention it earlier. It would make me look so suspicious, as if I had something to hide. I may well have been the last person to see her alive.'

'The last person to see her alive was her murderer,' Sarah said grimly. 'It certainly seems that a lot of evidence points towards you.'

'Sarah…' HJ looked from her to Tom, who'd been watching silently. 'Tom, believe me, I had nothing to do with it. Hannah was there all the time. She was furious I hadn't told the police and it was her that insisted I had nothing more to do with the After School Writing Club, or teach any junior classes after that. From then on I specialised in the seniors and exam classes. I was far better suited to those anyway.'

Sarah was still unconvinced. 'Did Rory confront you with all this?'

'Some of it,' admitted HJ. 'He was primarily interested in the family stuff, didn't really mention Shona. He wanted his programme.'

Sarah felt her voice very calm. 'You were alone with him, alone on Salisbury Crags, and he told you about his findings. You realised that the net was tightening.'

HJ looked shocked. 'Sarah, what are you suggesting? You couldn't believe that I had anything to do with…'

Sarah felt cold, tight. HJ was convincing but he was a showman. He'd always been an actor, which was what made him such an effective teacher. He'd admitted that Shona had come round to his house that night; Sarah had seen the poem, had seen how he was with young girls… All that stuff about the nanny was irrelevant, a red herring. And he'd been alone on the Crags with Rory.

She could see it in her mind's eye. Rory challenging him, HJ coming towards him, Rory falling back…

'Did you push him or did he just fall?'

Tom moved beside her and put her arm round her shoulders. Sarah shrugged him off and looked at her old teacher with disgust.

Kidd blustered. 'It wasn't like that at all! I wish I could prove it. Everything was being filmed, but unfortunately Rory's camera was damaged in the fall.'

'How very convenient.'

'Sarah, you're overwrought. This is ridiculous. You could equally well suspect Rory.' He paused. 'When I was reading *The Seagull* he did admit to me that he'd done something terrible in the past and that he was haunted by the memory.'

Sarah felt rage welling up in her. Kidd pressed on. 'You must admit that Rory, brilliant as he was, was not completely normal. In fact, I'm convinced that he suffered from a narcissistic personality disorder. You can see it in his charm, his philandering, his total refusal to accept the consequences of his actions, his appalling treatment of you...'

Sarah stood up and stopped Kidd's flow of words. 'How dare you? How dare you try to deflect attention from your guilt by slandering his name! I'm going to the police and I'm going to tell them everything, everything about Shona's murder and how *you* murdered Rory!'

*

Tom made Sarah a cup of coffee and brought it to her as she sat at the kitchen table. She was still shaking.

'That man,' she brought her hand down firmly on the table, 'trying to implicate Rory, who isn't here to defend himself. With everything he says Kidd just digs a deeper hole for himself. I'm more certain than ever he was involved in Shona's death, and then he murdered Rory when he challenged him with the truth. Can't you see it?' She looked defiantly at Tom. 'And when I speak to the police I'm going to tell them everything.'

Tom felt confused. Kidd was a good guy; he couldn't believe he was a murderer. In some ways he could understand the poem. He'd heard enough jokes about the delights of young girls from people who were in no way paedophiles. He thought back to some of the girls he'd been with in South Africa, their long blonde hair and slender brown limbs. Some of them were still teenagers, and he felt ashamed when he realised how little he'd thought about them as people. They were just a bit of fun.

And there were those pictures in his father's chest. They were far worse than HJ's poem. He'd wasted so much energy worrying about his father – and then he'd turned out to be innocent. He didn't want to make the same mistake with HJ.

*

The next morning Tom went out to buy rolls and came back with a bundle of newspapers. He laid them on the kitchen table. 'Archie sent me a text and said I should look at these before you saw them. Here they are – they're pathetic.'

Sarah picked up the first one, one of the red tops. It had a full-length picture of Mara O'Callaghan in a bikini, next to a story about 'three times a night Rory' who had comforted her after her appearance on his chat show. Mara explained that she had only come out in the press about this because she felt so guilty about Sarah. She hadn't known he was married and 'would never have gone to bed with him if she had known the pain it could cause.' The hypocrisy made Sarah crumple the paper in disgust.

A rival tabloid had a gruesome air-brushed photo of Jennie next to the headline. *Old Flame reignited at School Reunion.* Sarah tossed it away without even reading it.

Worse was a local paper with two grainy photos of her in her car. In the first she was alone as she drove towards the Cowgate and then there was another with Tom driving her back. *Grim-faced Sarah Dunbar leaves her £800,000 New Town flat for the first time since the revelations about popular chat show host*

Rory's secret families, returning several hours later with a mystery male companion.

She shuddered and looked out of the window into the wide cobbled street below. She couldn't see anyone. Who were these people and why were they spying on her?

Tom looked at the photos. 'Sarah, perhaps I should make myself scarce until after the memorial service? It's distressing for you to see this kind of thing.'

Sarah looked at him, shocked. 'No, I need you here.'

Tom coughed and went on quickly, looking uncomfortable. 'Actually, I know the timing is really not ideal, but I'm going to have to go back to South Africa. Now that I've decided to stay here in Scotland I must go and sort out a few things. And I have to tell Aunty Betty I'm going to stay in Scotland. She's the only person left I really care about in South Africa. It shouldn't take more than a week so I'll be back here very soon.'

Sarah stared at him, numb with disappointment. Having him in her life gave her the strength to face everything. She wasn't sure if she could manage on her own.

Tom put his arm round her. 'I can begin in the Canongate Centre at the beginning of December so this seems the logical time to go.'

'You're still going to work for that...' Sarah's voice became shrill.

Tom held her closer. 'I have to, Sarah. It's not my dream job, by any means, but I'm fast running out of money. I need a job and I need somewhere to stay and this seems to kill those two particular birds with one stone. I hope it won't be for too long, but I can't afford to stay at the Regent any longer, and I'll be glad to get out of Mrs Ritchie's floral hell-hole. She doesn't even offer me breakfast any more, as she 'never knows when I'll be staying'. She keeps giving me that *dirty wee stop-out* look,' he added, hoping to lighten the atmosphere with one of the insults from their youth.

'You can stay here,' said Sarah quickly.

'You know I can't, Sarah.' He looked into her eyes. 'There is nothing I'd love more but you have to think of your family, and the memorial service, and the papers,' he said, gesturing towards the photos.

'When are you going?'

'I've got an open ticket so I just have to see when there's a seat available.' He felt a heel, leaving Sarah now, but he had to go. 'The sooner I go, the sooner I'll be back.'

Sarah gave what she hoped looked like a brave smile although she felt empty inside. 'I'll miss you. Please come back very soon.'

CHAPTER 24

Tom landed at George Airport and drove his hire car along the beautiful Garden Route coast to Plettenberg Bay. Summer was starting here and the view of the waves crashing on the long beach at Wilderness was breathtaking. The purple mountains of the Karoo were silhouetted against the blue sky as sharp and clear as cardboard cut-outs.

When he arrived in Plett he drove to the Central Beach Bar. His old pal Jason was the manager and said he could crash there for a few days. He was leaning on the bar as usual and greeted him with the traditional African handshake. 'Hi mate,' he said, smiling broadly beneath his spiky blond hair. 'How's it going? Back for the Matric Rage then?'

They sat at the wooden table and benches on the warm sand and Tom took the cold Windhoek beer his friend offered. Tom explained he was just there for a short visit and not for the annual gathering of students letting their hair down after their exams.

Jason looked amazed. 'You're leaving us, just when Plett hots up,' he winked, 'in every way, and you're going back to gloomy Scotland.'

Tom nodded. He didn't want to say anything to Jason about Sarah or Shona. It was too precious to be reduced to bar-room banter. 'So what's new here in Plett, then?'

Jason got them both another beer and he brought Tom

up to date. Tom stared out over the azure sea sparkling in the sunshine and wished he were back in Portobello.

*

Sarah sat at Rory's computer, looking up DNA. She vaguely remembered reading about cold cases that had been solved years after the crime had been committed.

She read through Wikipedia and followed links to newspaper articles and campaigns which had thrown up miscarriages of justice. She could hardly believe what she was reading: there were so many cases where the wrong person had been locked up for unthinkably long chunks of their lives. This is what had happened to poor Logan Baird. She couldn't imagine what it must have been like for him, being incarcerated for so many years.

Fascinated, she read that murderers had even been discovered by tests on members of their families through a partial familial match. She thought of HJ Kidd. He was considered a model citzen and no member of his family was likely to have been involved in a crime, so they wouldn't be on the database. She was going to speak to the police. Perhaps they could get a DNA sample from him and then it would be proved.

She looked up as the light in the study became dimmer. Outside the high Georgian windows the greyness of the evening had crept subtly in. The fine sliver of the new moon was faint in the dusk and the street lights came on. Sarah switched on the anglepoise lamp and looked at her watch; she was surprised to see how long she'd been following links, reading newspaper reports. The afternoon had disappeared.

She got up and paced into the other room. The flat seemed very empty; she missed Tom. He was on the other side of the world, so far away.

Her mobile rang and she searched for it in excitement. Could Tom have felt the thought transference? She looked at the screen and saw that it was Nick.

'Mum, are you at home? I'd like you to meet Olly. Can I call round with him?'

Sarah felt her mood lift immediately. 'Of course.'

Nick carried on. 'I don't want to keep him hidden any longer and I think that the sooner you two meet the better.'

Sarah looked in the cupboard for wine and nibbles and wiped off a layer of dust she noticed on the coffee table. Hearing the doorbell she opened the door and heard voices and laughter as two pairs of footsteps came up the stairs.

Nick and Olly came through the door. They were about the same height and the first thing Sarah noticed was the ease of the body language between them. Nick kissed her and introduced Olly. He had unruly blond curls and an open freckled face with full lips and slightly prominent teeth. He smiled broadly; Sarah warmed to him immediately.

'I'm pleased to meet you, Mrs Dunbar.' He held out a good bottle of Italian red. 'I hope you have the glasses ready and then we can have a glass of this to cement our friendship.'

'Of course, there's always a glass ready in this house for a bit of good friendship-cementing.' Sarah took the bottle and Nick smiled gratefully at her before leading his friend in to the drawing room.

They sat down and raised their glasses. Sarah found Olly easy to talk to and noticed how relaxed Nick was, beaming at the two of them as they exchanged banter. Sarah felt happy. She hadn't consciously worried about meeting Olly, but now she knew that this was one problem she didn't have.

'Is there going to be a lunch this Sunday?' Nick asked.

Sarah hadn't really thought about it but nodded her head, pleased the decision had been taken out of her hands.

'I'd like to bring Olly along. How do you think Granny will react?'

Sarah laughed. 'I don't think she'll turn one of her beautifully-coiffed hairs. She seems to have taken everything in her stride recently.'

'That's great. I'm going to bring Olly to the memorial service.' He smiled at his partner. 'I want everyone to know how lucky I am.'

'I think that's right. Welcome to the family, Olly.'

'Thanks, Mum. It makes it all so much easier that you're so positive. Of course, Lottie and Liam are great, and Abigail, too.'

Sarah felt a twinge of annoyance at the mention of Abigail's name. Was she already so established in the family that she'd met Olly before Sarah had? She suppressed this unworthy feeling and asked Olly about his family.

'We haven't broken it to them yet,' Olly said ruefully. 'They're a bit old-fashioned and I don't know if they'll be as open and accepting as you are.' Sarah felt a glow of pleasure at the implied compliment and filled the glasses again.

The bottle was finished and another one opened before Nick looked at his watch. 'I'm sorry, Mum. We're going to have to go. We're going to the Traverse and the play begins at 8.00.'

'What are you going to see?'

'A new play from one of the Young Writers' Group. I can't remember what it's called.' He gave Olly a questioning look.

Olly shook his head. 'Me neither, but it will be interesting as we know a few of the writers and it's always good to support them.' He gave a wide smile. 'And we can have a few drinks in the bar afterwards.' He hesitated for a moment and then looked at Sarah. 'Would you like to come with us? I know there are still tickets available.'

Sarah felt touched by his offer but shook her head. 'I've had a really long day and fancy an early night, but I'd love to come another time. And I'm really looking forward to you both coming round on Sunday.' Nick stood up and Sarah took the cue. She hugged Olly. 'It's so lovely to meet you. Have a great evening tonight.'

Nick shot her a grateful look and hugged her tight before they both left, smiling together with Nick's arm falling naturally over Olly's shoulder.

Sarah sat down again with the remains of the wine. She was strong, she could survive, she had two lovely children and she could make it.

*

Running along the shining sea-washed sands of the Robberg Beach, Tom thought about the night before. He'd been to see Betty in the exclusive, and hugely expensive, nursing facility high on the cliffs looking down over the Piesang Valley. Her strong face had lit up when she saw him and she'd beckoned him to her with her awkward hands, puffed up with arthritis. She looked like an inflated version of her former self, pumped up with cortisone, but still with a wicked sparkle in her eyes.

When Tom had told her that he was going back to stay in Edinburgh her eyes glistened brighter and she smiled. 'I just want you to be happy. It's all I ever wanted. I often worried that you'd lost your way here in Plett.' She paused and her flabby frame was racked with coughing. She turned towards the window, her eyes looking far into the distance of memories. 'I remember you when you first came to Plett, a troubled boy if ever I saw one. You were a rascal, but I couldn't help loving you... You and your dear mother were my family after my darling Gus was gone. You were always so good to us two old ladies – I did worry that you stayed here because of us, didn't fulfil your potential.'

Tom felt awkward. Straight-talking Betty. He'd never heard her speak like that before; it was so unlike her. She was no-nonsense and down-to-earth, the very opposite of sentimental. She held her hands out to him and he'd grasped them, kissing them. Smiling, she drifted off into her own medication-filled world.

He'd looked down at her strong, handsome features, now blurred by illness, and felt another part of his old life slip away.

The tide was going out, leaving the sand smoothly wet, glinting in the low rays of the morning sun. His feet pounded on through the waves crashing in. The sun sparkled blue, green, yellow on the lacy fringes of water on the sand.

The high Fynbush-covered dunes ran along the length of the beach. There had only been a few fishermen's cottages here when Tom first arrived in Plett, but now the skyline was dominated by new concrete palaces, with turrets and balconies, built by rich businessmen from Jo'burg but remaining empty for fifty weeks of the year.

Nestling in a hollow he saw a couple of low wooden houses, with open terraces running along their length and corrugated iron roofs. One of them had been his home for all those years. It had belonged to Betty's family, which was one of the oldest in Plett, and she'd arranged the let. They were supposed to pay rent, but as Tom's father drank everything he earned on the fishing boats in the bars on Central Beach, the rent had been forgotten and after his death Betty had always refused it. Her family owned most of the properties along this coast and she was happy to help her second husband's relatives.

Tom's feet hit the sand with a rhythmic ferocity as he thought of Betty's nephew, Carl Van Wyk, a beefy lawyer from Pretoria who managed the family's properties. When Tom's mother died he'd sent Tom a letter telling him to leave the house immediately. Tom had asked him to transfer the tenancy to his name but he'd been told the property was to be pulled down and the land redeveloped.

Tom still felt the anger that had welled up in him when Van Wyk told him in his thick Afrikaans accent that he was to leave by the end of the month, and consider himself lucky that the outstanding back rent had been written off.

Tom was sure that Betty didn't know about this and wouldn't approve, but he couldn't bring himself to tell her, knowing how much it would upset her. So he'd stayed in Jason's backroom and started to make arrangements to leave for Scotland.

He thought about Betty. How old was she? She must be

about ninety and up until the last few months had been so active and alert. She'd formed a strong unlikely friendship with Tom's mother, Betty so dynamic and Annie so passive, but his mother's death had knocked some of the stuffing out of her. Tom thought back to Betty's words the night before and wondered if she had been saying goodbye.

His old house was still standing, but Tom knew it would soon be pulled down for another concrete monstrosity to be built. He carried on running. He wouldn't go to look at it – he was moving on.

PART II

The sun beats down and the air is mid-summer heavy. Shona and I are sitting on the wall of the prom, the concrete scratchy on my bare legs. We're wearing our shorts and suntops, the melting dribbles of ice-cream sliding down the cone and onto my hand, however quickly I try to lick it away. The air is sweet with the smell of candyfloss spinning onto sticks in aluminium tubs, suntan oil and the pungent tar melting at the edge of the promenade.

Portobello beach is scattered with family groups, reddening in the uncustomary heat of the sun. The air is broken by the barking of dogs and the lone cry of a child temporarily separated from his mother. My shoulders sting with the beginnings of sunburn as I look out over the crowds at the heat haze shimmering over the Firth of Forth.

As the heat beats down on my head I look around. I see Logan Baird in the shadows of the tenements, wearing his long dark coat despite the heat. I see Tom walking past us with two friends, drinking coke and laughing, ignoring us. Shona shouts something cheeky and they look round. One of them is Rory, sculpted cheekbones, dark hair curling softly in the nape of his neck. He winks at Shona.

My eyes are on Tom, his blond hair framing his face with the deep eyes and the wide mouth. I feel disappointment as my eyes follow the back of their heads growing smaller in the distance.

Faces loom nearer, HJ Kidd, recognisable but his features distorted like Batman's joker, taunting us. Images from the poem he read at school come back – but instead of the swallows, all that remain are the ugly bats, like broken umbrellas, hanging like old rags. Kidd's face melts into a grinning bat skull.

The sounds of the beach become louder as the face dissolves and

I'm alone on the wall. The space is empty where Shona was sitting and the air chills. My father's face stares down on me. I'm conscious of the brevity of my shorts and try to cover my bare legs with my hands. The smell of the tarmac lingers in my nostrils.

CHAPTER 25

Sarah sat up in bed and felt for the bedside light. The memory hung over her, with the briny smell of the melting tar in that hottest-ever summer of 1976.

She looked at her watch, only half past four but she felt strangely wide awake. She picked up the copy of DH Lawrence's poem *Bat* that she'd printed out from the internet. She remembered snippets so clearly from that lesson with Captain Kidd, the lesson when she found out that Shona was missing.

She read it through again. It was so vivid and beautiful, describing the swallows flying in the early evening under the Ponte Vecchio in Florence. She, Rory and the twins had once gone to Tuscany on a family holiday, and she'd loved that view. But reading to the end of the poem, the tone became more sinister as the poet realised the swallows had gone and been replaced by the ugly bats.

She walked restlessly into the kitchen where the shutters were not completely closed, allowing the street lights to throw fluid shadows onto the walls and units. On the kitchen table she saw her mobile phone flashing. *Missing you. Will be back in Edinburgh 20th xxx*

Tom was thinking of her and would be back in a few days. She texted back. *Missing you too. So looking forward to seeing you xxx. How banal*, she thought, but the words didn't really matter. It was the communication that counted. She held the phone close to her chest, somehow bringing Tom close to her in the only way she could. She missed him so much, wished he could be here with her. But he was coming back; coming back, *and* going to stay in Edinburgh.

She couldn't help but smile at the thought. She had to use this time when he was away profitably, get herself organised. The memorial service had been fixed for December 6th, and although the planning was out of her hands, taken over by BBC Scotland, she would check to see how it was getting on; she'd phone Lottie and arrange to have lunch with her, and contact her mother. And, of course, she had to speak to the police about Kidd.

She picked up an old envelope and started to write a to-do list on the back. She'd been numb for the past few weeks, in a daze. There were piles of envelopes on the hall table, letters of condolence. She'd been ignoring them, unable to face the words of comfort, praise, reminiscence, all of them avoiding the elephant in the room that Rory had been constantly, serially unfaithful to her.

She would have to find a way to acknowledge them. Archie had suggested a printed card with a photo of Rory that she could send out. She'd look for a photo today.

The unsettling memories that had disturbed her sleep began to fade as she felt the heady buzz of having 'a plan'. She looked at her watch. Too early to phone Lottie. Her daughter had been great after the accident and at the private funeral and she'd hoped that whatever had been troubling her had blown over. But she hadn't heard from her for days and she hoped everything was all right with her.

She sat down at the table with a mug of coffee and idly

picked dead heads off the chrysanthemums someone had sent. Tom. Her thoughts returned to him every few minutes. All this planning activity was just displacement; she was filling the space left by him. When he was there he filled her time, every moment was meaningful, everything was better with him.

Almost to her surprise Rory came into her mind. She was astonished how little she thought of him. Although it was only a few weeks since his death, he seemed to have slipped away into the past, leaving hardly a gap in her life. Of course, he'd never really been around much.

The phone rang, bringing her back to reality. She looked at her watch. It wasn't yet seven o'clock,

'Mum,' it was Nick's voice. 'Mum, you're not to worry, but I'm in the Royal Infirmary.'

'What?' Sarah gasped. Not again, she couldn't bear it.

'Olly and I were jumped by some neds last night and they gave us a bit of a kicking so we were brought here. But I'm all right, Mum. Just superficial wounds.'

'When did this happen? Why didn't you ring me immediately?'

'This is the first chance I've had really, because there were X-rays and things. Anyway, I didn't look too pretty, but they've patched me up now.' His voice cracked a little and Sarah could tell he was not as upbeat as he pretended. 'And Olly came off worse than me.'

'Oh Nick. I'll be right over. Is there anything I can bring?'

Nick gave an order for a few items of clothing and toiletries and Sarah quickly looked round the flat to see what she could take from there. She could go shopping for the rest later.

When she arrived at the main entrance of the hospital, she couldn't help but think of the last time she'd been there. Nick was on a different floor but the shiny clack of her footsteps on the corridors and the smell of disinfectant and polish took her back to that day they'd all visited Rory, the day he died. It was unbelievable that it was less than a month ago.

Tiptoeing quietly into the ward, she saw Nick lying in the bed nearest the door. She gasped in horror when she saw him, a bandage round his head, his face covered with stitches, one eye almost closed with a plum-coloured swelling.

He forced a smile and held out his hand. 'Thanks for coming, Mum.'

Sarah stifled the scream rising in her throat and tried to remain normal for his sake. She found a patch of skin to kiss and sat down next to him. 'Oh, Nick. What happened?'

'Jumped by a gang of thugs on Castle Terrace.' He strained a smile. 'But I managed to get a few punches in before they got us on the ground and started to kick our heads in.' His voice faltered and Sarah saw that he was putting on a brave front for her benefit.

'Are you in pain?'

'No, I'm fine.' He raised his left hand slightly showing the drip. 'They're keeping me hopped to the eyeballs.' He hesitated and Sarah saw a tear sliding from the corner of his swollen eye. 'It's Olly. They won't let me see him. They say he's all right, but he hasn't regained consciousness yet.' Sarah gulped. The picture of Rory lying still in his bed in the same hospital came into her mind and she knew that Nick was thinking of that too.

'I'll go and see if they'll let me visit him.' She looked at his injuries again. 'Did they catch the people who did this to you?'

'Not yet, but the police say they're looking at the CCTV images and they hope they'll be able to identify them. There has been a spate of homophobic attacks over the last few weeks and they've got a team working on it. Can you bring me some other clothes next time you come? They've taken the ones I was wearing away for analysis.'

Sarah gripped the side of the bed tightly. What was happening? Everything seemed to be crumbling around her. The words of the poem came back, where the swallows had turned out to be bats. Her beautiful life was being destroyed, tainted. The picture of a row of grinning bats hanging like dirty disgusting rags flashed before her eyes. She blinked and tried to seem as normal as possible for Nick's sake.

They talked a bit about the memorial service. Sarah suggested he could use his injuries as an excuse to get out of speaking at it, but Nick's eyes shone defiantly. 'I'm speaking at that service even if my face is still covered with bruises. I'm doing it for our family, for you.' He held her hand tightly, and Sarah felt her heart bursting with love.

Behind her she heard the efficient footsteps of a nurse who drew the curtains round, asking Sarah to wait outside.

Sarah went into the corridor thinking of Olly. She discovered his room number from the nurses' station and approached the door nervously. She hesitated, wondering if she would be intruding, but she plucked up the courage to knock at the door. She'd only met Olly the once but she liked him and he was Nick's partner. She wanted to show her solidarity; he was part of the family.

A faint voice came from inside and as she slowly opened the door she saw Olly lying in the single room, with an older couple sitting on chairs at the side of the bed. They turned and looked at her as she approached but didn't stand up. Sarah smiled and extended her hand; there was no reciprocating movement so she took her hand back and let it fall loosely by her side.

She kept her smile bright, 'I'm Sarah Dunbar, Nick's mother. How is Olly?'

The woman stared blankly at her with tired pale eyes and pursed her lips. Her husband, a short wide-shouldered man with a broad face and a monk's tonsure bald head, looked at her. 'I don't mean to be rude but we don't want you here. It's your son's fault that Oliver is here and from what I hear he got off lightly.' He raised a soiled linen handkerchief to his eyes. 'Oliver's unconscious and the doctors can't tell us when he'll come round.'

His wife blinked as if she was having difficulty understanding what was going on. Sarah guessed she was on very strong medication. She wanted to defend Nick but realised it would be pointless. She apologised for the disturbance and wishing their son a speedy recovery gently closed the door.

Her heart was thumping with embarrassment. She'd thought she couldn't feel any worse but she did now. The injustice of it inflamed her. She knew that Olly had been in the gay scene for longer than Nick, but he hadn't been able to tell his parents. Her annoyance quickly disappeared; she knew how she would feel if Nick were the one lying silent and unresponsive now.

*

Tom sat in the Central Beach Bar, feeling the sun on the back of his neck and the sand warm between his toes. He looked out at the sparkling horizon where the sea met the clear blue sky and sipped his beer. It was beautiful; he would love to bring Sarah here one day, so that she could share what had been such a large part of his life. He shook his head sadly. That was just a dream. He barely had enough money to fly back to Scotland. He would never be able to finance that.

Of course, he had a job now, he thought with a wry smile. After the initial euphoria, the thought of the Canongate Centre filled him with gloom. The living accommodation, filled with the cheap chipboard furniture, seemed to grow smaller, darker and meaner in his imagination. The work was dull and pointless, however much Kidd tried to dress it up as supporting an Arts Centre.

He looked at the long sweep of coastline and smelled the fresh smell of the Fynbos shrubs on the dunes mixing with the sea air. Life was cheaper here and he could always find work. He ran his hands over the smooth surface of the bleached pieces of driftwood he'd found on the beach. He saw beauty in the shapes and knew he could make them into works of art, which would sell well in the tourist shops up on Main Street. It was seductive, the thought of staying here.

Then he saw Sarah's face with her wide grey eyes, soft brown hair and her soft full lips. He felt a wave of lust, love, tenderness that nearly took his breath away. He had to go back to her, back to Portobello, where he belonged.

He felt his phone vibrating in his pocket. Could it be Sarah? He looked at the display and saw it was a local number. It must be the clinic. As he answered he felt a cold shudder; he should come to the hospital as soon as possible.

CHAPTER 26

Sarah was just gathering together some clothes for Nick when the phone rang. It was a Detective Inspector Chisholm of the Lothian and Borders Police wondering if it would be convenient for her to come to the Fettes Police Headquarters that afternoon to discuss the reopened enquiry into the murder of Shona McIver.

Sarah hesitated; she'd almost forgotten about this with everything that had happened. She was about to ask for another appointment, but stopped; she had to go to tell them everything she knew about HJ Kidd as soon as possible. She could fit the appointment in between hospital visits.

As she approached the enquiry desk at Fettes and gave her name, she couldn't remember ever having been in a police station before. She was sure she'd been interviewed at home when Shona disappeared and since then she'd never had any contact with the police. How sheltered her life had been; but now she was being sucked into a world she didn't know, a world of death and hospitals and police investigations.

DI Chisholm came to collect her from the waiting area and took her into a comfortable office, nothing like the interview rooms she'd seen on television.

He started off by offering condolences for the loss of her husband and apologised for calling her in now. They had not been able to trace many of the original witnesses and, as

305

she was one of the last people to see Shona alive, her recollections of the events of that day would be very valuable.

In answer to his questions, Sarah went through the events of that evening in detail, able to see the scene again in her mind. 'When she ran away she was excited, told me she had a secret. I didn't know then where she was going but I know now. She went to our teacher's house, to HJ Kidd.'

Chishom smiled encouragingly. 'Yes, we're aware of that.'

Sarah was surprised. She'd though she'd be dropping a bombshell. 'But surely that must place him under suspicion? He didn't tell the original investigation. He lied about what happened that night.'

'Mr Kidd has been to see us and was very open and candid about the events of that evening. We've also interviewed his wife, who corroborated her husband's account of the events. People often withhold evidence they think may place them under suspicion and that in itself is no proof of guilt. I can assure you that we are keeping an open mind about the case as we continue our investigation.'

Sarah was furious. 'You don't know what he's like. He fools everyone with his old school charm.' Then all her suspicions tumbled out: Kidd's behaviour at the After School Writing Club, the poem with the little pink tongues, his estrangement from his family. Chisolm let her tell her story without interruption, nodding encouragingly. Sarah's voice rose to a crescendo. 'Not only did he murder Shona, but I'm sure my husband's death was no accident.'

Chisholm watched her, without speaking. Sarah let her voice peter out and trail away. She looked down at her lap, feeling she'd said too much. The policeman took his glasses off and put them on the desk.

'Mrs Dunbar. I appreciate the strain you're under at the moment and I understand your concerns about the distressing circumstances of your husband's death. However, the focus of my investigation is the McIver case and we are following all possible avenues of enquiry. Our best hope of finding the murderer is a match for the DNA samples in the semen we took from the victim's cardigan. We've already interviewed Mr Kidd and with his permission we have taken a DNA swab which we will be comparing with those samples.'

Sarah felt she was being patronised. 'But don't you see that the two cases are connected? I'm sure Rory found out about Kidd's involvement in Shona's death and challenged him with it. That's why Rory fell. Maybe Kidd didn't actually push him, but I'm sure he was the cause.'

Chisholm pinched the bridge of his nose. 'Mr Kidd was interviewed by my colleagues after the incident and was a very helpful witness. Your husband's injuries were entirely consistent with Mr Kidd's version of events and, although there were no other witnesses, the camera being used has been found and the film, although damaged, is being analysed at the moment. I know it is hard for you but I can assure you that you will feel better and gain closure if you accept that it was just a very tragic accident.'

He hesitated, as if wondering whether to go on. Sarah leant forward, willing him to continue.

'In fact, your husband was one of the people who gave a statement after the murder of Shona McIver and we would certainly have interviewed him if he had not unfortunately predeceased our enquiry. Mr Kidd placed him as being in the park on the evening of the murder and he mentioned that Mr Dunbar had admitted to him the fact that he felt great remorse for an event in the past. It seems that something he had done was preying on his mind.'

Sarah felt rage building up in her. 'Kidd's trying to direct suspicion towards Rory to deflect attention from himself. You're not falling for this, are you?'

Chisholm gave a patient smile. 'Mr Kidd didn't make any accusations. He was just recounting his memories of the day of the murder and also a conversation he'd had, resulting from his reading of one of his pieces of work.'

'Which you only have his word for! Kidd is a very cunning man…' she found herself speechless with frustration. She opened her mouth but then closed it again. What good would it do to say anything more? Kidd seemed to have charmed them all. 'How long does it take to test the DNA?'

'Several weeks, I'm afraid. I am putting pressure on the labs to give me results as soon as possible but there's always a backlog of cases.'

Sarah's face fell and she went through the rest of the interview in a numb daze, answering Chisholm's questions about Shona, trying to remember which boys she'd liked, and other details of her interests and hobbies.

When she'd finished, Chisholm put his pen down and looked at her in a kindly way. 'Thank you very much for coming in and helping us with our enquiries, Mrs Dunbar. Be assured that we will do everything in our power to find the murderer of your friend.'

Sarah accepted his offered hand and allowed him to escort her to the door. She felt totally drained. Sitting in her car, she leant her head forward on the steering-wheel. She felt weak, as if she didn't have the strength to drive home, and more alone than she could ever remember.

Who could she speak to? The thought of phoning her mother came into her mind, but only very briefly. She hadn't told her mother about Nick yet, and remembering her hysterical behaviour when Rory died she knew she didn't feel strong enough to play the role of her mother's comfort and support today.

Lottie. She took out her mobile phone and tried to call her again. Lottie had gone to the hospital to see her brother, but had looked pale and shaky and had only stayed a short while. Now she wasn't answering her phone.

She needed the strength of Tom's arms around her. *Tom, come back soon.*

Her phone rang – it was Nick.

'Mum, great news. Olly's regained consciousness and he's going to be all right. They've allowed me to see him. He has to stay in hospital for a few more days, just to make sure, but I can come home today, provided I'm with someone. Can I stay with you, Mum? Will you come and pick me up?'

Sarah breathed a huge sigh of relief. Nick was going to be all right and he needed her. She drove straight to the hospital.

*

Tom arrived at the clinic and went straight to Betty's room, nearly bumping into Carl, who was hovering outside the door. Carl was about the same age as him, but since they'd first met as teenagers he'd always treated Tom as an inferior. He had the inborn arrogance of the spoilt only son of a rich Pretoria lawyer, educated at an expensive private college.

He stood in front of Tom, broader but not nearly as tall, with short legs and no neck, barring his way into the room. 'You can't go in there. My aunt is too ill.'

Carl's bullying arrogance annoyed Tom. 'I got a phone call. They told me to come immediately.'

'You've had a wasted journey then, because nobody's going in to disturb her last peace now.'

A nurse, a light-skinned Griqua with caring eyes and a determined mouth, stepped out of the room and looked at Tom. 'It's good you've got here, Mr McIver. Your aunt has been asking for you.'

Carl's beefy face became even more florid and he opened his mouth to say something, but Tom pushed past him and the nurse blocked the lawyer's path as she ushered Tom into the room.

Betty looked up at him with something approaching a smile hovering on her lips. Her mouth was moving as she tried to say something. Tom moved closer and lowered his head to her face. 'Go to Peter Roberts. Something for you.' The words came out slowly and painfully in rasping breaths.

'Aunty Betty?' Tom was not sure that he'd heard correctly. He pressed a kiss onto her spongy cheek and remembered what she'd been like when he was younger. She reached out and held his hand. A breathy rasp came out of her lips. It sounded like, 'Love you.'

'Love you, Aunty Betty.' He held her hand more tightly, then noticed a difference in her breathing. A look of peace came over her face and her whole body seemed to relax.

The nurse, who had been standing in the background, moved forward. 'She was waiting for you. She couldn't go in peace until you came.' She turned to Betty and muttered a few words. All that Tom could make out was 'Amen' at the end.

The door swung open and Carl pushed his way in. 'What have you done?'

The nurse turned round with an air of calm authority. 'Mr Van Wyk. Your aunt has died peacefully, very happy that she could say goodbye to her two nephews.'

'I'm her nephew. He's not part of our family.'

The nurse spoke with quiet determination. 'I spent a lot of time with your dear aunt and I know she loved you both. Now if you could please leave the room, there are some procedures that need to take place. Then you can both come in again to take your leave of her in your own way.'

The two men left the room. As soon as they were out of the door, Carl pushed Tom against the wall. 'Right, she's gone now so you can totally forget anything about being a member of our family.' As Carl spoke his voice became more heavily accented with Afrikaans and he lost control of his English. 'And don't think she have left you money because she don't. I have the testament and everything is left to me, to our family. Now go.'

Tom turned away and walked down the stairs. Carl had always been a bully, and Betty had showed her distaste for him when he came down for the holidays. He felt a tear coming to his eye; Betty had been his friend and now she was gone.

He walked slowly down the hill towards the centre of town. In some ways he missed Betty more than his mother. His mother had been soft, passive, unassertive, always lost in the sorrows of the past, whereas Betty had been strong, with a fierce sense of loyalty, loud and opinionated, not caring what other people thought. Uncle Gus had been her one true love and she had always stood up for him and his family against the pressure from her sister and brother-in-law. Now Carl had everything and Tom had nobody left in South Africa. Tom went to the Central Beach Bar and drank himself into oblivion.

*

Sarah stood in the kitchen, chopping onions, making creamy chicken and pasta, a special request from Nick. When he was young he'd always wanted that when he was ill. Sarah felt strangely content as she smelled the butter sizzling in the pan and blinked back tears from the onion. She missed having the children at home, missed having someone to take care of.

Nick was lying on the sofa in the snug with the duvet round him, watching the *Simpsons*. Sultan was lying next to him purring. He'd gone back to childhood. He was laughing at the cartoon, when his phone rang and Sarah heard a couple of words that suggested it was Olly.

'Mum, Olly's getting out tomorrow. Can he come here?'

'Of course.' Sarah didn't hesitate. She heard Nick making some arrangements and then he clicked his phone.

'He can get out after the doctor's round tomorrow morning. Can you collect him? He has to go home with someone and he really doesn't want to go to his parents. Apparently the police said something about homophobic crime and once they understood what that meant, they flipped.'

'Are the police doing something about it then? Have they got any leads?'

'Oh yes. As well as the CCTV, they're analysing three different types on blood on my coat.' He gave a lop-sided grin from the uninjured side of his mouth. 'I told you that I got a few punches in on them too so perhaps they can get a match from that. Olly and I had to give buccal swabs too, for exclusion purposes.'

Sarah looked at her son's face. Some of the swelling had gone down, but green and yellow bruising circled both eyes, replacing the purple. He would have the stitches out next week. She hoped he wouldn't be too scarred; he had been such a beautiful child and as a young man still had fine features. She pushed these superficial thoughts aside; it was just so fortunate the attack had not been worse. Nick wasn't certain, but he thought it was a gang of about seven or eight and CCTV footage had confirmed the numbers. With those odds they'd got off lightly.

She stirred the pan and looked at the amount. How many people was she cooking for? She seemed to have forgotten quantities. She looked at the pan again and thought about Lottie. If she cooked lots of pasta and put a bit more cream in there would be plenty for four. She picked up the phone and dialled Lottie's number again.

Liam answered. Lottie was just lying down but he took the phone to her. Sarah was shocked by the weakness of her voice.

'I'd love to have chicken and pasta, but I'm sorry Mum, I can't. I'm really not feeling well.'

'What's the matter? Have you been to the doctor?'

'Not yet, but if I feel like this tomorrow I'll go.'

Sarah began to suggest remedies but Lottie interrupted her. 'Sorry, Mum. I'm going to have to go.'

'Go to the doctor please, and phone me tomorrow and let me know how you get on.'

Sarah put the phone down. She felt so guilty. She'd been worrying so much about Nick that she'd almost forgotten about Lottie. She thought back to Lottie's accusations; she would always have said she loved her children equally but now she questioned herself. She'd go to Lottie's tomorrow and take her to the doctor.

She hit her forehead. She couldn't do it because she'd promised to collect Olly and had to wait for the call. She heard another laugh from the TV room and smiled, pleased that Nick could still be hugely amused by *the Simpsons*.

And her mother? She hadn't called her either. Because she felt such a failure on the 'good mother' stakes, Sarah picked up the phone, trying to build up some 'good daughter' credit.

Her mother took a long time to answer and when she did she sounded distracted and obviously couldn't wait to get off the phone. Sarah could tell she'd been drinking and wondered how much. She put the phone down and shrugged her shoulders. If her mother wanted to drink, she could.

Sarah looked into the wine rack. There were still a couple of bottles of red. While the sauce bubbled and the water boiled for the pasta, she sat down at the table and poured herself a large glass, gulping it back. Was *she* becoming dependent on alcohol? Enough things had happened recently to drive anyone to drink. She gave herself permission to have another glass.

She heard Nick laughing with the television again. She knew it was an escape from the events of the present, back to the simplicity of childhood and she was glad he could find comfort there. She thought about offering him a glass of wine but it wouldn't go well with the painkillers and – she grinned to herself – Nick, being a bit of a wine snob, would certainly not approve of red with the chicken.

She looked at her mobile phone again. Nothing from Tom today. She'd told him about Nick and Olly and he'd sent supportive texts, but since then there'd been nothing. She missed him. She typed in *Crap day. Need a cuddle x x x* and sent it off quickly before she changed her mind.

*

Tom woke up in the back room of the bar with his head throbbing. *Betty, dead.* He was amazed how empty he felt. She was the last one, the last connection to his family in South Africa. While his father was in an alcoholic haze and his mother in religious denial, he'd run wild and Aunty Betty had been the one who pulled him up, questioned him, challenged him. She and Uncle Gus were a perfect match; she was bossy and dominant and he was happy to be organised. They adored each other and Aunty Betty had missed him every day since he died.

He tried to raise his head and blinked against the brightness of the sunshine. He thought about how Betty would react to his current state. She'd be very practical, feed him protein and then ask him why he'd been so stupid. You couldn't fob her off with excuses, she would keep at him like a terrier until she found out what was wrong and then she always had sound advice. Thinking of her, he fried a couple of eggs and then forced himself out onto the beach. His head still throbbed and he had to squint his eyes against the brightness.

Aunty Betty's death had been peaceful but then her nephew... Tom's anger welled thinking of Carl's smug fatness. He hoped the funeral would be arranged quickly. He'd stay for that and then leave South Africa and Carl's greed behind him.

He must send a text to Sarah.

He felt in his pockets and had a feeling of panic. His phone was not there. He looked around the room and under the sofa, which caused a wave of nausea to wash over him, but it was nowhere to be seen. He asked Jason if anyone had found a phone and handed it in. Nobody had, so they both looked around the bar, but found nothing.

Tom began to feel panicky. When had he last had his phone? He knew he'd sent a short text to Sarah just after Betty died, to say he'd have to stay for the funeral... but after that? He must find his phone – it was his only contact with Sarah.

He thought back to those last moments with Betty, and he knew she'd said something important. It was there, hanging in his mind, just out of reach, but he couldn't remember what it was; not with the pain and haze of alcohol still misting his head. He took a deep breath and set off along the beach, determined to pound the unpleasant memories of the day before out of his system, before he went to the hospital again to find his phone.

CHAPTER 27

Sarah walked through Stockbridge towards the Botanic Gardens, glancing into the windows of the charity shops. It was one of those crisp November days with low bright sunshine and sharp clean air. Sarah felt happy and relieved; when she'd phoned Lottie to see how she'd got on at the doctor's, Lottie had sounded so much better and suggested meeting for lunch at the café in the Botanics. Sarah left Nick and Olly happily cooking together in the kitchen and looked forward to some proper time with her daughter.

As she approached the café, she saw Lottie sitting at a table near the window, her long curtain of hair swinging as she bent over her phone. She saw her mother and stood up; Sarah thought how sweet she looked with her blue tweed coat, her long legs in woolly tights and a tammy perched on the back of her head. She hurried towards her daughter and gave her a hug. Lottie looked pale, her face seemed thinner but her eyes were sparkling.

'How are you? What did the doctor say?'

Lottie smiled and held up her phone. There was a blurred picture on the screen. Sarah wondered what it was; it looked like a Google Earth view.

Suddenly it clicked. 'Is that what I think it is?' she asked.

Lottie smiled. 'Yes, congratulations, Granny. This is the first picture of your grandchild.' Sarah put her arms round her daughter and held her tightly, feeling tears welling up in her eyes; after all the terrible things that had happened finally there was some good news.

They sat down for lunch, but neither of them ate much. They were both too excited. Sarah looked out of the window over the mature trees of the Botanics as they talked about the practicalities for the birth, the date, the hospital, how Liam and Lottie's small flat could accommodate a nursery, and Sarah felt so happy.

Afterwards they walked through the narrow paths of the maze at the rock garden and Sarah was overcome with memories. She used to bring the twins in their double buggy round the gardens, watching their eyes follow the light flickering through the leaves on the trees overhead. It was the one and only thing guaranteed to stop them crying.

Despite the pale winter sunshine it was unmistakeably November in the gardens. Leaves crackled underfoot and Sarah could smell the peppery smoke of a bonfire in the nursery garden.

They walked over the Japanese Bridge. Everything in the Botanic Gardens was more commercialised these days, with a wedding venue at the gatehouse and bridal photo opportunities at this bridge. You even had to pay to go into the elegant Victorian glasshouses now, so different from the days when she remembered escaping showers with the twins there, breathing in the humid peaty air of the palm house and looking at the cacti in the dry cool air of the desert house.

She told Lottie how she and Nick used to stand with their noses pressed to the glass viewing panels under the tropical house, watching the fish swim in the pond above.

She wondered if they were still there. It was so long since she'd been to that part of the garden. Waves of nostalgia for an earlier, simpler time washed over her, and she was already imagining pushing her grandchild's pushchair through the gardens, recapturing the happiness she'd felt when her children were young.

Sarah was so excited she wanted to share her news with the world; Nick would be such a great uncle. And, to be truthful, she couldn't wait to tell Tom, to share her delight with him. She looked at her phone again, but there was still no message from him, nothing since the brief text saying he had to stay longer for the funeral. There had been no new flight details, nothing.

She looked at the giant monkey puzzle tree silhouetted against the gathering dusk in front of her and had a sudden feeling of panic. What if he never came back?

No, she mustn't worry. It was less than a day since he'd been in touch. It was just that before that they'd been texting every hour. She tried to comfort herself; he'd be busy with the funeral arrangements. But she did miss the ping of her phone and the comforting exchange of mundane messages.

Sarah and Lottie walked back to the flat along the cracked pavements of Stockbridge and Sarah looked again at the windows of the charity shops. She'd loved going to them when the twins were young, picking up Liberty print dresses and Osh-Kosh dungarees at bargain prices. Now she would be able to do that again for her grandchild. Her grandchild. How wonderful that sounded.

As they opened the door of the flat there was the sound of laughter and a female voice. Abigail was sitting in the front room with Nick and Olly; they looked up as Sarah and Lottie walked in.

Abigail stood up and Sarah hesitated. She was wondering about the most appropriate way to greet her when Abigail took the lead by reaching up and giving her a hug. 'Hi, Sarah. How are you? You look great.'

Sarah was strangely touched by this and noticed once again that, although Abigail was no conventional beauty, with her short spiky red hair and her stumpy figure, her eyes radiated a magnetism that was difficult to avoid. Abigail and Lottie embraced and then Nick patted the seat next to him on the sofa. 'Sit down, Mum. We're just talking about the memorial service.'

Sarah smiled. 'We can talk about that in a minute, but first Lottie has some lovely news.' Everyone looked at Lottie, standing with her hands resting over the front of her tweed coat.

Olly was the first to catch on. 'Lottie?' Lottie smiled and nodded. Olly raised his hands in the air and jumped up. 'I'm going to be an uncle!' All three of them gathered round Lottie, hugging and kissing her. Lottie was laughing and crying at the same time.

'This will be the first of the next generation. What a pity Dad will not see this,' Abigail said. Sarah realised with a jolt that this thought had never occurred to her; Rory had never seemed very interested in his own babies. She pushed that thought aside and allowed herself to get caught up in the excitement of the moment.

Abigail was still thinking along the same lines. 'Can we announce it at the memorial service? It would be a nice addition to the part about his legacy and what he leaves behind. I know they're going to mention the great contribution he made to the development of Scottish television.'

Lottie blushed and nodded. 'Of course. But I don't want to say anything myself.'

Nick looked at his sister. 'I'll speak for both of us.' He looked at his mother. 'Are you still sure that you don't want to say anything?'

'Absolutely sure.'

'We've been talking about it and we think that it's best if we come clean about the whole family thing. Then there'll be no secrecy, no scoop for the papers. Abigail's going to do that bit, as the oldest of the children.' Nick smiled across at his half-sister.

Abigail leant forward. 'There was one of the French presidents, Mitterand I think, whose wife and long-term mistress stood side by side at his funeral, together with his illegitimate daughter. It was a great photo and I believe that everyone had the greatest respect for his wife because of it.'

Nick joined in. 'We've talked about it with Archie and he too thinks that this is the best way to kill any revelations from what he calls wee scrubber opportunists. I'm going to talk about some of my memories of him as a dad, but none of the other children are going to speak.

'There are going to be readings by *Scotsman* and BBC colleagues and Archie's going to do a personal reminiscence – I've heard some of it and it's really funny and affectionate, too. There's also going to be an address from the Head of BBC Scotland,' added Abigail. She gave a wicked smile. 'Miranda thought she'd like to read a poem, but we squashed that one immediately. Trust her to want to make the occasion all about her.'

'But that old teacher, HJ Kidd, is going to read a poem he's written specially for Dad,' Nick added.

'No.' Sarah was shocked by the sharpness of her own voice. The other four looked at her in surprise. 'I don't want him there.'

Nick looked at her gently. 'Mum, he's written a poem especially for Dad. You know how important this last project was to him…'

'Kidd was there when he died,' Sarah felt a steely determination. She was going to win this one.

Abigail spoke softly, concern in her voice. 'That's one reason why he should read the poem. He's been in touch with my mum – they were old colleagues at Brunstane – and he's so upset about what happened. I think he needs to do this to reach some kind of closure himself.'

Sarah felt rage welling up inside her. 'What do you know about it?' She glared at Abigail. 'He hasn't been a friend of our family. I think he knows more about the death of Shona than he's letting on, and…' She felt hot, angry tears in her eyes. 'And he has the arrogance, the insensitivity, to suggest that your father might have been involved in Shona's death.'

'What?' There were sharp intakes of breath from everyone in the room.

'It's nonsense, rubbish, of course, but he's told the police that Rory was telling him about his guilt for something terrible he'd done in the past just before he fell.' Sarah saw the shock on the children's faces. 'That's another reason why I don't trust him. He's got something to hide about what happened between him and Rory on the day he died, and about what happened to Shona.' She gulped. 'He is not reading at the memorial service.'

Nick put his arm round his mother. 'OK, Mum. You've been so great about everything,' he shot a glance at his half-sister, 'and if you don't want him to read, he isn't reading.'

'You do believe me, don't you? You're not just humouring me?'

A look passed between Nick and Abigail. 'You've been through a terrible time. It's natural for all sorts of thoughts and suspicions to go through your mind. HJ Kidd seems like a good guy, as far as I can see, and the police are not stupid. They'll be checking up on everything, and with the wonders of DNA they can find out anything, just as I hope they will with those bastards that kicked my face in.' He gave a gentle laugh, trying to lighten the mood.

Sarah realised that she was coming across as slightly unbalanced so she followed his lead, looking at her son's bruises. 'I hope your face will have healed by the time of the memorial service.'

Nick gave a relieved smile. 'Whatever I look like, I'm going to stand up and be proud!'

Olly gave him a look full of affection. 'Actually I think it suits you. Gives a bit of character to your face.' Nick returned the look and threw a cushion in his direction, grinning as Lottie and Abigail laughed.

'Shows you're not just a pretty face,' Abigail said and Sarah found herself sitting back, envious of the easy familiarity they shared.

The laughter was interrupted by the door bell. 'That'll be the police,' said Nick.

Sarah looked up, surprised.

'They phoned up to say that they'd got some DNA

matches from the blood on my jacket, but they need to take more samples from me and Olly just to double-check. They asked us to come to the station, but when they heard we were both here they said they'd send someone round because they want to speak to you, too.'

Sarah opened the door and was surprised to see that DI Chisholm was one of the two plain-clothes detectives that stood there. She'd thought he was on Shona's case review, but maybe police worked on several cases simultaneously. She held out her hand and Chisholm introduced his younger colleague.

'Mrs Dunbar. There has been a development in our investigation. We have found a match, a partial match, to the DNA traces on Shona McIver's cardigan.'

Sarah felt a huge wave of relief. The case was going to be solved at last. She was just about to say, 'Is it Kidd?' but then she remembered what she'd read about DNA. 'A partial match? So that means that one of the thugs who attacked my son is related to Shona's murderer?'

Chisholm looked serious. 'Mrs Dunbar, the match appears to come from the sample taken from your son.'

The smile on Sarah's face froze. She heard the policeman's voice as if it was far away at the end of a tunnel.

'We would like to take a further swab from your son for confirmation purposes and, as his father's name has already come up in our investigation, we would like to ask you to provide a sample of your husband's DNA. A toothbrush, razor or hairbrush would be ideal.'

Sarah sank down into the armchair, her legs so shaky that she couldn't stand upright. *Rory?* Was Chisholm really trying to say that Rory was in the frame for Shona's murder? She couldn't believe it; Rory couldn't have been capable of murder. She'd discovered so many things about him since his death, but that couldn't be true.

PART 12

I'm caught in a tunnel. I can see my twins, babies in front of me. I reach out but my legs won't move. It's like running through mud, it's sucking me down. I look down – I'm only wearing a vest. I pull it down, but it's too short.

There's something behind me. I hear it and smell it but I don't know what it is. I'm filled with dread. The walls are closing in. I can't reach my babies and there's no escape. Looming in front of me I see HJ Kidd's mocking face. He's laughing; then the face metamorphoses into Rory. He comes nearer and places his hands between my legs. I feel the sensation and want to let go. The face changes to my father's, contorted with rage. Shame washes over me and the tunnel collapses. I can't breathe.

CHAPTER 28

Sarah woke up, shaking and gasping for breath. A feeling of panic filled her. Something was wrong: were Nick and Lottie all right? She wanted to get up and stand over their beds and watch them sleeping peacefully, like she had when they were babies. Nick was in his old room with Olly and she certainly didn't want to intrude on their privacy. What about Lottie, and the baby? She looked at her watch. Just after 3.00 – she couldn't phone now. She tried to breathe slowly, calming her thumping heart.

She switched on the light and sat up. It was just a dream. After the police had bagged up Rory's razor and toothbrush, taken samples from Nick and Olly and left, they'd all sat around, stunned. Lottie had been so white Abigail had driven her home to Liam. Nick and Olly were uncharacteristically quiet while they cooked the meal. They'd all eaten very little.

Olly kept saying, 'It must be a mistake. Crime scenes become contaminated, samples are mixed up.' Sarah appreciated his trying to raise their spirits, to find a chink of hope, but she was filled with dread. Could this be true?

She thought back to Shona. She was so pretty, and much more mature than her; she'd always liked flirting with the boys. Sarah could picture her so clearly; her long blonde hair, the beginning of breasts under her T-shirt, her slender brown legs. Could she have been with Rory that night? All the girls fancied him. Was that her secret? Was that where she was going that night?

She felt so confused, so desperate. She sat in the darkness of her bedroom, and picked up her phone. The screen was blank. *Oh Tom, please send a message…*

She'd never felt like this with Rory. They'd lived their lives in parallel, rather than together. Perhaps Rory had been unable to have a real relationship with anyone because he was always carrying the guilt, the burden of what he'd done as a teenager? Did he have a string of superficial relationships because he was afraid of letting anyone get too close?

Or maybe every marriage was equally hollow once you scratched the surface. She thought back to her own parents: she couldn't remember ever seeing them laughing together, or even really talking. It was always quiet in their house; her father was not to be disturbed and his food was to be on the table punctually. In return, her mother was allowed her treats, but there was never any sign of affection between them.

Sarah had never been able to talk to either of them. When Shona died they'd been annoyed if she'd ever tried to mention her. She could never have discussed her pregnancy or the abortion with her mother, and she realised that she kept up the pretence of the perfect marriage with Rory partly for her mother's sake. Marrying Rory was the one thing she'd done in her whole life that seemed to get any approval from her mother.

What did she even feel about Rory? She'd been thankful that he hadn't abandoned her when she was pregnant, grateful that there was no pressure to abort their twins. She'd done everything she could to keep him happy because she was secretly afraid she was too boring for him – and she was always relieved when he came home to her.

Now she realised how shallow their relationship was; when she saw the love between Olly and Nick, and thought of the easy, unquestioning support that Lottie and Liam gave each other, she realised how much she'd missed. She was glad that her children could experience love, although she'd never really known it herself.

Until now. Now, with Tom, she knew what a real relationship was; a relationship where you could say anything and didn't have to dance round on eggshells for fear of provoking a sulk; where you didn't have to play a role and keep up a façade; where you could be yourself and feel valued. *Oh Tom, why don't you contact me?*

She looked at her watch again and tried to get back to sleep but every time she closed her eyes her mind raced. Could Rory really have killed Shona? HJ Kidd's words echoed through her mind. When the teacher had said he had a personality disorder and called him a narcissist, Sarah had been beside herself with rage; but now, when she thought about it calmly, perhaps there was some truth in it. His superficial charm, the total lack of concern for the consequences of his actions, the easy lying, the need for admiration, the fires he'd set as a boy – it all added up.

*

Tom walked out of the clinic shaking his head. No mobile phone, but he'd found out some useful information – the funeral was taking place on Friday that week. Carl must have pulled a few strings to get it organised so quickly. Of course, he was now the biggest property owner in Plettenberg Bay, so he could probably do whatever he liked.

The funeral was to be held at the One World Church, in a lovely position looking out over the mouth of the Keurbooms River. Aunty Betty had a plot in the graveyard next to the church, where Uncle Gus was buried. She'd always said she was looking forward to lying down beside him again.

Tom just wanted the funeral over with so he could get back to Scotland as quickly as possible. He knew Sarah would be worrying because he hadn't contacted her and was kicking himself for not writing down her number anywhere, or at least bringing her email address with him. He'd done everything he could to find her landline number, pestering international directory enquiries, but she was ex-directory. In desperation he'd emailed HJ Kidd, partly to tell him he'd be back a few days later than originally planned, but also to ask for Sarah's phone number or email address. He hadn't received any reply.

He kept feeling for the pocket where his phone should be. It was awful not being able to contact Sarah, but he hoped she'd be able to feel his love for her, anyway. He felt so close to her, she must feel it.

He shook his head again. Thank goodness the effects of his hangover were wearing off at last – he hadn't felt right for days.

*

The day of Aunty Betty's funeral was as bright and sunny as every other day. Tom looked out the most sombre clothes he could find and went along to the church. He'd had no contact from Carl. He didn't know whether this was down to not having a mobile, or whether it was a deliberate snub on the lawyer's part, but Tom didn't care. He hadn't wanted to play a significant role in the service, anyway.

He knew Betty had written down her ideal funeral after Gus died. She wanted it simple; a celebration of her life and her love for her family and Plettenburg Bay. As she said to Tom then, it was not to be a sad occasion because she was going to be reunited with her beloved Gus.

The church was crowded with people Tom didn't recognise. Being over ninety, Betty had outlived most of her old friends from Plett, but as Tom looked around the church he wondered for a moment if he'd wandered into the wrong funeral. Then he saw Carl, looking smug and shiny, surrounded by a group of his clones: his circle from Pretoria.

The service was awful, nothing like Tom remembered Betty describing as her ideal. It was overblown and pretentious and all in Afrikaans. The music was pompous, with a singer wailing in a self-satisfied manner. Betty would have hated it.

As Tom followed the coffin covered with lilies – flowers that Betty disliked intensely – he didn't feel her presence at all. Only when he looked out to sea and saw the water sparkling over the Keurbooms beach did he feel her spirit.

Fly free, dear Aunty Betty. You were the best.

For the first time Tom felt tears pricking his eyes. He blinked twice and started to walk towards the centre of town. He shrugged off the dark jacket and knew that it was time to leave Plett.

He heard footsteps behind him and then a voice, 'Mr

McIver?' He turned round to see a tall, sandy-haired figure with a long aquiline nose. He didn't recognise him, but he stopped to see what he wanted. The other man extended his hand, 'Peter Roberts.'

Peter Roberts. In a dull spot of alcohol-destroyed brain cells it touched a chord. That was the name Betty had whispered just before she died, the name that Tom had been trying to remember for the last couple of days.

'I've been trying to contact you, but I didn't know if you were in the country or not. Somebody said you'd gone to Scotland.'

'I was there but I came back to say goodbye to Aunty Betty.'

Peter Roberts looked solemn. 'I'm sorry for your loss but I've got information that will be of interest to you. I'm a partner in Roberts and Cohn, Attorneys at Law, and we have a copy of your aunt's will.'

Tom shook his head. 'Her nephew, Carl van Wyk, has the will.'

Roberts smiled. 'He has *a* will, but you will find that the one in my possession is more recent.'

'Are you sure it's legal?' Tom raised his eyebrows. 'Van Wyk's a lawyer and you can be absolutely certain he will 'prove' that the one he has is the only valid one.'

'That's exactly why your aunt came to me. She'd been trying to amend her will, but Van Wyk wouldn't allow it, put all sorts of obstacles in her way. She came to me and we drew up a will that was identical to the previous one, but with one important difference.' He shot Tom a significant look. 'A very important difference for you.'

Tom wondered what was coming next. The lawyer

continued. 'Your aunt has left you the property you and your family inhabited for so many years.'

Tom looked astonished. 'I can't believe it. Aunty Betty never said anything about it.'

Roberts smiled. 'That was deliberate. She didn't want anyone to know because she was afraid that Van Wyk would find some way to change or contest the will. But I can tell you she was a very sharp lady and this will is absolutely watertight; we have witnesses, we have a doctor's report confirming she was of sound mind – and you now own the property on the dunes.'

Tom could hardly speak. 'I thought Van Wyk was pulling that down?'

'Oh yes, he's sold it, although he wasn't entitled to. You could challenge it if you wanted. Or you could just take the money.' He gave a wide grin. 'In that prime position the plot was sold for eight million rand.'

Tom gasped. 'Eight million rand.' He converted it quickly into pounds in his head: over £500,000.

Peter Roberts smiled again. 'Come into my office tomorrow and we'll sort out all the paperwork. And don't worry about Van Wyk. I would relish a fight but I suspect he won't challenge this because he doesn't have a leg to stand on.'

The sun was beating down on them and they moved into the shade of a yellow-wood tree. Tom looked at him, feeling numb with shock. Betty had done this for him. He couldn't believe it. Immediately he thought of Sarah. Now he could offer her something. Before he was a penniless bum, but now he could offer her a future. He, odd-job man, drift-wood sculptor, surfing teacher, beach bum, was worth half a million pounds. He repeated it out loud very slowly.

Half.

A.

Million.

Pounds.

He threw his head back and laughed.

CHAPTER 29

Sarah had fallen asleep again and woke up feeling scratchy and unsettled. After blinking a couple of times she realised what was wrong. The vague feeling of disquiet hanging over her crystallised into the awful reality: Rory, Shona's murderer? It couldn't be possible.

The phone rang. It was her mother.

'Now, I hope I'm not disturbing you, Sarah, and I know you have been very busy but I haven't heard from you for days. I haven't been very well, you know.'

A huge wave of guilt washed over her. She really had nearly forgotten about her mother. 'I'm so sorry, Mum, there's been a lot going on. Are you in today? I'll come and see you.'

'I'm always in,' said her mother, with a dramatic sigh. *Yes,* thought Sarah, *except when you're at the hairdresser or the Bridge Club or out to lunch...* She arranged to call round that afternoon.

Rory, a murderer? She couldn't escape the thought, and found it difficult to think of anything else. She showered and drank a large cup of coffee, trying to focus on the positive; there was wonderful news as well. Lottie and Liam were going to have a baby. She put her cup down. She knew what she was going to do. She'd collect Lottie, get some pastries from the French Patisserie in Stockbridge and give her mother a lovely surprise – tell her that she was going to be a great-grandmother.

Lottie was not at all enthusiastic when Sarah called to suggest the visit, but eventually agreed. Sarah picked her up, popped quickly into the patisserie, and then they set off for Corstorphine.

'Are you going to tell Granny about Dad?' asked Lottie.

'Oh, no. You know how much she loved him. It would break her heart.'

Lottie put her lips together in a firm line. 'She's going to hear about it soon enough, and perhaps it would be better for her to hear it from you. Now.'

'You seem very certain it's true.' An awful thought struck Sarah. 'He never did anything to you, did he?'

Lottie turned round and stared at her. 'Mum, of course not. He was never around.' Her voice remained very calm. 'And what if Dad *was* with the girl? That doesn't mean he killed her. Perhaps she wanted to be with him.'

'Lottie, Shona was thirteen.'

Lottie raised her eyebrows. 'Plenty of thirteen-year-olds have sexual experience.'

'Things were different in those days.' Sarah gripped the steering wheel tighter.

'Maybe it was an accident,' Lottie continued in a stubborn voice. 'They couldn't pin anything on him now he's dead.'

Sarah didn't know what to say. Lottie had always been the rational one, the one who treated her mother as if she was over-emotional and a bit naïve.

'And even if it *did* come out. What then? He was a teenager and there are plenty of other things he did in-between which were not exactly admirable. It's not as if he's got a shining reputation to tarnish.'

Sarah was shocked by the bitterness in her daughter's voice. Because Nick and Abigail had seemed to accept their father's numerous affairs and children so easily, Sarah had assumed that Lottie felt the same. Then she thought how Lottie had seemed to withdraw recently; this brittle shell hiding how much she was hurting. 'Your dad loved you very much.'

'Did he? He had a very funny way of showing it then.' Lottie's voice seemed to catch. They turned into the crescent of thirties bungalows where Flora lived. Sarah parked the car, but didn't go in. She wanted to sort this out now.

'And you know how much I love you, don't you?' Even to her, there was a desperate edge to her voice.

'I know, Mum, but it's just that you never seemed to face up to anything. I thought Dad treated you like a doormat, but I never dreamt he could be constantly betraying you in the way he did. You'll do anything to keep Granny happy, too, although she also treats you, and me, like dirt. I know you want us all to play happy families but it won't work. And I don't think that Granny's going to be as delighted with the news that she's going to be a great-grandmother as you imagine.'

Sarah gulped; she'd thought everything was fine again with Lottie and was shocked by the resentment that had obviously been running deep for some considerable time.

'I can't believe you feel like this. We'll talk about it more on the way back. You must make allowances for Granny. She hasn't been very well.'

Lottie set her mouth in a determined line. 'OK,' she said,

'but just for you.' She leant over and kissed her on the cheek. 'I know you love us, me and Nick, and you do try to do everything for the best.'

Sarah felt incredibly touched by her daughter's words and held her hand as they walked up the short drive to the front door.

When Flora opened the door, Sarah was shocked to see how thin her mother looked. As usual she was beautifully dressed, with shoes and scarf matching, but her clothes looked several sizes too large for her and her wrists protruding from her cardigan were painfully thin.

She greeted them with a perfunctory wave. 'At last. I haven't seen you for such a long time.' Her tone was heavy with reproach.

'Sorry, Mum. We really have been very busy, but we're here now and we've brought these for you.' She handed over the pastries. 'Shall I make a cup of tea?'

Flora indicated the sherry bottle. 'Well, as you're finally here, we might as well celebrate.' She got three crystal glasses from the glass-fronted cabinet.

'Not for me, thank you, Granny,' Lottie said quickly.

Flora looked crossly at her grand-daughter, so Sarah broke in. 'For a very good reason. We've got wonderful news – you're going to a great-grandmother.'

Flora's lined face crumpled into an expression of disgust. Sarah felt her stomach sink. Lottie had been right.

'I suppose it's that young man of yours. I would have thought you could do better than him, but I hope he's going to do the honourable thing. When's the wedding?'

Lottie's face had gone red but her voice was even. 'We're not going to get married just because of the baby. We don't

342

need to – we've known for a long time that we want to spend the rest of our lives together. You've never made any effort to get to know Liam, but he's intelligent, honest, decent, and he has integrity. I love him, he loves me… so that's all that's important. The baby has come a little earlier than we'd planned but we're thrilled. Even if you're not.'

Sarah looked at the furious set of Lottie's face and, hurried to change the subject. 'Shall I pour you a sherry, Mum?'

'Thank you dear.' Flora turned her back on Lottie. 'Do tell me about the arrangements for Rory's memorial service? I'm still not quite sure what I should wear.'

Sarah's heart sank a little further. Another dangerous topic. If the news of Nick's familial DNA match came out, the memorial service would be a disaster. 'They're going OK. Nick is going to talk about his father.'

Flora's face lit up. 'He'll do that so well. He's got such presence.'

'He'll certainly create an impression if his face hasn't healed by then,' Lottie muttered.

Flora gave a gasp of horror. 'What's happened to the dear boy's face?'

Sarah shot Lottie a warning look. 'We didn't want to worry you, Mum, but it's one of the reasons I haven't been to see you recently. Nick was involved in an… incident and he's got some facial injuries, but he's fine,' she finished hastily.

'Why didn't you tell me? He's my grandson. When you keep these secrets from me, it's as if I'm not part of the family.'

Lottie opened her mouth and looked as if she was going to say something, so Sarah hurried on, really not feeling that her mother was ready to hear her favourite grandchild had been a victim of gay-bashing. 'So much has been happening. They've also been looking into Shona McIver's death again and I had to be interviewed.'

Flora pursed her lips. 'Really, why are they raking that all up again? It's all so long ago.'

'They have to reopen the case because Logan Baird has been shown to be innocent.'

'So they say. But he was a danger to young girls, exposing himself to them.'

'That was never proved, Mum. It was just some silly wee girls wanting a bit of attention at the time. But, anyway, they have tests nowadays that prove it can't be him and–'

'–and they're looking at new suspects.' Lottie shot Sarah a rebellious look. 'Even our dad is a suspect now.'

Flora was pale before, but the colour completely disappeared from her face, leaving it grey. 'Rory? That's ridiculous. It couldn't possibly be him.'

Sarah knew that her mother was always very fond of Rory, but she was surprised by the vehemence of her response. She tried to rescue the situation a bit, her voice shaking. 'I'm sure it's just a mix-up but they found that Nick's DNA was a partial match to samples found at the scene of Shona's murder. Which suggests that the killer was someone from his, *our,* family. They came and took Rory's toothbrush to test it for DNA.'

Flora looked perplexed. 'What can they tell from that? He's dead.'

'DNA lasts for a long time. They're comparing it with some on Shona's clothes; you can use anything, a hair, a bit of skin, sweat.'

Flora turned even paler than before and stood up shakily. 'I'm afraid I don't feel very well. I think I'm going for a lie-down now. Thank you for coming.' She walked unsteadily towards her bedroom.

'Mum,' Sarah tried to follow her mother but the door was firmly closed in her face. She turned towards her daughter. 'What do you think you're doing, coming out with all that? She's an old lady.'

'She's an old witch. And anyway, being told is apparently what she wants.' Lottie mimicked her grandmother's voice. 'When you keep these secrets from me it's as if I'm not part of the family.'

CHAPTER 30

Tom sat on the bus from Edinburgh Airport feeling the excitement rising. All through the long night flight from Johannesburg and on the short shuttle from Heathrow, he'd been imagining the moment he saw Sarah again. He'd gone through his fantasy scenario time and time again, the embrace at the doorway, the kiss, making love and telling her about his inheritance. His heart felt full and pulsing in his chest, he couldn't wait to see her and tell her of his plans for the future.

First, he would buy a little flat in Portobello and go to Art College. That was what he'd always wanted to do and now he had the money to be able to do it. He knew it was not a fortune, but enough to keep him going if he was careful. He and Sarah would be able to spend time together, catching up on all the years they'd lost. He was amazed how romantic he felt, *him*, the old cynic.

When he got off the bus at Waverley Station, the skyline in front of him took his breath away, the silhouette of the castle and churches with the sky cloudy and brooding behind it. He was home.

He crossed Princess Street, pulling his suitcase behind him, and hurried down Frederick Street. As he crossed George Street he glimpsed the sea, and the smoky outline of Fife merging into the mistiness of the horizon. He and

Sarah would walk along the shore, hand-in-hand, he would support her and she would be his muse. After a decent time they'd move in together, perhaps even marry. As he turned the corner into Great King Street his whole body was tingling with anticipation. He ran up the steps and rang the bell, almost unable to contain his excitement.

There was no answer. It had never occurred to him that she might be out. He rang again, willing her to answer. He wanted to hear her voice through the entryphone system, he wanted to run up the steps two by two and hold her in his arms.

After ringing for a third time he realised she wasn't going to answer and he wondered what to do next. He hadn't got a Plan B. He shivered; there was a light drizzle in the air and he was still wearing the light denim jacket he'd worn out of South Africa, quite unsuitable for November in Edinburgh.

He remembered a café in a converted bank on the road towards Stockbridge; he'd go and have a cup of coffee and try again later. He yawned. He'd hardly slept on the plane with his long legs cramped in front of him and he'd been in the same clothes for twenty-four hours. In his disappointment, he began to feel the weariness.

He was walking down Circus Place when he saw Sarah's car coming in the opposite direction. He waved, but Sarah's eyes were fixed straight ahead. His stomach lurched as he saw her profile, serious but even more beautiful than he remembered. He turned and hurried back up the road, his suitcase bouncing on the uneven pavement.

As he turned into Great King Street he saw she'd parked the car and was concentrating on putting her key into the lock of her front door. He hurried up the steps. She didn't notice him until he was directly behind her, but then she half-turned and her face lit up. She reached out and buried her head in his shoulder, her whole body shaking with sobs. The welcome was not the one Tom had anticipated. He stroked her hair. 'Shhh…' he whispered. 'It's all right.'

He took the key from her hand and opened the main door, before leading her gently upstairs. They reached the door of the flat and Sarah held him tight. 'I've had such an awful time. It's been a nightmare. I've missed you so much.'

'I'm here now.' He held her close and led her to the drawing room. 'Tell me what's happened.'

Between sobs, Sarah told him about Nick being attacked, the DNA and the suspicions about Rory.

Tom sat bolt upright. 'There must be some mistake. Rory couldn't, wouldn't…' He thought back to those days after Shona's body was found, when everyone was considered a suspect. Never, ever had it crossed his mind that it could possibly be Rory.

Then from deep in his memory he heard Rory's voice. *'Wait until your little sister is a couple of years older. She'll be a real goer.'* He'd been furious at the time, filled with rage that Rory could talk about his sister in that way. Had something happened between them?

'And I've just been at my mother's. That was a disaster too.' Sarah described what had happened, and the escalating hostility in the car on the way home. 'Lottie's so bitter. I'd never realised. This should be a wonderful time, with the baby coming, but she said our family is a sham and she doesn't want to be part of the big pretence any more. And she called me a doormat.'

Tom suppressed a laugh; Sarah looked shocked. 'It's not funny.'

Tom raised his eyebrows. 'I'm sorry to laugh, and I wouldn't exactly call you a doormat, but you do tend to put everyone else's feelings and needs before your own.' Sarah pouted and gave him a playful thump on the chest.

'It's one of the many things I love about you: your kindness, understanding and empathy for other people, but,' he raised his hands in mock defence, 'you have to learn to be a bit more selfish, sometimes.' He leant over and kissed her. 'And you need someone to care for you and spoil you a bit. You've looked after other people all your life and now it's your turn for a bit of TLC – and I'm your man. I'll always be here for you; I'm never going away again.' And as he said it Tom knew it was true.

'Thank you,' Sarah leant over and kissed him on the lips; then she straightened and shook herself. 'Oh, I've just been talking about myself all the time. How are you? The last thing I heard from you was that your aunt died. I'm so sorry.'

'Aunty Betty was over ninety and happy to go and join my Uncle Gus. And,' his face broke into a wide smile, 'I'm not a beach-bum any more. She left me something in her will and now I'm half a millionaire.'

*

The low morning sun was shining into the drawing room as Sarah was hoovering. She caught herself humming; she felt so happy, was sleeping well, and wasn't haunted by those dreams and memories. Since Tom had come back, she felt reborn, blossoming like a dried-up flower, nurtured back to life.

They'd fallen into a comfortable daily routine: Tom got up and went for a run while she did a bit about the house and when he came back they had breakfast together. Then the rest of the day they just pottered around, finding out more about each other and enjoying doing nothing. Sarah had never felt so happy.

Tom would be back in a minute. She put the hoover away and was laying the kitchen table when the doorbell rang. That would be Tom with the rolls. She pushed the buzzer and left the flat door open as she started the coffee.

'Hello, Mum.'

She looked round. It was Lottie carrying a bag of croissants.

'Lottie, how lovely to see you.'

Lottie rushed towards her mother and hugged her. 'I'm just on my way to the Health Centre, but I had to come in and speak to you.' She stood back and looked her mother in the eyes. 'Mum, I'm sorry I was such a bitch the other day. I don't know what came over me, saying such awful things. Blame it on the hormones! I've even been crabby with Liam – and he's the best-natured person in the world. In fact, it was him who said I should come and see you and apologise, because I was fretting over it so much.' She kissed her mother. 'You know how much I love you – and I know you're going to be a wonderful grandmother.'

Sarah pulled Lottie tight. 'You know I've always loved you, since the day you were born – and I can't wait to be able to meet your little one, and have as much fun with her, or him, as I did with you and Nick. And you know if there's ever anything you need, any help, I'm here.'

Lottie kissed her again. 'I know, Mum, and perhaps that's

one reason I took you for granted. Because I always knew you'd be there. But when I think of everything that's happened I just realise how lucky I am. Mum, you're the best.'

The doorbell rang again. This time it would be Tom. She wondered how she would explain him to Lottie, but realised she didn't care.

The door opened and Tom came in, panting in his running gear, clutching a paper bag of rolls. Lottie looked at him and smiled. 'Hi, Tom. I'm just going – have an appointment at the doc's. Hope you're hungry because there's loads to eat – I brought croissants too.' She turned to her mum and gave her a smile. 'Have a great day, you two and see you soon.' And with a smile and a wave to both of them she disappeared through the door.

Tom smiled at Sarah and raised his eyebrows. 'Well, it seems as if that's one of your worries crossed off the list. I knew the kids would be all right – they just want you to be happy.'

Nick and Olly came round that evening with a bottle of wine. Sarah didn't know if they'd been primed by Lottie, but they made no comment about Tom being there and acted as if his presence was totally natural. They had a lovely evening, with lots of laughs and several bottles of wine. When they left Sarah fell into bed with Tom, feeling thirty years younger and happier than she could ever remember.

*

The next morning the phone rang early. Sarah saw it was her mother. They hadn't spoken since that dreadful visit with Lottie so Sarah was pleased her mother had taken the initiative.

'Are you in this morning, Sarah? I've got something very important I want to show you.'

Sarah agreed to see her mother at ten and told Tom to go for a longer run today. She'd decided that she was going to face up to her mother and tell her the truth, but still didn't feel comfortable with Tom being there. She'd spent her whole life keeping things secret from her mother and it was going to be hard to be honest with her for once.

When the doorbell rang she pressed the buzzer without checking, expecting to hear her mother coming up the stairs. She was surprised to hear two sets of footsteps and see DI Chisholm and a female officer coming round the corner of the stair. Chisholm shook her hand, introduced his colleague and strode into the flat.

Sarah hardly dared think what was coming next. 'Have you checked the DNA?'

'We have. Your husband's DNA was not a match for the sample found on the victim's cardigan.'

Sarah gasped; she felt a huge weight had literally been lifted from her. 'Thank God. I knew it couldn't have been him.' Sarah's mind leapt to the next possibility. 'So was it HJ Kidd?'

DI Chisholm exchanged a weary look with his colleague. 'Mr Kidd's DNA has also been tested and as a result he has been definitely excluded from the enquiry. Incidentally, we've been able to process the film that was in the camera at the time of your husband's accident and the evidence thereon is entirely consistent with the version of events given by Mr Kidd.'

'But who then?' Sarah held her breath.

DI Chisholm cleared his throat. 'Although your husband has been eliminated from the enquiry, the fact still remains that your son's DNA is a familial match to the murderer. Therefore, we have to investigate other members of the family.'

'But Rory was an only child and his father was an invalid at that time.'

'We also have to look to your side of the family. Do you have any brothers, Mrs Dunbar?'

Sarah gasped. Someone from *her* family? Her legs felt weak. There was nobody, except… No, it was unthinkable. She sat down on the sofa, feeling the eyes of the two police officers on her. Her mind was racing. In *her* family. There could only be one person…

CHAPTER 31

Tom ran along the seafront at Portobello. He'd had to go out. It was strange – Sarah didn't care who knew he was there, but when her mother said she was coming over she reverted to being a secretive teenager. The thought of Sarah made him smile. She was such a mass of contradictions, on the surface so composed, yet underneath so insecure.

He ran along the sand and looked up at the red tenement where he'd lived as a child and thought of Shona again. Could it have been Rory? Could he have arranged to meet his little sister? Maybe, it wasn't impossible – he knew what Rory was like – but it must have been an accident. He'd never have done anything to harm Shona on purpose.

Shona. Somehow being a murder victim had sucked her of all personality, she had become an innocent angel in everyone's minds, the smiling face on the posters. Talking to Sarah had made her a real person again. She'd told him some tales he hadn't heard before, like the afternoon Shona had persuaded Sarah to skip off school with her. There was no getting away from the fact that Shona was naughty, but she was so sweet she could always get away with everything. Tom smiled at the memory.

Looking up he saw a FOR SALE sign on one of the tenements further along the prom. That would be a possiblility; he'd love to live here, completing the circle. At the end of the month he had to move into the Canongate Centre. He wasn't at all keen on the idea now, but he felt a commitment to Kidd, who'd offered him the job when he was virtually penniless. The thought of the spartan accommodation filled him with gloom, but he'd go and work out his notice and hope he'd find someone to take over the job.

Because he was rich. He could still hardly believe it. After years of always being short of money, he now had more money than he'd ever dreamed of. It was difficult to get used to the idea, but Peter Roberts, the lawyer from Plett, had contacted him to say that that although Carl had challenged the will, it had been officially ratified and the money would be released by the end of the year.

Running further along the beach towards Abercorn Park and HJ Kidd's house, he saw the old teacher and Hannah stepping out of their front gate, carrying shopping bags. Tom stared straight ahead and kept on running. He hadn't contacted HJ yet to tell him that he was leaving the job as soon as possible. He'd been putting it off.

Out of the corner of his eye he saw them walking slowly along the prom. HJ Kidd was stooped, far more than he remembered, and Hannah almost seemed to be supporting him as they walked arm in arm. Although he didn't want to, Tom decided he must go and speak to him. He didn't want to risk them seeing him and think he was ignoring them.

He ran over the beach, up the steps and stopped in front of the Kidds. HJ raised his head. Tom was shocked; the old teacher's face was grey and lined and his eyes looked dull. He seemed to have aged ten years. Even his voice seemed to have lost its power.

'Oh, Tom, you're back.' The teacher hesitated, 'There's something I have to tell you. Bad news, I'm afraid. There will be no job at the Canongate Centre. They're going to close the Arts Centre down.' His voice cracked in disappointment.

Relief flooded through Tom's body, although he tried to hide it because HJ was so obviously upset. He muttered a few sympathetic remarks.

'The building's being taken over by the Grassmarket Community Project. They've decided our concept is out of date.' Hannah smiled gently in encouragement and HJ went on expressionlessly, as if reading from a policy document. 'The Grassmarket Community Project offers a mixture of social integration activities, like cookery, woodwork, art and music, giving opportunities for people who have been marginalised by society to volunteer and work there.'

Tom sensed a huge 'but' coming. 'It sounds great; would you be able to continue with the poetry group there?'

HJs face seemed to crumple even further.

Hannah took over, firmly. 'Unfortunately poetry does not fit in with the concept of the project.'

Tom looked at HJ's face and saw the pain in his eyes. 'But you could continue the group somewhere else?' He caught the look in Hannah's eyes and realised he'd said the wrong thing.

Hannah glanced protectively at her husband. 'HJ is going to concentrate on his own work from now on, and enjoy his retirement.'

HJ looked up at Tom hopefully. 'Have you heard anything about the investigation? I was interviewed but I haven't heard anything more. I had hoped that my DNA sample would exclude me and that there would be an end to this most distressing matter.'

Tom wondered whether he should say anything about Rory but decided against it, despite seeing the pain in the older man's face. If the police hadn't said anything, it wasn't his place to give out information. He shook his head.

HJ reached out his hand. 'I just hope for your sake that we'll be able to find closure. I'm sorry I was unable to help you financially, as I'd hoped.'

Tom smiled. Of course, HJ Kidd didn't know. He shook the older man's hand warmly. 'Thank you for all your help, but actually I'm OK for the moment. I've come into a bit of an inheritance.'

*

Sarah's legs gave way and she sat on the Chesterfield, still trying to come to terms with what DI Chisholm had said.

The doorbell rang. That would be her mother. She mustn't come in. Sarah couldn't let her be confronted with the monstrous suspicion that was crossing her mind. The two police officers nodded to her and she went to the entryphone.

'Mum, I'm sorry, it really isn't convenient at the moment. Can you go for a cup of coffee and come back in an hour?' Although her heart was pounding with panic, she was surprised that her voice came out normally.

'Let me in, Sarah. I *have* to speak to you.'

'Mum, it isn't possible. The police are here.'

'That's very good. I would very much like to speak to them. Sarah, open the door.'

Sarah hesitated and then pushed the buzzer.

Her mother came up the stairs, looking thinner than ever in her designer clothes, clutching a large Jenner's bag to her chest. Sarah was shaking but introduced the detectives. Her mother responded politely; everyone was observing the social niceties. DI Chisholm led them all into the drawing room.

'Mum, the police are here about Shona's death.'

'I know, and that's what I want to talk about. Ever since that Baird was freed I've been troubled. But now that Rory is a suspect, I've had no rest.' Her voice was shaking but she struggled to compose herself. 'It wasn't Rory. I know.'

Sarah gasped, frightened by what her mother might say next. Mrs Campbell opened the Jenner's bag and took out a blue leather box. She opened it carefully, revealing a pair of silver-backed men's hair brushes nestling in the blue velvet lining. Sarah recognised them from the dressing table in her parents' bedroom. Her father was never a vain man, but he had always brushed his thick luxuriant hair with them, one in each hand.

'These were my father's and he gave them to my late husband.' Flora spoke with precision and calm. 'They are among the few possessions I took from the Portobello flat when I moved. When Sarah told me about Rory and this DNA thing, I looked at them and saw there are still one or two of my husband's hairs there.'

All the eyes in the room were fixed on her. DI Chisholm was about to say something, but Flora waved him aside. 'Rory was not the murderer.'

Chisholm nodded to the female detective, who took a notebook out of her pocket. 'Can you tell us the whole story, Mrs Campbell?'

The old lady took a deep breath and began. 'This is so

difficult. I made myself forget it, pretended it never happened.' There was a bright spot of colour in the middle of each cheek, but otherwise her face was deathly pale. 'I remember that terrible night. He went out to look for Sarah and came back, covered in mud and full of rage. He was always a religious man, but after that he was obsessed. He was always praying, always at the church.' Sarah noticed that her mother couldn't say her husband's name.

'That was the night Shona McIver disappeared?' Chisholm asked gently.

'Yes, but it never crossed my mind that he could've had anything to do with it. He was a man of God. And they found the murderer very quickly.' She took another deep breath. 'Then six years later he had his heart attack. We were alone in the house. He was so frightened. He was shaking, saying he was going to hell, to eternal damnation because of what he'd done.' The old lady looked up and continued speaking, her voice quiet but firm. 'I didn't know what he meant. Then he said he had to confess or he would burn in hell for ever. He made me listen to what he had done, the terrible crime he had committed.'

Everyone was silent.

'He said he found her in the park alone. She stopped to talk to him and smiled at him. He said she was so beautiful he just wanted to hold her.' Her voice faltered. 'Then the devil took him over.'

Sarah stared at her mother. Her brain felt as if it was imploding.

Flora looked round the room. 'He couldn't control his passion. He said it was an accident. He didn't mean to kill her. He was too strong.' She took out a lace-trimmed handkerchief and screwed it up in her hands. 'In that last moment he cried out for forgiveness.' A shocked silence hung in the air. 'And then he died.'

Nobody dared to speak until Chisholm broke the moment. 'Why didn't you say anything about this at the time, Mrs Campbell?'

'What would have been the point? That other man was in jail.'

Sarah couldn't keep silent. 'But Logan Baird has been in prison *all this time*.'

Mrs Campbell jutted her chin forward. 'Everyone said he was a danger to young girls.'

Sarah leant forward to say something but Flora looked her in the eyes. 'I did it for *you*. Can't you see that? If people had found out you were the daughter of a murderer, you'd never have married, we'd both have been totally ostracised from society.' Sarah was about to explode but Chisholm gestured to her to keep quiet.

'Mrs Campbell, you should have told the police this at the time. Your actions were responsible for an innocent man being imprisoned for very many years. Nevertheless, I'd like to thank you for telling us now. Thank you too, for bringing the brushes. They will be useful for the conclusion of this case.'

'Sarah told me that you can get that DNA thing from a single hair.'

'That's right. Now, if you would be so kind as to accompany us to the station we will be able to get a full statement.'

*

360

Tom opened the front door gently. 'Sarah?' He'd sent a text message to see if the coast was clear, but there'd been no reply.

The flat was silent except for the ticking of the grandfather clock in the hall. Tom checked the kitchen and then looked into the front room. Sarah was standing silhouetted against the high casement window, looking out at the dark sky, heavy with threatening clouds.

'Sarah? Is everything all right?'

She turned towards him, her face pale and drawn.

'What's happened?' Tom stepped quickly to her side and put his arms round her, feeling the tension in her body.

Keeping her eyes lowered, Sarah told him everything that had happened, in a low clear voice. There were no tears, just a dazed bewilderment.

Tom listened without speaking, surprised at his own reaction. He was shocked that Sarah's father was the murderer, because he'd seemed so upstanding and correct, a bastion of the Free Church, but mainly he just felt relief. Relief that it was all over, that the truth was known at last. Now he wanted to look to the future, because for the first time in his life he knew what he wanted and where he was going. He wanted to study art and be with Sarah.

Sarah paused, then straightened herself and looked at Tom. 'Have you got the spare keys to the flat?'

Tom was puzzled by the change of subject; he felt in his pockets and nodded.

'Keep them. They're yours. This is your home now.'

Tom's mouth fell open. This was what he wanted more than anything, but he'd been prepared to wait. 'Are you sure, Sarah? We haven't even had the memorial service for Rory yet. People will definitely be shocked.'

Sarah brushed her hair back from her face. 'For the first time in my life I feel certain about what I want. I've spent my whole life trying to keep other people happy, doing what I thought other people, especially my mother, wanted me to do. But she was living a lie and so was I.' She looked defiantly at Tom. 'I don't care what anyone thinks. The twins really like you, and they're the only people whose opinion is important to me.'

Tom took the keys from his pocket and held them up. 'Well, if you're really certain, I'm honoured to accept.' He gave a mock bow.

They laughed, and at that moment the sun pierced the clouds, and streamed in through the window, capturing them in its glow. The shadows of the past, which had hung over them for so long, were clearing at last.

ACKNOWLEDGEMENTS

The idea for this book has been in my mind for over thirty years, since I was teaching at Portobello High School in Edinburgh, but I would never have got round to actually writing it without the inspiration, encouragement and support of a great many people. You are too many to mention individually, but I'd like to thank you all very, very much – you know who you are!

Some of you, however, must get a special mention. Firstly, my wonderful family and friends, who read the early drafts, gave me feedback and motivated me to carry on – John and Alec, Heather, Taina, Pauline, Clare, Gillean, Michael, and Rolf H. Special thanks also to Fiona and Mary Sarah on South Uist, and Gabriele and Gabriella in Plettenberg Bay, for introducing me to these beautiful places. Huge gratitude also goes to my writing friends, Sarah Ward and Tana Collins; my editors, Frances Richardson and Sam Kruit; my tutors and fellow writers on the Arvon courses and everyone at Matador.

This is a work of fiction, but I have 'borrowed' a few incidents, sentences, or houses from real lives. They are too numerous to list here, but I'd especially like to thank my English teacher, Tony Barringer, who introduced me to 'Bat' and awakened my love of poetry, and Rowena, for her superb organisation of the Ilkley Grammar School reunions. And always remembering dear Rolf S and Alex B.

The book is set in Portobello, Edinburgh, the Outer Hebrides and Plettenberg Bay. I have played a little fast and loose with their geography and institutions, but I hope I have remained true to the spirit of these beautiful places I love.

ABOUT THE AUTHOR

Alison Baillie (Massie/Taylor) was brought up by Scottish parents in the Yorkshire Dales. After studying English at the University of St Andrews, she spent a year in Finland and then taught in various Edinburgh secondary schools, including Portobello High. She later moved to Switzerland, where she taught until her retirement. She now spends her time reading, writing, travelling, walking in the mountains, being with her family and friends, and going to crime-writing festivals.

If you'd like to contact her, please visit:

www.alisonbaillie.com

She'd love to hear from you!